"I WANT TO T[AKE] ME, NAKED AN[D...]"

The catch of passion in his voice thrilled Alana. She should stop him, but the fleeting impulse was soon forgotten . . . she loved him.

Rand lowered her gently onto the riverbank, spreading the blanket on the soft moss. Above her, the purple sky was pierced by rivets of stars, and the moon glowed softly. Beneath her, she felt the heartbeat of the river, pulsing as clearly through her as the full, strong current of her own heated blood.

"For me," he growled softly, his arm pillowing her head, "you're the first, the only woman in the world. Here, by this river, in my valley, I claim you as my own. Now, in this wild place, you'll belong to me, and I to you."

She needed nothing more. . . .

For Alan, for always,
and
the Elk Valley nieces: Tammy, Holly, Nicki
and especially, Allana.

I would also like to thank Jill Bates-Smith, teacher
of the deaf, for her advice on training deaf
children.

SHELTERING BRIDGES

Bobby Hutchinson

A SuperRomance from
HARLEQUIN
London · Toronto · New York · Sydney

All the characters in this book have no existence outside the imagination of the Author, and have no relation whatsoever to anyone bearing the same name or names. They are not even distantly inspired by any individual known or unknown to the Author, and all the incidents are pure invention.

The text of this publication or any part thereof may not be reproduced or transmitted in any form or by any means, electronic or mechanical, including photocopying, recording, storage in an information retrieval system, or otherwise, without the written permission of the publisher.

This book is sold subject to the condition that it shall not, by way of trade or otherwise, be lent, resold, hired out or otherwise circulated without the prior consent of the publisher in any form of binding or cover other than that in which it is published and without a similar condition including this condition being imposed on the subsequent purchaser.

First published in Great Britain in 1986 by Harlequin, 15-16 Brook's Mews, London W1A 1DR

© Bobby Hutchinson 1985

ISBN 0 373 70166 7

11-0486

Printed and bound in Great Britain by Cox & Wyman Ltd, Reading

CHAPTER ONE

"IF YOU'RE HAPPY and you know it, clap your hands." The flying fingers of the young teacher in blue jeans at the front of the large room signed the nursery song to her group of attentive pupils. Her rings flashed in the late June sunlight, while the words she made in sign language were copied by the small hands of the deaf students. Communicate, the Vancouver Private School for the Hearing Impaired, was having its end-of-term assembly.

From the back of the room, the silent song and the unified movements of hands and fingers sent a shiver of emotion coursing through the tall, slender body of the young woman standing just inside the door. Deaf children were like a spontaneous ballet, she mused. Her own long, ringless fingers automatically joined the children's with fluid, graceful movements. The signs she formed came as naturally to her as did speech to the young clerk now tapping hesitantly on her shoulder, drawing her attention away from the children and the assembly.

"Ms Campbell, your secretary says to tell you there's someone waiting to see you in your office."

Wearily, Alana ran a distracted hand through her untidy crop of short, burnished red-blond curls, disturbing them even further. She glanced enviously at the relaxed and happy group who were giggling now at the motions the song demanded. "If you're happy and you know it, rub your nose." Small hands squashed tiny noses. "If you're happy and you know it, then your face will surely show it." Reluctantly, Alana slipped out the door and into the hallway.

What, she wondered, did *her* face show? She grimaced at the thought. Certainly, this job as supervisor that she'd fought so hard to attain wasn't making her happy. Why, why, why, she pondered as she strode down the chalk-smelling corridor, had she not realized sooner that promotion wasn't always progress? Teaching deaf children was what she did best, what made her happy—but instead of doing that, her time was now spent attending boring meetings, doing the necessary public relations work, answering mountains of correspondence and using vast amounts of youthful energy trying to tactfully deal with the small group of elderly administrators, all male but one token—and silent—little woman.

They'd all felt she was too young for the job. They'd told her so when she'd applied two years before. If only she hadn't become furious with the injustice of being judged on the basis of age and sex. If only she'd honestly examined the job itself, and realized it wasn't what she wanted anyway.

"You're hoist with your own petard," her father used to tease whenever her temper overcame her reason, landing her in a jam. With this job, she'd hoist herself, all right. She passionately envied the teachers she hired, like that woman back there, doing the job she ached to do: building bridges that attempted to span the worlds of the deaf and the hearing. Very shaky bridges at the moment, she mused, considering the school's current financial situation. It was ominous, at best—the government was cutting back funding for special education.

Her slate-gray eyes were narrowed with frustration as

she burst through the outer office door. She lifted one arched brow enquiringly at Grace, the friend who was also her secretary. There were no appointments scheduled this afternoon, she was sure.

"A Mr. Randall Evans is waiting to see you, Ms Campbell," Grace announced formally, nodding her newly blond head at the open door leading to the inner room. "His son Bruce is with him." Grace's wide, deceivingly innocent eyes took in Alana's scowl, and her manicured fingers flew as she signed, "He's good looking, so smile a little. You're not getting any younger."

Alana's frown disappeared, and she had to grin at the mischievous contrast between the prim spoken message and the silent warning. It was typical of her friendship with Grace, begun years before when Alana was first teaching a night-school class in sign language to help pay her university fees. Her earnest students were stumbling with rebellious stiff fingers, answering her practice question, "Why do you want to learn sign language?" The answers were all serious, well meaning, high minded. Except for Grace's. A vibrant redhead at that stage, she had signed fluently, "So when the dentist says, 'That rubber dam isn't really bothering you, is it?' I can tell him about his damn rubber dam."

They'd had coffee after class, and soon Grace had invited Alana home to meet her madcap family. From her widowed mother, Margaret, down to the youngest eight-year-old brother, the family were all as delightfully outspoken, impetuous and loving as Grace. Alana was immediately adopted, fed, lectured and worried over as one of Margaret's brood. It had made all the difference to the lonely girl Alana had been then.

Now, Grace's hands moved again, this time pointing

to the front of the narrow blue skirt Alana wore. It was streaked and wet with muddy splotches and small dirty finger marks. Her white crepe shirt also bore traces of a child's tears. Its top button had popped off, leaving a larger amount of snowy lace camisole exposed than had been intended. At lunchtime, a pupil had fallen on the cement steps in front of the school. Naturally, Alana had picked the small boy up and cuddled him. Since neither she nor the child had a handkerchief, the blouse had suffered. Grace rolled her eyes in mock horror and despair.

"Can't you *try* to stay clean?" her fingers teased while her decorous secretary voice said primly, "I'll hold your calls for you, Ms Campbell."

Alana gave the blue gabardine over her slender hips a tug and a casual brush with her hand, shrugging eloquently at Grace and rolled her eyes. Clothes could be replaced. Children couldn't. She headed through the open door.

The man stood with his back toward her, cradling a small boy on one forearm. They were looking out the window that made up the northern wall of the room. Hazy blue north-shore mountains formed a soft backdrop for the dark waters of the inner harbor with its tankers and ocean liners. It was a glorious panorama that always helped Alana put the problems of her job back into perspective.

She paused, noting the Harris tweed jacket resting comfortably on shoulders that blotted out an unreasonable expanse of window. Had her office shrunk suddenly, or was this man really as immense as he seemed at first glance?

"Mr. Evans?" she asked politely. There was time to

glance at soft wood-brown hair curling nearly to the collar of his jacket, and to note very long legs encased in gray flannel, before he turned, setting the child down, gently straightening the tiny denim jacket. Fluidly, he rose and moved close in front of her, offering his hand.

"Good afternoon, Ms Campbell. Please call me Rand." He *was* big, with a deep voice. Her fingers were engulfed in a callused grip, huge and rough and strong. Dark eyes—brown? black?—studied her intently. The harsh angular planes of the stern unsmiling face were framed incongruously by the mass of hair, and he wore a well-trimmed mustache. His hair seemed the only part of him even remotely out of control, she found herself thinking as she slanted her eyes up to meet his somehow challenging gaze. Looking up at men wasn't something she often did. The two-inch heels on her navy pumps made her an even six feet: he towered over her by at least four inches. She drew her hand quickly from his grasp, unnerved by his cool inspection and, strangely, by his nearness. Her glance dropped to the small boy now resting wearily against his father's knee, scuffing one miniature runner back and forth across the rug. Children, she understood. This one looked about three. Impulsively, Alana dropped to her knees on the soft green pile, putting herself at the boy's eye level. She extended a hand, but he ignored her after one swift glance from hostile blue eyes shaped just like his father's. He had the same softly textured hair, thickly curling around his head like an aureole, except his was white blond. The shape of the tanned small face, too, was his father's, even to the deep cleft in the stubborn chin.

"Hello Bruce," Alana said gently, grateful for Grace's careful prompting. But the child made no response at all.

Alana's professional eye noted that the boy wasn't wearing hearing aids. Was he deaf? Most of the children brought here were—but deafness was an invisible handicap. Bruce ignored her grandly. There were traces of recent tears in silver streaks down his plump cheeks.

Alana stood, gesturing to the comfortable armchair, and as soon as Randall Evans sat down, she became horribly conscious of the still damp and now wrinkled skirt, the fresh run in her hose, the absolute certainty that any makeup she might have absently applied that morning was gone by now. From his lower vantage point, he took in every detail, studying her openly, especially noting the gap created by her missing button. Heat made her skin prickle. The blush crept up her neck. Surely at twenty-seven her blushing days should be long over, she cursed irritably, taking hurried refuge behind her desk and banging her thigh painfully in the process.

"Ouch," he said softly, not missing her clumsiness or even politely ignoring it. For the first time, a faint gleam of amusement showed in his unwavering gaze. Alana sank into her chair, wanting to rub her throbbing leg but resisting heroically, resenting this arrogant male facing her.

"Now," she said icily, "just what did you want, Mr. Evans?"

He was lifting the child onto his knee, and while his attention was distracted she took a good look at him. Deeply tanned skin, the kind that came from exposure to the elements rather than sunbathing. Strong, aquiline nose, hard-looking mouth. Deep lines etched across his forehead and at the corners of his eyes, although he looked only about in his midthirties.

He caught her inspecting him and she felt a new flush rise to the roots of her hair. Stop acting the idiot, she cautioned herself furiously. He stared first, didn't he? Defiantly, she tilted an eyebrow at him, holding his gaze.

"I came to offer you a job, but now that we've met, I see it would never work. Professor Lane, at the University Hospital, led me to believe you were—well, that you weren't quite so young. Frankly, I expected the supervisor of a school to be older. Although, Professor Lane seems to consider you one of the best teachers of deaf children she knows." He shrugged, as if her supposed talents were overshadowed by other, less admirable qualities—such as her age.

He also seemed totally oblivious to the irritation in her voice, or the sarcasm of her tone when she snapped, "I don't remember applying for any job with you. Obviously, I have a job. But," her tone became ominous, "had I applied, you would have no grounds to reject me because of my age." Her darkening eyes spat angry sparks at him. "Have you never heard of Human Rights, or age discrimination?" Her voice rose, but his rumbling tones remained maddeningly cool and even.

"I run a business, I'm aware of the rules of employment. In this case, they don't apply. Bruce needs a tutor. The doctors have just finished a week-long session with us. They agree that Bruce is profoundly deaf." The words were level, their tone revealing no bitterness, no pain—seemingly, no emotion at all. He might have been discussing the weather. But the casual arm around the boy's body tightened and flexed, and the huge hand clenched into a fist against his son's body. The tight-lipped smile beneath the mustache was sardonic, however, and the tone still light.

"That's *all* they agreed on. One suggested I put Bruce immediately in the provincial boarding school. Another suggested sending him to a program in Los Angeles. Teach him to talk, one insisted. No, teach him sign, the other argued. Finally, the only one who made sense to me was Dr. Lane. She said find a tutor who'll use every method available to teach Bruce language, and do it at home." He rubbed his chin gently on the top of Bruce's curls, and the boy twisted around to grin up at his father, who immediately smiled back. It was such a nice smile, boyish and innocent, softening the grim sternness of the man and tilting his heavy eyebrows up at the outer corners.

The exchange touched Alana, and she forgot to be angry. What he was telling her was typical of the confusion surrounding deaf education. Methodology so often obscured the needs of the child. It was one reason she'd worked so hard to help make Communicate a success. The school was one of the few she knew of, dedicated to offering small deaf children total education—using sign language, speech training, visual aids, imagination, pantomime; in fact, any and every method its teachers could devise to do what the name, Communicate, promised.

"She said the big problem would be finding a special tutor for Bruce," Rand said. "I have no idea how to find someone suitable. Could you suggest anyone? Older, reliable, but with similar qualifications to yours?"

Alana's quick temper flared anew at the man's cool assumption that he could first explain how unsuitable she was and in the next breath ask her to help find someone else. He managed to make it sound as though good teachers were simply waiting around for a chance to work for him. "Older and reliable." Why did society think the adjectives inseparable? And what was it about this particular man that caused one violent emotion after another to wash over her? A new thought struck her.

"Perhaps it's none of my business, but shouldn't your wife be involved in choosing a tutor for your son?"

Traffic on the street below sounded faintly, and Grace's typewriter clattered from the other room. The noise of parents arriving to collect their offspring and the laughter of excited children sounded in the halls. Alana found herself tensing as she waited for his answer. His voice was once more devoid of all emotion, and icy cold.

"I'm the only parent Bruce has, Ms Campbell." The stark words held no explanation, and Rand Evans offered none. Divorced, widowed... Maybe, Alana found herself hysterically imagining, this cold, imperturbable man had given birth to his son himself, like the proverbial seahorse. But the admission that he was single disturbed her. Her glance flickered to the small restless boy in his arms. Poor little kid. Handicapped, and no mother. But a single father as handsome... sensual... overwhelmingly male? Whatever, this man surely wouldn't be alone very long. And the way he had looked at that missing button was certainly not the disinterested glance of a celibate man. Rather, his eyes had seemed to scorch her. She shivered a little. Arrogant, that was the name for him. High-handed and arrogant. Coming here, insulting her first and then blithely asking her for help. Why on earth had dear Dr. Lane sent him here?

Probably, Alana deduced, as a direct result of their luncheon several weeks ago when her perceptive friend—and former Professor of Speech and Development—had listened patiently while Alana poured out all her dissatisfactions with this job. "Go back, my dear," Dr. Lane had suggested. "Simply resign, and go back where you belong. Working directly with deaf children is a job you were born to. You have a great gift, Alana. Use it!"

A warm rush of affection for Dr. Lane stopped the cool dismissal on her tongue, and instead she asked, "What else does this tutor you need have to be besides older and reliable? Male, perhaps?" The sarcasm of her tone once more brought the one-sided smile to the rugged face, but again no trace of real humor was apparent in the deep-set eyes. He settled the child, stretching out one muscular leg, moving the boy to the other.

"Willing to live in an isolated valley where the nearest town is twenty miles away, and then boasts one tavern for entertainment, mostly patronized by loggers and miners. Obviously, someone more interested in teaching Bruce than in leading an active social life."

The bitterness in his tone caught Alana's attention. "If the isolation is a problem," she suggested, "have you considered moving to a larger center, where Bruce could attend—"

"Bluejay is our home, Ms Campbell." There was no mistaking the finality underlying the deceptively quiet voice. "I know it's difficult for a city person to understand the attraction a place like Bluejay holds. The mine I own and operate is located there—I'm not moving. That's exactly why I'm searching for a tutor for Bruce." Irritation was evident in his tone, and Alana reacted to it.

"I do understand," she said coolly, "but I'm afraid I can't help you." She rose abruptly. "I'd just be wasting your time. So good afternoon, Mr. Evans." She was glad of the desk between them. He definitely disturbed her. She waited for him to get up, to leave, to dispel the palpable tension in the small room. But he didn't move.

"Please, sit down," he said wearily. "I'll try to explain." The words came out on a sigh, and Bruce stirred sleepily, turning his curly head restlessly to find a spot on his father's chest to comfortably fall asleep. Must be like pillowing your head on a rock, Alana thought fleetingly as she sank down in her chair. The room seemed very warm.

"Bluejay is in an isolated corner of British Columbia, about seven hundred miles east of Vancouver. I'm a coal miner, the way my father and grandfather were before me. My mine's small compared to the huge developments in that area, and there's no way it would operate successfully if I lived anywhere else. As it is, we're having serious problems because of the economy. Mining's what I know best, what I choose to do." He shook his head and the soft curls moved and resettled. "Sending Bruce away is out of the question." The muscular arm around the boy's body tightened protectively, mute testimony again of deep emotion. "And I know from past experience how impossible it is for women to adapt to the type of life I have." His head turned away from Alana, gazing out the window where an ocean liner glided over mirror-clad waters, heading out to sea. When he looked back, it was as if his eyes had absorbed the ocean's calm, deliberately masking all feeling. The man was a master at controlling emotion. What happened when that Herculean control slipped, she found herself wondering? The women who found it impossible to adapt—was it the environment or the man they found impossible? Was he talking about Bruce's mother?

"Do you see why working at Bluejay wouldn't satisfy a...city person, like yourself?"

Once again, his eyes lingered, taking in the unruly copper curls touched with gold by the late afternoon light, the straight small nose with its sprinkling of freckles, the tilting eyes with their long straight lashes. Before Alana could reply, Grace appeared around the door, blond hair freshly combed, makeup very recently and carefully applied—all in honor of Rand Evans, Alana suspected. Irrationally, she felt annoyed, especially when he grinned up at Grace so charmingly, revealing white, slightly crooked teeth, which only added to his rugged good looks.

"Can Anne come in just for a moment to tell you goodbye?" Grace asked, posing her plump, sensual body in the doorway. She motioned to the child hidden behind her. Anne was six, an impossible blond tomboy whose elbows and knees wore constant scabs, an effervescent smiling child whom everyone loved, and who returned the affection wholeheartedly. She clutched a homemade stocking doll in one hand, and as Alana came out from behind the desk, the girl bounced into the room, throwing her arms around Alana's waist in a hug. Then, freeing her arms, tucking the doll handily in an armpit, she signed with lightning speed, "I come to say goodbye for the summer, Ms Campbell. I go home now for two months."

Alana crouched down at the girl's level, uncomfortably conscious of being very close to gray-trousered legs and huge shiny black loafers. She formed her answering message with her fingers close to her face, saying the words aloud as she signed them.

"I'll miss you, Anne. Have lots of fun this summer, okay?" The girl planted a noisy kiss on Alana's cheek. She waved the doll excitedly under Alana's nose. "Grace gave to me," she signed, and with a cheery wave, ran out. Alana got to her feet, shaking her head and smiling widely. Grace probably had given similar small gifts to every single child in school today.

Rand Evans's eyes had been riveted on the exchange between her and Anne. "The way you talked with her," he blurted. "Is that how Bruce will have to learn to talk?" It was obviously a subject he hadn't yet thought about.

"Sign language, yes. We teach both sign and speech here, but at first, most children just learn to sign. It gives them immediate communication, a key to a very confusing world." Her glance rested on the now-sleeping child he held. "Signs are a gift of love, I've always thought." Leaning back on the edge of the desk, she smiled at him, relaxing with the subject she loved. Why was his gaze so compelling, holding her in an almost physical embrace?

"Love, Ms Campbell?" His scoffing tone surprised Alana. "Necessity, perhaps. Convenience, certainly," he added. "But love...?"

She leaned toward him slightly, gesturing at Bruce. She needed to make him understand. "The deaf live in an isolated and very lonely world. A teacher struggles to break the barrier of that silence. When a deaf child first tries to share his thoughts and feelings through the use of sign, his teacher is receiving a gift of love."

Rand was silent, listening intently. Then he flashed

her that unexpected, disarming, little-boy grin. "I see why Dr. Lane recommended you so highly." His voice sounded almost admiring. Alana dared to meet his eyes, and instantly the strange prickling awareness sprang to life between them. She knew he felt it too, because he awkwardly gathered his son close, and stood up, filling the office with his presence, making her feel she should hide behind her desk, out of the range of his powerful aura. Instead, annoyed with herself, she stood her ground only inches from him. He smelled faintly of soap, cigarettes, warm sleeping child, subtle aftershave.

"I'll come by tomorrow morning. Perhaps by then you'll be able to suggest something. I haven't much time to get this tutor affair settled." He speared her with a glance. "Dr. Lane did assure me you'd help."

Blackmail, now. His nerve was colossal, almost equal to his attractiveness. She opened her mouth to tell him so, but he was already disappearing out the door, with Grace dancing attendance.

Alana had no time to recover before the flamboyant entrance of yet another broad-shouldered male.

"Johnny," she gasped with delight as he swung her up and off her feet. His handsome face was split by a wide grin, and she wrapped her arms around her brother's neck, thrilled at this unexpected appearance after several months. But he set her down abruptly and moved to the window.

"What did that guy want, Alana?"

Exasperated and amused at her brother's protectiveness, Alana rolled her eyes heavenward. "Johnny, this is a school. The man has a deaf child. He needed some information."

"I didn't like his looks—" He turned, and Grace was entering the office, her approving and speculative eyes going over him.

"Mr. Evans left this paper with his address—in case you need to contact him," she purred, not taking her eyes from Johnny. Alana glanced at it—the Granville Island Hotel. Did he think she was planning on spending the evening rounding up tutors for him?

"Introduce me to this lovely lady, Red," her brother was ordering, "or I won't take you out to dinner after all."

TWO HOURS LATER, Alana sat across the table from John, reveling in the early-evening calm just before sunset, watching tugs and pleasure craft float past the outdoor restaurant. When Johnny announced he was taking her to Pelican Bay, the popular new "in" spot overlooking False Creek, she'd hesitated only a moment. It was, coincidentally, the restaurant serving the hotel where Rand Evans was staying. With all the eating places in Vancouver, why did Johnny have to insist on that one? She really didn't want to see the disquieting visitor again today. But it was Johnny's night, and Alana gave in to him. Of course, there had been no sign of Rand Evans anyway. Granville Island was large, and teeming with people. Alana was at ease and happy.

John tipped their bottle of white wine, measuring a careful half into each stemmed glass. Catching Alana's eye, his long fingers spelled out a toast their father had often used. "Good wine, good food and absent friends." Silently sharing memories of the man they'd loved so deeply, they lifted glasses in tribute, oblivious to the curious stares John's finger language attracted from other diners.

They sat on cedar decking, nearly overhanging the river. Sophisticated waiters bustled in and out of the swinging doors while high overhead, a constant busy rumble signaled the heavy flow of traffic crossing the Granville Street Bridge. John shook his head in amazement.

"When the Force first posted me to Vancouver, this whole area under the bridge was a welter of warehouses and smelly sheds. I can't believe all this has sprung up so quickly."

Before dinner, they'd wandered through the market where open stalls offered a hypnotic array of fresh produce. Colorful eggplant, cabbage, beets, purple onion, squash, lettuce and carrots rioted close beside pineapples, mangoes, grapefruit, honeydew. Down the aisles of the huge roofed area, long glass-fronted refrigerators held squid, oysters, halibut, live lobster, shrimp, whole pink salmon. The market was a tribute to Vancouver's unique blend of the exotic and the ordinary. Even the air was a feast of odors, freshly baked bread of every type, coffee ground to order, flower stalls redolent of freesia and daffodils, bagels hot from ovens. And everywhere, elbow to elbow, people of every nationality were lining up at food stalls for spinach pie or lasagna, tasting a grape from a fruit vendor offering advice on what to buy. A turbaned old man in silk pajamas had lectured Alana seriously about avocados. "Not the large, not this time of year. Goodness gracious madam, no flavor. Buy the small."

"He's sizing you up for his harem," Johnny had warned. "I'll have to see what he offers for you." Alana punched him on the arm.

Outside, wooden boardwalks led past theaters and art

galleries, pottery shops and bookstores sharing quarters in what had been, as John remembered, old warehouses. Granville Island had become a meeting place for residents and tourists alike—there were several hotels and numerous restaurants like the one where Alana and Johnny now sat.

Sipping the slightly tart wine, Alana studied her brother, noting the changes since she'd last seen him. "Your hair is longer," she remarked. "And I thought the Mounted Police didn't allow beards. Or mustaches."

"C'mon, Red," he teased, using the nickname that had driven her into screaming, kicking frenzies when she was a child. "All this trimming suits me, don't you think? The RCMP needed a sex symbol in their ranks, and I'm it! Photographers, interviews—" He stroked the Fu Manchu mustache ostentatiously, leering at her, his hazel eyes twinkling.

"Idiot. Tell the truth. I'll bet they've kicked you out for breaking too many hearts." With his tall, lean athlete's build packed into a smartly tailored uniform, and his off-green eyes, chestnut hair, and wicked grin, John left a string of women behind him after years of being transferred here and there. Surprisingly, most of them had remained his friends, writing letters that were forwarded to him, pink and purple envelopes smelling of perfume. Alana had seen them, tossed carelessly wherever he was staying, their postmarks like a road map of Canada pinpointing his Mounted Police career. She shook her head at him, short curls bouncing around her ears.

"Johnny, seriously, how come you're out of uniform? Are you working here now? I haven't seen you in so long, and I do miss you. With dad gone..." She swallowed hard. Their father had died in a logging accident the year before. There were no other close relatives, so that left just her and John. Their mother had died when they were entering their teens, John twelve and Alana nearly eleven. She'd been a wonderful mother, warm and funny and caring, a teacher of the deaf like Alana. Always an unusually close family, their mother's death had left the children frightened and bereft. Despite his own heartbreak, their father had spent the next years making a home of each logging camp he worked for, so his children could be with him for their summer holidays. Only looking back did they realize how meticulously he'd planned their time together—fishing trips, hikes, camping and picnics they'd believed spontaneous ideas of their own. Alan John Campbell had been unique—a perceptive, thoughtful man who devoted his life to his children.

The usual tidal wave of emotion washed over Alana—sorrow, horrifying guilt and remorse, the empty aching loss his death had brought. She forced it down, pushing it like a terrifying jack-in-the-box deep into her subconscious mind, slamming the lid, making her voice steady as she queried her brother.

"Will you be working here, Johnny?"

Their waiter arrived just then, bringing freshly caught pink spring salmon stuffed with shrimp, buttery golden biscuits, lettuce salad with creamy blue-cheese dressing in a huge wooden bowl. He fussed with their wine, served the salad and finally left. The sun was almost gone, dipping behind the mountains in a fanfare of scarlet and crimson.

John had caught a note of longing in her voice. He

sounded apologetic as he began, "Lana, I've started a job I've wanted a long time. I've been on a training course—it's special duty, working undercover." He stroked the drooping mustache, watching her eyes grow large and concerned.

"What...where—" she began, and he held out a hand to stop her.

"I can't tell you much—undercover work is on a 'need-to-know' basis." He took a mouthful of salad, chewing appreciatively. "Good salad. Anyhow, as long as I'm undercover I won't be able to contact you. And I'm not sure where I'll be." He hesitated, anticipating her reaction to his next statement. "Lana, if you should happen to see me here in Vancouver, on the street or somewhere...well, you're going to have to ignore me. Pretend you don't know me. Let me get in touch with you instead." He calmly took another huge mouthful of salad, chewing methodically, avoiding her eyes.

Alana's mouth felt papery and dry. "Johnny Campbell, this must be dangerous." All Alana's reservations about her brother's career surfaced forcefully.

Alan Campbell had been the proudest of men when his son was accepted to train for the Royal Canadian Mounted Police, but Alana had always felt a nagging sense of dread about Johnny's chosen vocation. His occasional offhand comments about some of the more violent aspects of his work frankly terrified her. There seemed no meeting place between his world of criminals and violence, and hers of children and teaching. She was certain undercover work was dangerous—probably *the* most dangerous area of that cloudy criminal world her brother confronted with such zest.

Knowing her thoughts were always mirrored by her

too-mobile features, she didn't even attempt to hide her dismay. "It *is* dangerous Johnny, isn't it?" she insisted. He still refused to meet her eyes. "Why do you have to volunteer for these things?" she moaned.

"Let's just say it's challenging," he finally said. "And I've told you before why I want to do this. Life's an adventure." His tone became teasing. "You're way too young yourself to be so stodgy. And before you blast me, close your mouth, Red. People are staring. This assignment isn't life threatening, and I get a fat expense account which is paying for this lovely meal you're not eating. Eat, eat, Red. You're getting downright skinny." He eyed her figure in its slim red cotton mini dress. "Well, you're not too bad—yet. But with that sharp tongue, I'll never get you married off if you lose your looks."

She refused to be distracted by his teasing. "What if something happens to you, Johnny? You're my only brother, you're the only relative I have," she said plaintively. "Tell them you want to transfer to the traffic detail. That way, you'd be around if I need you."

"If you ever need me, just leave a message at headquarters here. They'll make sure I get it, wherever I am. And I'll come." His gaze sharpened. "You're not having any trouble with that so-called doctor you were engaged to, are you?" His tone was ominous, and she flushed, hating to be reminded. She shook her head emphatically. "Of course I'm not. Even if I were, I could handle it. I've never seen him again, after... Johnny, I'm capable of managing my own affairs. Glen Lewis was simply a bad mistake in judgment."

"Everybody's entitled to one mistake. Just don't let an idiot like him sour you on men, Alana. There's a lot of us good guys around." He smiled gently at her.

Unbidden came the vivid image of Randall Evans, tall, powerful—gently cradling his son. Soft hair, hard eyes, cool, arrogant, irritating. And somehow, her intuition whispered, as emotionally injured as she was. What were his shuttered eyes hiding? More than just the natural pain of finding his son handicapped by deafness. Why on earth should she be thinking of him now? She struggled to fix her attention on what John was saying.

"Is she married? Steady boyfriend? Divorced?" He shook his head at Alana's confusion, repeating patiently, "Grace. Your secretary. I'm interrogating you for details. Now pay attention." He tapped her knuckles playfully with his fork.

For the next half hour, as the dusk turned to night and the golden carriage lamps around the deck came alight, they bantered back and forth. Alana firmly warned John off her friend unless his intentions were strictly honorable, smiling wickedly to herself as she said it. Nothing would put Grace off faster than honorable intentions. Grace had barely survived an early, disastrous marriage—she wasn't about to risk another involvement. With the support of her family, she'd taken secretarial training and become independent. Too independent, Alana suspected at times, watching her friend wind one handsome male after another around her soft fingers, retreating rapidly when the situation threatened to become serious. Grace and Johnny were really very much alike, Alana mused. Charming, earthy, humorous—and elusive.

Their final cup of coffee finished, Johnny excused himself to go and pay the bill. Alana lingered close to the railing near the water, idly enjoying the dancing play of lights in the dark depths. She glanced over her shoulder, watching for Johnny, and instead, caught a profile view of...blast it! It *was* Randall Evans, just entering the deck dining area.

Her heart began to pound inexplicably, and Alana wondered if he'd glance over and see her. He wore a dark suit, its expensive, well-tailored lines sculpting his massive yet trim frame. He turned to speak to a waiter behind him, and Alana's breath caught at the beauty of the nordic-looking blonde who'd been hidden on his far side. She wore a black silk jump suit, bloused at the waist, its neckline dipping brazenly deep so her lack of a bra was immediately apparent. Incredibly long legs ended in high silver sandals. Her face was perfectly made up, its small features almost doll-like. It was a beautiful, but not an animated face. As Alana stared, unable to look away, the woman suddenly stumbled awkwardly, causing Evans to shoot out a steadying arm, wrapping it securely around her slender waist. The intimate gesture caused an ache somewhere in Alana, a stab of...envy, perhaps?

John suddenly appeared at Alana's side, skillfully maneuvering them out a side exit, fortunately not noticing Alana's heightened color or her slightly shaking hands. There was absolutely no reason to be upset just because Randall Evans, a man she'd met only once, happened to be out for an evening with a beautiful woman. What was the matter with her?

John settled their parking fee and unlocked the doors on his old silver Thunderbird. Alana numbly climbed in, berating herself silently. A man as vital as Rand Evans would naturally have an address book full of beautiful women's phone numbers. It was stupid and gauche of her to respond to his physical presence the way she obviously had today. First flushing and stammering like a schoolgirl, and now feeling ridiculously and incredibly betrayed because he was having dinner with another woman. At least he hadn't seen her. She hadn't been forced to speak to him or be compared in her bargain basement cotton to the perfect creature in black silk.

"You're not still brooding about my job, are you Alana?" John asked, and she jumped guiltily. He was threading his way through heavy evening traffic in the direction of her Kitsalano apartment. She ought to be worrying about Johnny, rather than about a stranger.

"No, no," she mumbled, then shook herself and chatted about everyday matters for the next ten minutes.

"Have to hurry, Red," Johnny said as he pulled up to her apartment building and glanced at his watch. "I'm back on duty in ten minutes." He ruffled her curls, made a gentle fist and tipped her chin. "I worry about you, Red. I don't want you hurt again." He kissed her cheek, then gave her a brotherly squeeze that almost cracked her ribs. His eyes flicked once more to his watch. "Gotta go. Be good, little sister. Remember, if you need me—"

"Notify headquarters," she finished for him. "They'll put me on the waiting list." She leaned across the seat and hugged him once more.

"Don't let the dragons get you, okay, Johnny?" Her voice was shaky as she slid quickly out of the car, slamming the door and hurrying up the concrete walk to the building. He honked jauntily at her. She turned and forced a smile. He signed, "Love you, Red," through the windshield, and before she could answer, he gunned the engine and sped off down the street.

Slowly, feeling let down, sad and lonely, she climbed the stairs and unlocked the door to her bachelor suite on the second floor. Switching on a lamp, she went to the stereo and flicked a button. Soft music filled the room. Working as she did so near the world of silence, music was a luxury, the one area that many of her adult deaf friends mentioned when asked what they missed most by being deaf. Tonight, though, the soft, melodic strains failed to soothe her as they usually could. Her mind was a tumult of concern about Johnny's undercover work, disappointment that he wouldn't be around for the summer... all interlaced with the most vivid and disturbing images of the stranger named Rand Evans. Well, it didn't matter.... Alana had no intentions of seeing him again—after tomorrow.

GRACE EYED HER SPECULATIVELY when Alana rushed in late the next morning, carrying her Adidas bag containing her jogging gear. The plump blond silently handed her a cup of coffee, then waited until it was half gone before she announced, "I know this is adding insult to injury, but the board has called an emergency meeting this morning at ten. I tried to call and tell you, but you'd left already."

Alana groaned. Her head ached from the wine the night before. She'd spent a restless night, not falling asleep till just before the alarm rang. Her eyes felt scratchy. In the night, she'd planned in detail how she would conduct this morning's meeting with Rand Evans. Then, she would take a very long lunch hour and spend it jogging around the park. She kicked the bag containing her shoes and running gear in disgust. A board meeting could last hours and hours. Besides, she wasn't dressed for it. Some perverse demon had prompted her to don her oldest faded jeans and a shapeless green shirt—she'd anticipated no other visitors this final day of school with all the children gone and only paperwork to catch up on. Well, it was either her jeans or her jersey running suit. A grim smile touched her mouth as she imagined the reactions of the stuffy committee should she turn up in short shorts and a singlet. A nagging feeling of foreboding about this unexpected meeting stole over her as she gathered various reports together that they might want to review.

"Mr. Evans also phoned before you came in. He said he'd be here about eleven," Grace called just as Alana hurried out.

"Phone him and cancel. I won't be available." That settled that, at any rate. "Tell him I can't be of help to him, and I won't be in this afternoon, either." She sped off down the hall, feeling strangely let down. A pang of guilt struck her, thinking of the child with his halo of blond curls, and Dr. Lane's misplaced confidence in Alana's ability to help. Undoubtedly, Bruce needed a tutor. Well, there were bound to be elderly, efficient teachers around who would meet with his father's approval. Alana just didn't know of any. But good jobs were scarce, and undoubtedly Rand would pay well; he cared deeply about his son.

Alana opened the door to the board room, smiling determinedly at the assembled sober faces arranged around the table, noting their dark business suits, their correct pale shirts, their knotted ties. And the one proper gray shirtdress. Smiling, she sat down.

A SHORT HOUR LATER, her smile had disappeared. Maybe forever. The board meeting had been uncharacteristically short and to the point. Her nagging doubts over the past months' budget sheets should have warned her.

Communicate was closing permanently. The government grants had been withdrawn as a result of general cutbacks, and there simply weren't enough private funds to run the school. Student fees had formed only a minuscule portion of the budget—Alana had been proud of the fact that Communicate didn't cater only to the children of the well-to-do. The students would be directed to the provincial school, and Alana's duty was now to inform the three teachers she'd hired that they no longer had jobs in September.

The concerned board members had expressed effusive praise for the work she'd done, and woodenly, she'd thanked them. As she left the board room, her stomach was nauseated, her hands icy. Communicate had represented a dream for those involved in deaf education, a huge step ahead in technique and application. Now, it was only a dream—a dead dream.

Unlike Alana's teachers, Grace took the news philosophically. "There's always work around for secretaries," she said stoically, when Alana told her. "But how about you?" It was late to apply for a September teaching job—most of them would have been filled months ago.

Alana shrugged, then rolled her head from side to side, aware of the tenseness in her shoulder muscles and the feeling of total defeat she experienced as she reviewed the morning.

"Grace, I'm going out for a run right now," she decided impulsively. "I won't be any use around here anyway, the way I feel." An overwhelming need to escape overcame her, a need to run until her mind could sort everything, make new plans, overcome the desperate sense of depression growing within.

Pushing the office door shut, she stripped off her clothes, yanked on the white jersey singlet, the brief white running shorts with their attached panty. She relished the free, sensuous feel of the silky cloth against her skin, trying to stop the events of the past hour from running nonstop through her brain.

Jamming her feet into well-worn gray track shoes, she quickly left the building by the side door, anxious to avoid any board member still around. Soon, her battered green Toyota was nosing its way across the city on its regular route to the place Alana liked best to run— the six-mile seawall surrounding Vancouver's unique thousand acre Stanley Park.

Twenty minutes later, she was pushing against a giant cedar tree, stretching her calf muscles, bending and arching her pliant runner's body to warm it. The intoxicating smell of seaweed and ocean washed over her as she began a slow trot. Moving steadily, her body soon found its own rhythm. The seawall curved in front of her, ocean on one side, park drive on the other, all but deserted at this hour. Passing the Vancouver Yacht Club, she drank in the heady blueness of the sky, the gentle waves bobbing the myriad brightly colored yachts up and down like toys, the sunshine glancing off glass walls of high-rises across the narrow inlet separating the park from the city's heart. Alana increased her pace slightly, concentrating on breathing evenly, in-out in-out. Gradually her thoughts gentled, sensation taking over. Running was the best tranquilizer in the world, she exulted.

The deep voice from close behind her left shoulder startled her, made her falter in midstride. She would have gone down if a huge hand hadn't grasped her upper arm.

"Careful, there. Lovely down here, isn't it?" asked Rand Evans companionably. He was puffing slightly, and his hand still gripped her bare upper arm. She wrenched away.

"What—" her breath seemed to come only in short gasps "—what do you think you're doing here?"

Today he wore a navy suit with a deep-blue shirt. He'd loosened his tie, and it hung rakishly off to the side. His suit jacket hung over one shoulder, suspended on two fingers. The deep-set eyes she'd thought might be black showed now to be a rich chocolate brown, fringed in thick brown lashes. His shirt sleeves were rolled back, revealing softly matted hair down corded, muscular forearms.

"Grace told me where to find you." He seemed surprised she'd had to ask. "She's kindly keeping Bruce for me while I'm here."

Damn, damn Grace, Alana fumed. She felt suspiciously close to tears. Running was *her* time, her way of getting free of just such tensions as he represented. Unreasonably, instantly, she felt murderously angry with him, as if he were to blame for all the morning's problems. He was studying her face and she felt the tears spring to her eyes, her lips quiver.

"Is something wrong, Ms Campbell?" he queried.

His own words from the previous day now rang in her brain. *I'd hardly expect you to understand.* Even if she were willing to relate all the things that were wrong, he wouldn't understand. He was an egocentric male who only cared about finding a solution to his own problem—in fact, he fully expected her to solve it for him. He was here expecting it, when she needed to be left alone. How dare he pretend concern for her problems?

For some irrational reason, the memory of the icily beautiful woman he'd had on his arm—in his arms—the night before added to her growing fury.

"What are you doing here?" she demanded again, hearing her voice quiver with anger.

"We have something to discuss, don't we?"

A small breeze off the water chilled her. The warmth from the short run was disappearing. Why was she standing here freezing, allowing him to control her? Here, she wasn't Ms Campbell, supervisor of Communicate, conscious of public relations. After this morning, she was free anyway. The too-young, probably unreliable Ms Campbell. She owed this man nothing.

Taking a fast step away from him, she turned her back and began to run again, increasing her speed with every step. Dressed as he was, he'd never follow—not wearing an expensive business suit and thin-soled Italian loafers.

After the first hundred yards, she dared a glance over her shoulder. To her utter horror, there he was, a scant eight feet behind, jacket bouncing over his shoulder, thick feathery brown hair blowing in the breeze. He smiled widely and raised a friendly palm to her.

Whirling away, she began to run in earnest, far faster than usual. On her left, totem poles rose in stately columns. To her right, the inlet widened. Two joggers in blue warm-up suits came toward her, their curious eyes intent on the man behind her and his strange choice of jogging gear. A stitch tore at her side, eased, grabbed again, forcing her to gulp shallow breaths. Running too fast, her brain warned. But, incredibly, she could still hear him right behind her, his leather soles scraping the cement.

Two more runners were approaching, grinning broadly as they swept past. One hollered, "Give the poor guy a break, lady. Let him catch you."

She was now uncomfortably aware of what her back view must consist of, the running shorts cut high on her buttocks—it was almost as if she could feel his eyes on her body. And he was saying something, grunting the words out between gasping breaths. "Wanted to make you a proposal over dinner...no time, have to leave at four-thirty today...damn you, woman, will you *stop* a minute and *listen* to me?"

But she could no more stop now than explain the unreasonable panic making her run away from him. She broke into an all-out gallop, a panicked flight, and she heard him curse foully. And she was jerked almost off her feet as calloused hands grabbed both shoulders, arresting her in midstride. For a minute, she knew they would both fall, and then his strength righted their balance.

"Get your hands off—" Panting heavily, she twisted, trying to break his hold, but the hands biting into the soft flesh of her shoulders were like iron clamps. Effortlessly, he turned her to face him. His tie was gone. The buttons on the blue shirt were open halfway down. The soft mat of brown curling hair on his chest moved up and down with each gasping breath. Alana's own heart was pounding madly, half from the insane exertion of the last moments, but half with his nearness. His body heat radiated over her in waves, and she smelled his clean, warm, panting breath on her face with its faint tobacco tinge. His jacket had dropped at their feet, and his deep-brown eyes glared fiercely down at her. Before she could think or move, he drew her fully against him, roughly sliding his arms down from her shoulders until she was trapped in his embrace. The buttons of his shirt pressed through the flimsy singlet she wore. She tried frantically to twist her head away from the face descending over her own, blocking out sun and sky. But one of his hands moved quickly to grasp her head, large fingers spreading to easily cradle her skull, hold it immobile, forcing her lips to meet his own.

After that first rough contact, his anger seemed to dissipate—and with it went her own. The kiss gentled, deepened, lips nibbling, teasing, tasting, and abruptly she stopped struggling. The hands she'd used to pummel the solid wall of masculine chest paused, hovered, slipped beneath his arms, making her shudder when they came to rest in the intimate, damp warmth. It became a kiss of discovery, of introduction, an embrace that drew a deep and hot response from the depths of her body. She could feel the thundering of his heart against her breasts, the almost searing heat of his flesh through her clothes and his. Her nipples hardened, warmth suffused her lower body, and she lost any will to resist. Sensation, like a separate dimension, engulfed her and she was aware only of this moment, the pleasant roughness of his trousers against her bare legs, the pressure of each finger touching her scalp, the corded muscular arm encircling her back, the salty taste of healthy sweat from his skin.

A girl's high-pitched giggle made her pull abruptly away from him, her face suddenly scarlet. This time he released her instantly, looking down at her with an expression that must have mirrored her own surprised confusion.

Two young teenage girls stood nearby, openly leering at them, licking chocolate ice-cream cones between bursts of giggles. Reluctantly, at Rand's savage glare, they began to edge away. Alana stood immobile, dazed.

He rubbed a hand across his neck, and burst out, "I'm sorry. God, I'm sorry. I lost my temper, chasing after you like that, and then—well, I guess I lost my head as well."

Now Alana was burning with embarrassment remembering the extent of her response. She took refuge in anger.

"What's wrong with you, chasing me that way?" Her voice was high and shrill. An old man walking past looked at her disapprovingly, and she lowered her voice. "Is that how you get whatever you want, by using brute force?" Somehow, she had to dispel the effect of that embrace, put the whole incident into perspective.

The look he shot her was veiled, and a muscle jumped in his cheek as he clenched his jaw. But his tone was once more controlled, almost distant when he answered. "I said I was sorry. I'm not a rapist. I was mad, frustrated—I turned up at your office this morning, ready to apologize for the way I behaved yesterday." He rubbed a hand through his hair as he bent to pick up his jacket.

"I was going to ask—beg you—to consider tutoring

Bruce just for this summer, until I can arrange a more permanent situation." He held out a palm toward her as she opened her mouth to refuse point-blank.

"Hold it...hold it. I know what you're about to say. Give me a break, please, let me explain a bit before you race off again. God, I'm a smoker, I won't live through that twice." There was a trace of a twinkle now, and the hard mouth under the mustache curled up. Alana closed her mouth firmly, resisting an urge to giggle. She folded her arms across her chest. Defense against the breeze? Or an attempt to cover the erect nipples poking through her singlet.

"Besides, I'm not dressed for this," he went on ruefully, lifting one elegant loafer and pointing to the scuff marks scarring the toe. "You definitely have me at a disadvantage," he concluded, his glance running like molten heat down her brief white shorts, high cut on tanned thighs, skimming down the long muscular runner's legs whose slender curves had been sculpted and defined by exercise. She hugged her arms closer to her chest, turned and began walking briskly along the winding path.

He strode easily beside her, his attention seemingly intent on a tug inching its way out of the harbor. High above their heads Lion's Gate Bridge hung suspended from the sky. They walked in silence.

Then he began.

"My son," he said simply, "is the center of my life." There was a well of bitterness under his control. "I'm thirty-five years old. Until last week, I thought I could deal with anything life could hand out." He thrust his hands deep in his trouser pockets, coat carelessly tucked beneath his arm.

"Last week I found out for sure that Bruce is deaf, that no operation, no amount of money—nothing is going to make him hear. These have been pretty tough days to get through. You see, to me he's not a 'three-year-old male, deaf from unknown causes.'"

He was quoting the medical reports she saw so often, the impersonal folders outlining personal tragedies. Now there was anger in his voice, and Alana found herself admiring his honesty, understanding so well what he meant.

"God damn it, he's...my son. I must help him, any way I can." They strode on, and she didn't look at him. The vehemence faded, and he went quietly on. "Yesterday, I watched you with that little girl. Dr. Lane was right. You have this thing with children. With deaf children." Alana could tell it still hurt him to use the word.

"The doctors say Bruce is too withdrawn, too remote for a child his age." Now there was an undertone of fear. Did Bruce have other problems, besides deafness? Or, as often happened, had he just created a world for himself where he felt secure?

"There are...complications in my life that undoubtedly have affected him." He stopped suddenly, pounding one clenched fist into the other palm, ignoring the intrigued glances of couples strolling past.

"I know Bruce is intelligent. I know that with training, he would be just as—as happy as that little girl is. But who the hell is going to teach him?" He seemed to collapse, his shoulders slumping. He began to walk, his hands again shoved deep in his pockets.

Against her will, against every shred of common sense, a wealth of compassion was growing inside Alana, becoming mixed with all her conflicting emotions about the man at her side. The challenge of this child excited her, she admitted to herself. He was undoubtedly right about the boy's intelligence. Deaf children were often withdrawn, cut off as they were from the world of sound. She felt instinctively that Bruce simply needed training. How challenging, how miraculous it could be, watching such a child unfold, respond! Direct interaction with small children was the very thing she'd missed these past two years. And that was why she'd been so dissatisfied with her job.

Also, her curiosity was piqued by the ominous-sounding valley Rand described as so unsuitable for women. It aroused her obstinate nature, made her long to prove him wrong because he was so sure he was right. And, one part of her argued, he had suggested a contract only for the summer. Her job at Communicate was over. Who knew if she could find another on such short notice? She'd saved some money, but not enough to last for months, certainly. Johnny was gone, heaven knew where. And hadn't he just last night accused her of being too stodgy? Her ties with the city this summer were tenuous at best.

The only disturbing factor was Rand himself, and this insane physical response she had to him. Hormones, she decided, striding along, not hearing even the gulls screaming overhead. The response of a too-healthy body curbed by a Victorian set of principles. The Victorian Virgin, Glen had sneered. She shivered, thrusting the memory back down with the others.

A gull who suddenly swooped in front of her made her aware that they were marching along, faster and faster, silently and separately lost in their private thoughts, oblivious to the winding seawall, the sound of the water slapping gently just below them.

Impulsively, she reached out a hand to his warm and furry arm.

"Why don't you try to make me an offer I can't refuse?" she asked mischievously, knowing her slanted eyes were flirting up at him.

He stopped and swung toward her so fast she stepped back, startled. The intense joy on his features made her feel suddenly humble, and the amount he instantly named as monthly salary was more than she'd earned at Communicate in two months. She met his eyes boldly, stretched out her hand to shake his, firmly ignoring the sensory pleasure of having her fingers engulfed in that monstrous paw.

"A two-month contract?" His smile was dazzling, the worry lines between his eyes smoothing, eyebrows doing their unique uptilt.

When they were walking again, he said, somewhat embarrassed, "Ah, what happened back there—" his thumb jerked over his shoulder "—I guarantee you it won't happen again."

For one mad moment, she almost changed her mind. Except that when his eyes met hers, they made a mockery of the guarantee, and she knew she had to go.

CHAPTER TWO

THE REMAINING DAYS IN JUNE passed in frenzied preparation. Alana had her apartment, her car, her plants, her friends—a million details to arrange and settle. Finally, Grace solved three at once by subletting Alana's apartment herself for the summer.

"I'm twenty-three," she announced. "It's about time I gave mum a break, so she can decide what she wants to be when us kids grow up." She eyed Alana hesitantly. "You'd better insure the car and the plants—I've been told I have a black thumb and a heavy foot."

Waving goodbye to Grace after a hair-raising ride to the airport, Alana agreed. Grace had even managed to intimidate a Vancouver taxi driver, consequently Alana had been relieved to arrive at Vancouver International in one piece. The air-conditioned coolness in the terminal building was lovely; this early July morning was a scorcher.

Two hours later, Alana stepped onto the concrete open runway in Cranbrook. The sun's intensity seemed to etch the surrounding landscape in sharp relief. Tiny wooden airport buildings and runways were plunked haphazardly down, in what seemed a green forest meadow. Beyond, stretching in every direction were the snowcapped peaks of B.C.'s rugged Rocky Mountains.

The short flight had left her unprepared for this total

change in landscape. Soft coastal gray pastels had been exchanged for this spectrum of deep-blue sky, variegated greenness of trees and purple mountains. Alana supposed the altitude, much above sea level, must be responsible for the way her heart was pounding as she entered the door of the terminal.

A smiling young passenger in a business suit held the door for her. As soon as her eyes adjusted to the softer lighting in the large, open room, she scanned the crowd anxiously for Rand.

He'd phoned the previous week, explaining that her trip was all arranged—tickets were waiting to be picked up, and accommodation was ready at his ranch. He'd added carefully that his housekeeper would make her comfortable, and Alana blurted, "Was she the lovely woman you were with at the hotel restaurant?"

The question had popped out. Instantly, Alana was horrified she'd asked; more so every second the humming silence intensified. At last, Rand had replied, "You saw me that night?" At her mumbled "yes," he replied shortly, "I was with my ex-wife. Is there anything else you want to know?" Alana couldn't think of a thing to say.

He told her there would be a car at Bluejay for her use, that he would meet her at Cranbrook and drive her the rest of the way, some hundred twenty miles.

His husky distant voice on the phone had unexpectedly brought back all the intense pleasure of the embrace in the park, the very texture of his lips on her own. Alana had burned with embarrassment for her gauche question. Why let him know she'd even noticed him? She'd nervously ended the conversation before asking all the questions she'd planned.

And now, where was he? The crowd was thinning rapidly. She didn't even know the exact location of Bluejay Ranch. What had possessed her, agreeing to be collected here like a parcel?

Her old brown suitcase and three new soft canvas bags she'd bought were circling forlornly on the luggage roundabout. Bending, she heaved one off. Before she could rescue the next, the same blond man who'd held the door appeared at her side, neatly scooping the rest and depositing them at her feet.

"There's a place to sit over there." He had a pleasant voice and a friendly smile. He picked up her bags, strode over to some chairs where his luggage was piled, and set hers beside it. His dancing blue eyes behind round spectacles admired her simple navy-blue shirtwaist. She immediately ran nervous fingers through her copper hair, setting it on end.

He gestured at the nearly empty room. "Ever see a place evacuate this fast? There must be a penalty for lingering over fifteen minutes."

Alana stood awkwardly beside her bags. Damn Rand.

"Obviously your ride's not here, either. Care for a coffee while we wait?"

His grin seemed so open and friendly. Alana smiled back at him, sinking down in the seat he indicated. "Yes, please, I would." She fumbled in her bag for change, but he was already at the counter, his slightly paunchy figure moving surprisingly gracefully. He was quite tall, about her own height. His sandy hair insisted on falling over his forehead, and the glasses gave him a studious look. He had soft, well-cared-for hands, Alana noted as he handed her the cup of steaming liquid. Settling comfortably in the next chair, he said companionably, "I'm starting a new job in a town called Elkford, west of here. Dr. Monroe was supposed to meet me, but he seems to be late." He openly studied her, adding admiringly, "Lucky break for me, I'd say. My name's David, David Williams." He extended the hand not holding the coffee, his quirked eyebrow plainly questioning.

She told him her name, adding that she also was beginning a job. "Only for the summer," she amended. Maybe much shorter, if Rand didn't soon show up. The parking lot outside the huge front windows was now almost empty.

"I'll be working at the medical clinic in Elkford," David volunteered, after Alana confirmed that her destination was near his own. "I'll bet we meet again." The idea obviously pleased him.

"You're a doctor?"

"A very recent one," he nodded. "Finished my internship at Vancouver General, applied for this job and got it. My goal is to be a family physician in a little place where everyone knows everyone and two-thirds of the population don't suffer stress-related illness. I *like* simple ailments—tonsilitis, colds, that sort of thing." He brushed back the lock of sandy hair and smiled again.

She liked David Williams, Alana decided. Could he have met Glen, she wondered? But the suave Dr. Glen Lewis would never have bothered with a young intern who couldn't benefit him in any way. Alana had realized long after the relationship ended that part of her own appeal to Glen had undoubtedly been her healthy paycheck and her willingness to spend it freely.

"Most of my classmates figured I needed psychiatric help, coming way out here," he was saying.

There were doctors, and then there were doctors, Alana pondered. This one wanted all the challenges his profession allowed, and Glen had wanted the prestige the title afforded. It gave her a glow of satisfaction to realize that thinking of Glen no longer twisted her stomach into aching knots. Somehow, in the months since she'd broken their engagement she'd stopped feeling destroyed by him. The realization made an unconsciously warm smile curve her cheeks into dimples, and sparkle the slanted gray eyes. David leaned a bit closer, his face alight with admiration and interest.

She was still smiling softly at David when she sensed someone approaching and glanced up to find Rand towering above them, blackly scowling at her, his deep-set eyes flicking angrily from her to David and back again. His huge frame seemed to dwarf David's smaller build, and his white polo shirt and beige cotton slacks were streaked with dirt and grease. A dark smear ran down the side of his face, disappearing into his mustache. He looked hot, thoroughly out of sorts and altogether forbidding. The muscle development in his upper arms bulged beneath the cuffs of his knitted shirt. Without a single word of greeting, he motioned at Alana's pile of luggage.

"Yours?" he growled.

Stunned by his rudeness, she could only nod. He swept the bags up, tucking some under his arms as though they were empty, adding impatiently, "Let's get a move on, then. It's late."

As though being late were her fault. As though he didn't give a damn whether she'd arrived or not. She felt bright flags of angry color flame in her cheeks. Getting to her feet, she thanked David warmly—very warmly—

for keeping her company while she waited, for getting her coffee, for helping with her luggage. Let Rand cool his heels while she delayed, for a change.

David was obviously puzzled as he shook her proffered hand. She could almost see him wondering why she was going off with this—this boor. But all he said was, "It's been a pleasure talking with you, Alana."

Rand hadn't waited. He was halfway across the room, stalking toward the door with long strides, not glancing back once to see if she were following. He shouldered the door open, and then waited silently until she caught up and preceded him out. Her white open-toed sandals slid clumsily underfoot in the coarse gravel of the parking lot. He passed her, still silent, heading toward a dusty dark-blue truck with an enclosed back. By the time she stumbled up, he had tossed her suitcases in, and stood with the door open, waiting impatiently. What in heaven's name was wrong with him?

His soft mop of curly brown hair was gleaming in the sun, and the stained white shirt clung sweatily to his shoulders and chest, emphasizing their deeply muscled strength. He seemed to gaze past and through her remotely, as if her image didn't register. The unusual care she'd taken with her appearance this morning added tinder to the flame of slow-burning fury building in her the past few moments. She took a deep gulp of mountain air in an effort to cool down, and then she exploded.

"You listen here, Mr. Randall-Bloody-Evans. I've flown here in good faith to work for you, and I won't be treated like this. The very *least* you can do is be polite." If the gravel hadn't been so treacherous, she would have stamped her foot with rage.

Now he looked at her. The deep-brown eyes were centered on her hot face. She narrowed her eyes at him, shooting arrows of anger. "You—you haven't so much as said hello to me, much less welcome. It was *you* who were late, not me. And—"

"Get in." The words were ominously quiet. The glare he gave her was as angry as her own. Stubbornly, she stood immobile. The heat of the midday sun throbbed into her along with the awareness he managed even now to create.

Without warning, one long brown arm swooped behind her knees, the other cradled her back. He crushed her for an instant against his chest, long enough for her to feel the rocklike hardness of him against her. Then he hoisted her in, her dress slipping indecently high on tanned thighs.

"Buckle your seat belt." His eyes were definitely on her legs. In another moment, the engine caught, gravel spun wildly, and he backed, turned and accelerated onto the highway.

"What is *wrong* with you?" The cry boiled out of her as she scrambled furiously to pull down her dress in the narrow bucket seat. Her back and legs tingled maddeningly from the sudden assault of his arms. Outside, the landscape flew past in a blur of country color.

His window was open, his hair blowing wildly. One arm looped casually out and up, the other rested lightly on the wheel. He spoke without turning his head.

"I'm damn good and hungry, that's what's the matter with me."

It was the last thing Alana expected to hear. She gaped at him in astonishment. He stared straight ahead, and recited, "There was an emergency at the mine this morning—a generator conked out. I missed breakfast and got a late start. Halfway here, the damned rear tire went flat. There went coffee break...and my clean shirt. I promised I'd be here to meet you when the plane arrived, and I'm a man of my word." His hand thumped the window frame in frustration.

"The next thing I knew, I got this." He waved a blue speeding ticket under her nose. "When I finally arrived, ready to apologize, you were having a great old time charming some dude." This time, his dark gaze traveled all down the narrow blue linen dress, noting the slit in the side that bared long legs covered in sheer panty hose. It traveled up to the golden cross she'd fastened at her throat, over the mussed copper hair.

Eyes safely on the highway once more, he added enigmatically, "I should have remembered beautiful women always find a man to take over."

"Mr. Evans," Alana burst out, exasperated with him, "I find—"

"Rand," he interrupted. "I'm not spending the entire summer with Mr. this and Ms that. Rand—and Alana, agreed?"

She tilted her chin up and nodded. Once.

Half an hour later, at a roadside hamburger stand called Burger Bob's, Rand finished his second double with everything, plus half of hers, ordered them both more coffee and lit a cigarette with a contented sigh. He stretched his legs as far as the table allowed.

Her remaining half burger lay nearly untouched, witness to the nervous knot twisting in her stomach. The man across from her was anything but reassuring, and each mile the truck had covered emphasized the ruggedness of the country she'd come to. The softness of the coastal rain forests bore no resemblance to this foliage. Here, the forests were sparser, grass yellow from the sun's intensity. She felt a stranger to this country, and to the man she'd come to work for.

Sipping her coffee, she listed the few facts he'd revealed about himself. He owned a coal mine in an area few had ever heard of, a mountainous bridge bordering British Columbia and Alberta. Alana had studied a map, pinpointing this remote southeast corner with its sprinkling of small towns.

He had a ranch, a son and an ex-wife. He was foully bad tempered, especially when hungry, and could devour massive amounts of food. He affected her the way no man had before in her life.

He was staring at her, and she hoped fervently he had no idea what she was thinking. "Going to eat that?" He pointed at her food. She shook her head, and he paid the smiling young waitress and placed a warm hand on Alana's shoulder to guide her through the door, amused when she jumped a bit and moved quickly out of his reach. Before he opened the truck door, he screwed his eyes shut and repeated, "Alana Campbell, I'm sorry for being late. Hello, I hope you had a pleasant flight. Welcome to the Kootenays." Eyes open again and twinkling wickedly, he demanded, "Doesn't that at least rate a smile?" She couldn't resist. The man was impossible. A giggle escaped her, and then they were laughing together.

She was much more at ease after that, although his size seemed to dwarf the cab of the truck, and she could feel his body too close beside her own. She blurted the first question that came to mind as a distraction from his nearness.

"Why do they call this the Kootenays?" They were

traveling through wooded hills, with very few other cars on the road.

"After its first residents, the Kootenay Indians."

One of his arms again casually crooked up and out the window. Alana noticed how his eyebrows tufted up at the ends, how the softly curling sideburns sculpted his well-shaped ears. He glanced over teasingly. "How much do you really want to know? Local history is a hobby of mine."

"Go ahead," she urged. "I'll fall asleep if I'm bored." She was as much intrigued by his low-timbered voice as the history lesson.

"Deal," he agreed, then cleared his throat in a parody of an officious professor.

"My grandfather came here from Wales, a mining engineer hired by the railway. That was in 1898. Anyway, old gramps kept a journal. From that, I learned a lot of trivia about this area, as well as some history, and a few details grandma never found out about, fortunately." He winked lewdly at her.

They were passing a sign that indicated a branch road. "That, for instance, goes to Fort Steele, the first North West Mounted Police post established west of the Rockies. Grandpa Evans was only impressed by Fort Steele because of the camels he saw there." Rand chuckled.

"Camels?" Alana was sure she'd heard wrong.

"Camels." He was enjoying this fully. "Camels were brought to B.C. about 1862. Twenty-three of them, to Esquimalt Harbor, on Vancouver Island, to be used for carrying supplies up to the Cariboo during the gold rush. They ended up all over the province, poor things. Grampa Evans saw what must have been one of the last, being used by a French Canadian prospector as a pack animal."

Rand's eyes were alive with interest and the harsh lines around his mouth had softened. He was a quite different man from the forbidding stranger he'd been an hour before. Alana watched the expressions flit across his strongly featured face, watched too as the scenery changed almost minute to minute as they drove deeper into magnificent and rather frightening mountain passes. They followed a wide and tranquil river along the valley bottom and climbed abruptly to where the highway clung along the rocky side of a mountain.

"There's a local legend that says an Indian Chief put a curse on this valley when a white man killed his daughter. Old-timers here insist the entire area still suffers from it." His voice was more serious now, the bantering gone.

"Fires and rockslides have wiped out whole towns, mine explosions have killed hundreds of miners, the entire town of Fernie once burned to the ground."

Alana shuddered. "Why do you stay, when mining's so dangerous?" Her question seemed to bring a sudden chill to the conversation.

"Modern safety procedures have taken a lot of danger out of the job," he replied finally. "But the Evans Mine is my heritage." His face became remote again. "I'd hoped Bruce would take over after me, as I did after my father. Of course, that's not possible now."

"Just because he's deaf?" As always, Alana was quick in her defense. "Bruce is capable of doing almost anything he sets his mind to, Rand." She hoped she was right. "Don't you think he should be able to choose for himself? You can't decide his life for him, deaf or not. Maybe he isn't cut out to run a mine."

The work-roughened hands tightened on the wheel at her challenging words. When he flashed a sidelong glance at her, his eyes were angry. She studied the narrow mouth beneath the mustache, remembering the taste of him, his strength, his powerful body. He was a man who wanted things his own way. Just like his hands, which guided the truck so effortlessly over the twisting mountain roads, firmly in control even at high speed, so, she suspected, would he seek to control his environment—bend it to his will. His son included, she realized with a sinking feeling—his son... and her? For all his veneer of sophistication she sensed in him a primitive spirit, as different from the suave young lawyers and teachers she'd occasionally dated as this wild country was different from the civilized, rain-washed city she'd left behind this morning.

Was he adaptable enough to become a part of the silent world in which his son was fated to live? Alana's adopted world, where graceful symbols flew from hand to hand to eye, bypassing mouth and ear. Could Rand adopt it, too?

He chose not to respond to her challenge about Bruce. Instead, he named the villages they passed quickly through, Wardner, Jaffrey, Galloway, Elko. Their two-lane road seemed now hewn from the gray rock wall, clinging above a gorge. The guardrails seemed scant protection against a drop into the valley far below.

Soon, though, they were once more on the valley floor beside a tumbling river. Small farms and meadows smelling of clover flashed past as the valley widened. The town of Fernie took only moments to enter and leave, the snowcapped peaks of the surrounding mountains forming a cradle to hold the quaint steeply banked roofs and old church spires.

"If you're tired, we can stop for coffee," Rand offered, but Alana shook her head. With each mile, she was growing more apprehensive, unable even to guess what sort of surroundings awaited her at Bluejay. The country seemed to alter so quickly. Rand must have read her feelings on her face. It irritated her, this transparent countenance she had. "Don't ever play poker, Lana," her father used to tease.

"Having second thoughts about a summer with us mountain folk?" Rand drawled now.

"I grew up as a part-time country kid," she said defensively. "Some of my childhood summers were spent visiting my grandparents' farm, outside of Toronto."

He waited for her to continue. When the silence grew, he demanded, "Well? What type of farm? Do you still see them?"

Shaking her head, she felt the short curls bounce. "They died when I was in my teens, within a year of each other." She turned to the open window, so her face was hidden. Sometimes she felt deeply her lack of family. She'd tried to contact Johnny before she left Vancouver, with no success. It had made her sharply and painfully aware of how alone her father's death had left her. She absently ran her hand through her hair, enjoying the wind playing over it.

Rand seemed determined to probe her family tree. "What about your other grandparents?"

She shook her head again. "I never knew them. Dad was sent away to school at a very early age, and he never really went home again. There were... family problems." From the little her father had told her, his Scots parents sounded both narrow-minded and cruel. "It was my Finnish Gramma I adored. She taught me how to knit, she told me stories. Why, she even taught me how to argue effectively." She glanced mischievously at him, and he smiled. Alana fingered the Nordic gold cross at her throat. It had been one of Gramma's legacies. "She even tried her best to teach me how to cook. It didn't work, though." She laughed. "Gramma used to tell me my slanted eyes—and hers—were caused by being out in the snow and northern lights so much. We were descended from the Laplanders, the people in Northern Finland who herd the reindeer. Gramma said they had to squint all the time, and finally their eyes, and ours, just stayed this way. Of course, I believed her. I used to spend hours holding my eyes as wide open as I could, hoping they'd open more. The kids used to tease me."

"I hope you've given that up. They're very exotic, those eastern eyes of yours. And very beautiful."

This personal turn to the conversation suddenly made her warmly uncomfortable. Self-consciously, she reversed the questioning.

"You spent your childhood here?" she asked, gesturing out at the countryside. "It must have been a wonderful place for a boy to grow up."

She was surprised when he shook his head. "Nope. Only my summer vacations. I went to private boarding school, in Vancouver." He named an exclusive academy, run in the English tradition. "Then I went on to UBC, for my engineering degree."

They'd attended the same university, he and she. Years apart, probably. It pleased her, to share this tiny kernel of common experience with him.

"It was a lonely childhood," he added gruffly. "That's one of the reasons I don't want to send Bruce away to school. Kids belong at home, with their parents." The line of his jaw tightened, and a tiny muscle twitched.

Then he pulled out to pass a logging truck, and they were entering a town. Welcome to Sparwood, the Clean Coal Capital of Canada, read a huge sign.

"Clean coal?" It seemed such a contradiction in terms, Alana had to laugh. They wound slowly through the modern small village, set between the ever-present hovering peaks. The highway wound close beside a mountain whose entire side was being strip-mined, the shiny black coal seams visible. Huge machines and trucks were coming and going, and clouds of black dust filled the air.

"All the coal from both surface and underground mines in the area is washed, loaded on trains and sprayed with a latex finish so it can't blow away."

They crossed a bridge spanning the Elk River. The valley was surrounded by mountains, sprawling giants whose green sides were patchworked with black scars from surface mining. Remembering a movie about the raping of West Virginia, she asked, "Are they left that way, torn apart?"

"No." Rand shook his head. "We progressively reclaim areas with seeding, tree planting. My father was one of the early environmentalists, and he insisted on controls."

There was a caustic note when he mentioned his father. Alana was curious about the influences that had formed Rand. His passion for history, his education—obviously, he was far from being the simple coal miner he often portrayed.

They turned abruptly off the highway to a well-traveled secondary road. "We'll be home at Bluejay in half an hour," he said. "Jenny will be wondering what's become of us."

Alana felt suddenly apprehensive. Would this Jenny be friendly? Was she young, pretty? Stealing a glance at Rand, she assessed once more the stern profile, lean weather-tanned cheeks, hard jaw line. Rand's blatant and disturbing virility made her next, neat conjecture seem both rational and all too logical. Jenny was probably his mistress. The old-fashioned term made Alana grimace. She should update her vocabulary, and maybe her outdated morality as well. That conclusion kept her both silent and unappreciative of the spectacularly wild and empty countryside on these final miles.

Too soon, Rand slowed the truck, turning from the paved Elk Valley Road onto a rutted gravel track winding through thick pines. A rural mailbox marked the turn. It read Bluejay Ranch.

Sunshine fell in dusty shafts through the trees. Gravel bounced under the truck wheels. Rand stopped to open a log gate, carefully relocking it behind them. With an uneasy feeling of foreboding, Alana wondered what they locked in, or out. Was the gate symbolic, a barrier between this isolated ranch and the entire rest of the world? He probably had livestock, she chided herself... but only forest stretched around.

A rustic wooden bridge spanned a shallow stream. The track made a sharp turn into a winding descent. The forest stopped as though an invisible line marked its boundary. Alana drew in her breath sharply.

Before her was a meadow, mint green with spring grass, the foreground of a scene any artist might have coveted.

In the purple hollow at the base of a mountain an emerald-green jewel of a lake shimmered like a gemstone in the bosom of the valley. Its mirrored surface was tranquil in the afternoon heat, reflecting the sun and sky. Around its edges were pine trees growing almost to the water on every side but the one closest to Alana.

There, rough grass carpeted a natural stand of silver birch, giving way in turn to wide manicured lawns interspersed with shrubs and roses. In their midst sprawled a two-story log house, its deep gray-brown mellowed with age and weather. Up one side ran a stone chimney. The roof was gabled, and covered with cedar shakes.

In the meadow were outbuildings also of logs. Several horses grazed tranquilly inside a pole fence. The gravel trail passed beside the meadow, ending behind the house in a cleared area close to a double garage.

There Rand braked to a halt, sitting for a moment with both hands folded wearily on the steering column. Then he turned toward her with a smile flooding his face. Her hand was engulfed in his. Shaking it in a strangely formal and appealing gesture, he said, "This is Bluejay, Alana. I hope you'll feel at home and happy here."

For a long moment after that, he seemed as reluctant as she to draw away from the tingling warmth of his palm pressed closely to her own.

CHAPTER THREE

AT LAST he broke the contact. She opened the door and stepped out, aware of silence—and then of birds, twittering and calling from the branches of the pines and poplars in the nearby woods. She stretched, muscles cramped from the ride, drawing in deep breaths of air free from exhaust and industry, loving the warmth of the sunlight on her skin.

From nowhere, a huge black dog bristling with fur and fury seemed to explode toward her. His teeth were bared, and he growled ominously low in his throat. Alana scrambled for the truck door, ready to leap in.

"Tad!" Rand ordered. "Cut it out, you old phony." The dog became a tail-wagging bundle of friendly tongue and welcoming yaps. "Down," Rand ordered laughingly, for now the animal was jumping madly first on him, then on Alana.

"Meet Trefusus Antropus Denningham, the First. Tad, to his friends."

Alana gaped at Rand, and then at the dog. Rand looked slightly abashed. "Well, he reminded me of certain boys at school," he explained. "All bark and no bite, with fancy double-barreled names."

An instant later, Bruce was racing to greet his father. Rand strode forward, scooped the boy up and lifted him high in the air, laughing at the child's wriggling delight.

"Hello there, tiger," he crooned, settling Bruce comfortably on his forearm. He turned so Alana could greet her new pupil. Once more she marveled at the strange whim of nature that had chosen to draw the child's features so like the man's. Even the eyebrows, still delicate on the small face, were tilted gently up at their corners, just like Rand's when he smiled. She watched for the fleeting instant the boy's sky-blue eyes rested on her face before they dropped shyly, hiding behind the long gold-tipped lashes. Reaching out, she gently took one small grubby fist in her own and squeezed a greeting, before he yanked it away. Then Rand set Bruce down, to stand with feet planted wide in exact mimicry of his father, balled up fists shoved deep into pockets in miniature blue jeans, sheltering behind his father's long legs.

Impulsively, Alana dropped to her knees on the grass in front of Bruce, careless of the blue linen dress. Again she waited patiently for the boy's eyes to rest on her, and the instant they did, she began slowly and gracefully to make signs with her fingers, repeating the message vocally as well. She held her fingers beside her face so Bruce would see both.

"Hi, Bruce," she spelled and said. "I am Alana. I want to be your friend." The dancing motions of her hands captured his attention. Fascinated, he stared at her and then smiled shyly before he quickly looked away. Getting to her feet, Alana was elated. It was a beginning.

Glancing just then at Rand, her breath caught. On his face was such a mixture of pride, fierce tenderness, vulnerability and passionate love for his son, it could leave no doubt as to his adoration for the boy she'd come here to teach. His eyes sought her own, the warmth of his gaze like a stroking hand, and she shivered despite the heat of the day.

His attention shifted. Alana turned to meet the curious dark eyes of a short, stocky man balancing on a single aluminum crutch, his right pant leg empty, pinned up above the knee. His lined face was weatherbeaten, ruddy from exposure to wind and sun. Tendrils of iron-gray hair escaped the brim of the worn cowboy hat he wore pushed to the back of his head. He looked about sixty, Alana guessed. She smiled tentatively.

"Tom Saunders, Alana Campbell," Rand introduced. "Tom's foreman here at Bluejay."

Tom nodded, wiping his hand down his jeans before he offered it. The rough brown paw with bent and broken fingernails sawed up, down, and dropped her own abruptly. Obviously ill at ease with her, he turned brusquely to Rand.

"Pumps goin' again, Boss. Had to replace the cylinder, though. Did ya pick up another intake valve?"

Soon, he and Rand were deep in discussion of motor parts and Bruce was helping tear open the box dragged from the back of the truck. Ignored for the moment, Alana watched Tom, noting how swiftly he moved in spite of the missing leg. He swung the suitcases easily out of the truck, using his crutch to prop the door open. Even with his disability, he was a graceful, well-coordinated man, and strongly muscled.

"So, Boss, finally you made it home. I nearly sent out a search party you took so damn long," called a shrill, sing-song voice. Rand greeted the woman hurrying toward them, his face wearing a wide, affectionate grin. She was short and plump, the top of her head barely reaching Alana's shoulder. Oriental, she had smooth golden skin and an oval face, and eyes shaped like Alana's. But the color was different—instead of Alana's gray, these were shining, unwavering black. She might have been anywhere between forty and sixty; it was impossible to tell.

She seized Alana's hand in both her own. "You are teacher for our Bruce. I am Jenny Chan. Glad to meet you." The words were warm and welcoming, but there was reserve and a keen intelligence behind the assessing look she aimed at Alana. Long black braids liberally sprinkled with white were wrapped carelessly round and round her head in a coronet. She wore a man's green flannel shirt like a jacket, over a printed red housedress. On her feet were tennis shoes and white socks.

"Bet you're stiff after all that driving. Did Boss even stop to give you coffee?"

The sparkling eyes were inspecting Alana minutely. Jenny would watch and wait, Alana suspected, before giving her entire support and approval to Bruce's teacher. The rush of words could be an effective cover for caution.

Alana felt both embarrassed and relieved. Certainly, this wasn't Rand's mistress. But neither did Jenny act or sound like any housekeeper Alana had ever met.

Jenny's next rapid-fire announcement solved part of the puzzle. "I was Bruce's nurse from the day he was born, and—hey, Boss, should I tell her the truth?" Jenny giggled, delighted at Rand's sudden attempt to look remote and stern. "I raised him, too!" Her thumb jerked in Rand's direction. "From the time he was knee-high to a grasshopper. And was he one stubborn kid. Him and Bruce, they gave me these gray hairs, chasing after both of them."

Rand had colored at Jenny's disclosure, and he waved a quelling hand at her. Alana was delighted. Maybe with Jenny around, she might get some information concerning this man who seemed so evasive about anything personal.

"We'll bring up the bags," Rand said. "Jenny, if you're finished relating the story of my life, take Alana up to the house."

Unperturbed, Jenny set off at a half run, talking all the while. "The pump broke, we had no water, but it's fine now, so I made lunch, and he never turns up, just when I clear away, wouldn't you know it, but the coffee's hot, and if you're hungry—"

A chickadee sang its name monotonously somewhere close, and there was a flash of brilliant blue as a blue jay ventured to the railing of the wide porch, fronting the house. There really were blue jays in this enchanted place! Neat flower beds were laid out against the softness of the aged logs of the house, and daffodils and purple crocuses bloomed. Rose bushes bordered the path where Jenny led, buds beginning to color pink and coral and yellow. The very air was heady, and bees buzzed loudly. Rough cedar boxes spilled geraniums along the porch railings, scarlet and bright green.

Jenny rambled on not expecting answers, leaving Alana free to absorb her surroundings.

They were now mounting the wide wooden steps to the veranda. Comfortable old chairs and a large round table covered in oilcloth hinted at casual outdoor meals, and a battered wooden rocking horse crouched in a corner. Jenny threw open the wide front door, and Alana stepped first into a short hallway, then into an impressively large, informal living room.

Jenny led the way down the long room where a mixture of overstuffed couches and handsome antiques seemed bathed in a sepia tone because of the log walls. The faded atmosphere almost gave the room an air of neglect. A winding staircase was visible through a corridor.

"Up here, Ms Campbell, is your room." Jenny maneuvered past a small tricycle blocking a doorway and stopped short.

"Ms Campbell..." she began.

"Please, call me Alana."

"Alana. My Bruce gets in so much mischief. I try to teach him, don't leave toys here, turn off water taps, don't play with fire. Very hard to keep him out of trouble." The dark eyes were anxious and questioning.

Carefully, Alana explained, "Kids who are deaf learn by doing. Most of what they do we classify as mischief. Actually, they're learning the only way they can." She smiled reassuringly. "He'll get much easier to handle as his language improves."

Following Jenny up the curving stairway, she felt a stab of apprehension. The assessment had hinted at behavior problems. What if she'd taken on more than she could handle? The summer could become a nightmare.

Jenny turned right, down a short hall where a stained-glass window poured color over the faded gray runner. After indicating a bathroom, Jenny opened the next door.

"Your room, teacher." Then she bustled back down the stairs.

Alana stood in a large, bright bedroom, slightly musty smelling. Walking to the windows, she found the room overlooked the front of the house and the lake.

There was no sign of other houses. Primitive magnificence, and total isolation.

On long-ago fishing trips with her father, Alana had experienced this same overwhelming feeling of being almost an intruder to nature. Her sudden transition today from bustling, sophisticated Vancouver was unsettling in a similar way, as well as making her lonely for those childhood days now lost in time.

She whirled away from the window to study her room. She wouldn't think about her father now...she couldn't let herself. *Concentrate on this lovely, spacious room, Alana.*

The log walls had been painted a pale lemon, and several small floral prints hung in tidy arrangement. The long window wall was curtained in yellow gauze, which allowed the sun free access, and the bed was a lovely white-painted iron affair. She sank down on it. The past chaotic weeks combined with today's tension to create a sudden bone-wearying exhaustion.

She jumped slightly at the tap on the door. Rand came in with her bags, setting them in a heap on the rug and studying the room.

"This was my mother's room," he commented. "When she graced us with a visit. We close off the rooms we're not using with just Bruce, Jenny and I. Tom has a place of his own, a mile or so away."

Alana didn't ask, but wondered at the relationship between Rand and his mother.

Rand walked to the window, passing close beside her. She was conscious of his body, the breadth of his shoulders as he brushed past. Grasping the bottom of the frame, he raised the window high, letting in the freshness of the summer day. "Needs a good airing in here."

His glance swept the room once more, pausing on an ornately framed photo on the wall beside the bed. The austere-looking woman in it wore a high-necked blouse, which seemed to force her chin unnaturally high. Her expression was stern but the black-and-white picture couldn't hide the softness of the hair curling around her forehead, escaping the knot high on her head in floating tendrils. Distinctive hair—Rand's hair, Bruce's hair.

"Your mother?" It was an obvious guess, and he nodded, lifting it down from the wall, blowing dust from its edges.

An ironic half smile floated across his face. "She was the forerunner of today's liberation movement. She's a businesswoman, runs a consulting firm she inherited from her father. She lives in London—has ever since I was small. She wasn't happy here, so she went back to England. Hated Bluejay. Couldn't stand the isolation." His voice became caustic. "It's a problem Bluejay seems to have. The men won't leave, and the women won't stay."

"Jenny's stayed a long time," Alana ventured.

"Jenny's different," he said, and she caught his eyes studying her in the tilted mirror of the oak dresser opposite the bed. The blue linen was hopelessly crushed, her sandals scuffed, the red-gold curls defiantly—typically, she knew—on end. How could he make her so conscious of how she looked, and of her body? She brushed a hand across her hair and he watched, a half smile tilting his lips. He moved abruptly to the door, carrying the picture with him and passed close to her. Reaching a finger out, he rubbed at a smudge on her cheek. The spot glowed, their eyes locked and held. Then he was gone, and she could hear his footsteps going quickly down the stairs, his deep voice calling a question to Jenny.

She felt utterly exhausted and looked longingly at the wide bed, covered in a hand-sewn quilted spread. The decision was made. Tossing her handbag off the bed and onto the soft gray carpet, she tugged off her sandals and wriggled her toes with relief. After a moment, she struggled out of her panty hose as well, letting them float down into a wispy heap on the rug. Hateful things, panty hose, hot and itchy. Bare legs were much better. She relaxed, leaning back on the downy pillows. The breeze caressed her, and somewhere below the open window Tad was barking. Trefusus Antropus Denningham. Her mouth quirked with amusement. Bruce's high-pitched toneless laughter sounded.

Curling her legs up comfortably, she pondered how best to reach the little boy, interest him, hold his attention. Regretting the months spent away from teaching, she admitted that although she was sad at the closing of Communicate, she could only feel immense relief at never having to attend another board meeting.

Her thoughts veered to Rand. She'd come closer to knowing him today. But he was such a jigsaw puzzle of a man, angry and aloof one moment, charming the next. Mischievous, endearing—remote, forbidding, stirring up emotions she would rather leave undiscovered.

The curtains swayed gently in the breeze. She closed her eyes, vowing to rest just a moment. Instead, she fell heavily asleep.

Disoriented, she woke to a soft humming noise and a fast rhythmic thumping. Opening her eyes reluctantly, she saw the muslin curtains slightly fanning and what looked to be afternoon sunshine on her wall. She turned her head lazily, and was pleased to see Bruce's white-blond curls where he sat, back to her, cross-legged on the carpet. Tad lay against him, tongue lolling, tail steadily thumping the floor. Bruce softly hummed, intent on whatever he was doing.

Delighted the child would seek her room, Alana swung her legs to the floor, and leaned over to watch Bruce play.

"No," she cried out, horrified. "Bruce, stop!" But of course he couldn't hear her.

He had found and emptied her handbag, discovering the marvels of her smaller makeup bag. Its contents were smeared all over his face in a mad clown's mask of assorted color. Tad's fur was also well covered with lipstick and traces of eyeshadow. What brought Alana to the boy's side in one jump were the matches he held and the charred remains of a tissue package. Other papers from her wallet were just beginning to smolder.

"No," she hollered again, snatching the smoking bundle and hastily dropping it, pounding it with her empty handbag to extinguish the flame just igniting.

Bruce cowered away, lipstick vivid around his frightened eyes, green eyeshadow in patches on his cheeks and hair. He scuttled away on all fours, rounded gaze intent on her. Opening his mouth wide, he let out a roar that brought Tad to his feet, ears back and growling low in his throat. His paws were coated liberally in rose nail polish. As Alana backed away from the dog, Bruce's roars grew in volume. The door burst open, and Rand erupted into the room.

"What the hell is going on?" he began, marching across to the group. Bruce's roars became even louder with the appearance of his father, and Tad disappeared under the bed.

Rand swooped on the matches, touched the remnants of ash now ground into the rug. He glared menacingly first at Alana, then at Bruce.

"I—I fell asleep, and—" Alana heard herself stammering and stopped. Rand had now turned to Bruce, swept him off his feet in one lithe motion, turned him over and delivered several hard swats to his backside. Bruce's howls increased to shattering proportions, and Tad sent out muffled barks from under the bed. Alana's angry voice added to the uproar.

"Don't you spank that child!"

Jenny appeared at the door, hands covered in flour and a white apron tied around her middle. Shooting an accusing look at Rand, she stretched out her arms and Bruce flew into them. Jenny carried him off, his sobs subsiding as they descended the stairs. Rand dragged a reluctant Tad out from under the bed and none too gently shoved him out the door. Then he advanced on Alana, jaw grimly set and hands on his hips. She did her best not to retreat, glaring angrily right back at him.

"You didn't have to spank him," she accused icily. It was a punishment she'd never had to resort to, and didn't believe in.

"What do you suggest I do instead—let him burn the house down?"

"Violence is no solution." She lifted her chin defiantly. He was standing far too close to her.

"Violence?" His voice rose in amazement. "You've led a sheltered life if you think those swats were violence, Alana Campbell." He moved closer still. She steeled herself not to move back, although he now was only inches away.

"In my entire life, my father never laid a hand on me. Discipline *can* be civilized, *Mr.* Evans."

"Bruce is going to grow up civilized, and if it takes a few spankings to accomplish that, then he'll be spanked." Each word was drawn out menacingly, and his eyebrows met in a scowl. He spoke with exaggerated patience. But Alana was too righteously angry to notice that dangerous patience, or the heightened color in his face.

"Civilized!" she shrieked. "You think beating a small child is civilized? A huge bully striking a helpless baby? That's civilized?" She snorted and whirled away, turning her back on him disdainfully. "Well, I've got news for you. You're about as civilized as... as a tree trunk. You don't deserve—"

The tirade ended in an involuntary shriek as she caught a glimpse of him moving swiftly toward her. His chest was heaving with rage, his eyes determined slits. She was trapped between the man and the bed. The man was murderously angry, his words shivering through her like a stereo with the bass turned full.

"You were hired to tutor Bruce, not lecture me. I'll thank you to remember that!" He didn't touch her, but she felt scorched anyway.

Taking one faltering step back, she sat abruptly when the back of her knees caught the edge of the mattress. He effectively trapped her there. Feeling definitely at a disadvantage, she glared up at him, chin jutted forward, hoping her lips weren't going to tremble. His words dropped on her like stones.

"For the short time you'll be here, I suggest you keep your opinions about my character to yourself. Here, I run things. Like it or not, you'll do well to remember that."

Too outraged at his arrogance to care about being frightened, she struggled to get up. Putting his hands firmly on her shoulders, he pressed down and held her there easily.

"You don't look so civilized yourself at the moment. With such a fiery temper, a few spankings would have done you good." Now a spark of humor flickered across the rugged face. "Your father was far too easy on you." He allowed his eyes to travel slowly over her, lingering on the sparks of hair rumpled and on end from sleep, the soft pink mark on her cheek from the pillow's fold, her hopelessly crushed blue dress riding high above bare knees. His eyes flamed for a pulse beat, and she drew her breath in sharply. An animal savagery seemed to burn between them for an instant, before he replaced it with cool amusement. Dropping his hands from her, he turned casually to the door.

"Dinner will be in half an hour."

Drawing a long, shaky breath, Alana pounded her fists on the soft quilt. "Damn you, Rand Evans," she spat viciously, and jumped with fright as he stuck his head around the doorjamb and drawled, "Randall *bloody* Evans, wasn't it?"

Jumping up to slam the door after him, she stood shaking with rage. Then she took a furious kick at the heap of rubbish still strewn all over the floor. Her bare toe connected painfully with a perfume container. Black ashes and ruined makeup flew to every corner of the room. She spent the next ten minutes scurrying around on hands and knees, trying to recover what was left of her makeup, silently using all the bad words she could remember; Johnny had taught her an awesome quantity over the years.

She hurriedly took a quick bath in the bathroom's claw-footed tub, wrapped hastily in her velour robe, and ran back to her room. When she next encountered Rand, she would be well prepared.

Rummaging through her suitcase, she found lacy scraps of satin bra and panties, midnight-blue raw silk pants and an emerald-green pullover blouse from Vancouver's Chinatown area. It was tissue silk, and the hand hemmed edge of the long shirt skimmed her buttocks. Tying on the matching belt, she felt the sensuous fabric cling to every curve. There. Comment on her grooming, would he?

Then came makeup, and she grimaced. Tad and Bruce had thoroughly used most of her meager supplies. Finding a copper-shaded lipstick with a good piece of it still intact, she smoothed it over her lips, and the result was fine; glossy, understated. Her eyelash curler was unharmed. She rolled her straight gold-tipped lashes carefully, twenty seconds right, twenty left, and peered in the mirror. Take that, Rand. The still-stormy gray eyes had thick, delectably curly lashes to frame their almond shape.

She used her hairbrush with a zeal that made her scalp tingle, and she was ready, except for shoes. Another suitcase scramble produced navy slim-heeled sandals. Enough armor. Shrugging her shoulders, drawing a deep shaky breath, she headed for the stairway.

In the living room, soft music drifted from an old sideboard converted to house an extensive stereo system.

"Care for a drink?" The lazy question came from the depths of an armchair, which had been turned to face the windows and the superb view of the lake. Evening sunset shimmered into the room. She knew Rand had watched her hesitant descent. His eyes flicked over her, recording detail without comment. Alana's eyes gleamed dangerously back at him, her cheeks still dusty rose with fury under her golden jogger's tan.

Nervously, she smoothed the wings of copper hair that waved up and away from her temples. Her senses registered the impact of Rand's attention as it moved slowly down from her wide shoulders, over the small rounded breasts. Uncomfortably she knew her nipples were showing through the flimsy silk. His gaze was palpable, tracing narrow ribcage, slender hips, long runner's legs. Bravely, she stood her ground, challenging him. But when at last his eyes met hers, there was no sign of the raw anger she'd inspired only an hour earlier.

So that's how he wanted to handle it. No confrontation, no resolution. Head held high, she smiled politely.

"A drink?" he asked again.

"Rum and Coke."

She moved gracefully to a sofa and folded herself into it. He mixed the drink and handed it to her.

"Tom will be along soon, and then we'll eat. He joins us whenever Jenny can persuade him." Rand even sounded friendly.

Relieved that she wouldn't be dining alone with Rand, she relaxed, taking appreciative sips of her rum. Tom seemed a neutral enough subject.

"Will Tom be fitted for a prosthesis soon? It must be hard on him, managing with a crutch."

Rand took a long swallow of his own drink. "Tom lost his leg five years ago, in the same mining accident that killed my father. He was a pit boss in the Evans Mine, and mining was his life." Rand swirled the amber liquid in his glass. "There's no way he'll even consider an artificial leg."

Surprised, Alana looked full at him.

"For heaven's sake, why not?"

Rand shrugged. "Stubborn, mostly. He tried one in the beginning, had problems, and refused to try again. He'd always been an underground miner. Even with an artificial leg, he couldn't go back underground. So he makes do with a crutch."

Jenny bustled in then, giving Alana a warm smile.

"Bruce had supper and his bath, and now he's fast asleep."

The comment was obviously meant to reassure her, and Alana was grateful, relieved to know the scene in her room hadn't upset the little boy too much. Alana's offer to help with dinner was firmly refused, and in another few moments Tom came in, his gray hair slicked down, his brown-checked shirt freshly ironed.

"Evenin'," he greeted them, shy dark eyes sliding across Alana's smile and away.

"Beer, Tom?" Rand offered.

"Sounds good." Tom sat down and the three of them awkwardly lapsed into silence for the endless ten minutes it took Jenny to finish preparing the food. Alana considered and rejected each subject that occurred to her, and nervously gulped her drink. The two men made no attempt at conversation.

It was a huge relief when Jenny called, "Dinner's ready."

The dining room adjoined the kitchen, and a circular golden-oak table was laid with a gleaming white linen cloth. The window here looked out on Jenny's kitchen garden, already green with lettuces and neat rows of sprouting seedlings.

Rand held Alana's chair politely, brushing her arm with his own, and she sat hurriedly, bumping the table. She felt as stiff and uncomfortable as Tom looked. Jenny bobbed up and down, from table to kitchen, serving.

Jenny was an amazingly good cook. She served clear zucchini soup, flavored with curry, fresh garden salad, hot homemade rolls. Lake trout stuffed with wild rice and herbs brought exclamations of praise from Alana. Flavor, color and taste were exquisite.

Jenny patted Tom's arm. "Fish are thanks to Tom, he caught them. Not hard to cook fish, once they're caught."

Tom's face lit up at the compliment. Obviously, fishing was a passion. Delighted to find an opener, Alana pursued it.

"Did you catch them here in Bluejay Lake, Tom?"

"Yup, the other evenin'. They were bitin' good, not like that trip we took up the North Fork, eh, Boss?" He shook his head in disgust. "Boy, did we get skunked on that one."

Rand's eyes twinkled and Tom began to relax. "It was too close to spring breakup, Tom. The streams were dirty. And besides, you brought the wrong lures," Rand gibed.

"Listen to him, trying to worm out of it now. Why, I brought the best lures—"

"What kind, Tom? What were you using?" Alana sipped the white wine. Rand answered, his tone and words annoyingly condescending. "All the usual fishing gear—we had fly rods, spinning reels, light test lines—" He made it sound as though he were instructing a kindergarten class in fishing.

"Yes, but what type of flies?" The men were watching her now, and surprise showed on their faces. Jenny was grinning, anticipating something.

"Coachmen, mostly," Tom supplied laconically.

Still sipping her wine, Alana said idly, "Dad used to lead the fly with a small Gibbs spoon if the water was cloudy."

Rand stared at her as if she'd just sprouted another head.

"You don't use a spinner when you're fly fishing." The reprimand was blunt.

"Yes you do, if the water's dirty," she defended sweetly.

Tom's sudden whoop of laughter interrupted them. "By the lord Harry, Boss, you got yourself a fishergirl here for sure. I was gonna say the same myself, we shoulda tied a spinner on those lines, so's the fish could see it. Makes sense. By Harry, teacher, who'da figgered a city gal like you woulda known somethin' like that?"

Tension entirely gone, Tom launched a discussion of the merits of certain kinds of flies, and Alana asked him if he tied his own, adding that her father had taught her how at one time, but she was rusty.

From there on, Tom was in his element, and Alana was his buddy. Jenny winked broadly at Alana several times, thoroughly enjoying Tom's ease.

Finally, Tom glanced at his watch. His eyes widened in disbelief. Grabbing the crutch Jenny picked up for him, he thanked her for the dinner.

"Got to do chores, teacher, but anytime you like, come on down to the cabin and I'll show you how to tie that Malibu. And, Boss, we gotta plan a trip into Polkaterra Lake this summer, so this gal gets a taste of some real mountain fishing." Punctuating the words with nods of his head, he hurried out, crutch swinging with every step.

"Night, teacher." The title was warmly affectionate.

Jenny was patently delighted. "I never heard Tom say so much all at one time. He took a shine to you, teacher." She bustled off to make coffee, and Rand studied Alana until she shifted uncomfortably.

"So you're a fisherman, too?" He moved his head slowly back and forth. "Couple of hours ago, I'd have guessed fishwife. How many other talents are hiding under that shiny hair?" The gibe was gentle and Alana smiled, thoroughly enjoying herself. The soft golden light of early evening crept in the open French windows near the table. The peace of the landscape and the fun she'd been having talking with Tom had made her forget totally her anger at Rand.

"More wine?"

She hesitated, then nodded. Time enough tomorrow for restraint. Jenny poured strong cups of steaming hot coffee, refusing Alana's offers to help clean up.

"There's a dishwasher, does all the work for me," she declared.

Rand picked up their wineglasses, and led the way to the roofed porch facing the lake.

"It's much cooler out here, and the mosquitoes aren't too bad yet."

Sinking into a cushioned rocking chair, Alana breathed the heady mountain air into her lungs, feeling slightly tipsy from the wine. Rand stretched both legs out before him in a chair that matched hers, crossing one moccasined foot over the other. He tipped his curly head forward, lighting a cigarette by snapping his thumbnail on the head of a wooden match and cupping the flame protectively.

The wild and rugged beauty of the landscape suited him. Here, he seemed at one with his environment, while in the city he had emanated tension. Breathing a stream of smoke from his nostrils, he said peacefully, "So you consider me a child-beating, uncivilized boor."

Caught offguard, she stammered.

"We...well, we...we seem to have very different ideas about discipline." That seemed bland enough. But why did he have to bring this up just when she was beginning to feel at home?

"What would you have done with Bruce this afternoon?"

It was a loaded question, and she thought carefully before she answered. The issue was crucial, because discipline would come up, working with Bruce closely. There would have to be some sort of agreement with Rand.

"I'd have shown him how upset I was, insisted he clean up the mess, tried to find a way to make him understand how dangerous matches and fire can be. Maybe later I'd give him a chance to experiment with fire in a safe way. Kids that age are always fascinated with fire."

His answer was mocking, derisive. "Calm, cool, controlled. How very admirable, to have such control."

The peace of the past few hours seemed to be deserting her as rapidly as the light now fading over the lake.

"Losing control solves nothing. It just teaches a child violence is acceptable." Suddenly her words sounded prissy. After all, she had to admit honestly that two swats on the backside were hardly child beating.

"Maybe," she went on slowly as a new thought surfaced, "Bruce just needs to have more contact with other children. Does he have many friends his age? Perhaps there's a preschool nearby he could attend—" She got no further. Rand sat forward on his chair, his body suddenly tense.

"Bruce doesn't need other children around, teasing him about his deafness, making fun of him. Forget that idea, right now." He rapped a fist on the chair arm, emphasizing his words. "That's precisely why I hired you, to avoid sending him where he'd be mocked or hurt." He stubbed his cigarette out in a can lid beside him. "I went to boarding school. I remember how cruel kids are to each other. Bruce stays right here at Bluejay, at least for the time being."

Flabbergasted, she sputtered, "You surely can't intend to—why, he needs other children, he..." The man was absolutely impossible. A mental image of the locked gate painted itself on her mind. Why didn't he install a moat and drawbridge, for heaven's sake.

Before she could tell him so, Jenny appeared, coffeepot in hand.

"More?" She poured, and then yawned widely. "Pardon, it's bedtime for me. I'm not as young as I was. I'll keep the pot on warm, if you want more. Good night." She paused in front of Alana. Hesitantly, she said, "My Bruce is a very good boy, really, teacher. Today, he's just excited, same as all of us. Not many visitors come here to Bluejay, so he was curious. You will see, teacher, he is very smart and tries to be good."

Embarrassed, Jenny fled. Her concern touched Alana deeply, reinforcing the very thing she'd been trying to explain to Rand. It was essential Bruce venture out of this protected world his father had created for him—it was a vital part of his education. And more than anything, she wanted to help Bruce escape the cocoon of silence nature had imposed. Would she have to fight Rand to accomplish that? He was Bruce's father, and he was her employer. He was also the most irritating, stubborn and irrational man. It was a huge challenge. Was she up to it?

Rand's elbows rested on his knees, head tipped forward so that in the growing darkness she could only see the thick brown of his hair. The sigh was exasperated. "I'm still trying to accept the fact that he's deaf," he admitted. "I feel my own kid is locked away from me. I can't talk with him, tell him stories, reason with him, the way I'd planned to—the way I thought a father should. It nearly drives me—" his fist slashed the air impotently. He raised his head, and his eyes burned into hers. "Have you the faintest idea what children in a small town are like? This is a mining town, a rough-and-tumble area. The kids are no better or worse than kids anywhere, but these kids have probably never seen a deaf kid before. Bruce would be a novelty, a—a scapegoat. Here at Bluejay, I can protect him."

Rand's raw anger and bitterness shook her, and part of her responded to what he was saying. Weakly, she tried again, struggling to find the words she needed to make him understand.

"Hiding Bruce won't make him hear.... His deafness won't go away. A problem doesn't just evaporate." She'd learned that herself, the hard way. But she couldn't tell him that now. "The earlier he learns to adjust to society, the easier it will be on him. On you, too."

"That's probably true. But for now, we'll try this my

way." There was finality in his voice, and she temporarily gave up. His next words were cool and businesslike.

"I'll need a full list of any supplies you need for his training. Anything. The hearing aid the doctors recommended should be arriving this week. If there's anything else..."

So money's no object, mused Alana bitterly. But what if Bruce needed what money *couldn't* buy—other children, contact with people. Uncharacteristically, though, she held her tongue.

For the next half hour, she outlined her general lesson plans. Rand listened closely, questioning, making astute suggestions. It was obvious he spent a great deal of time with Bruce, and he was able to give her valuable tips about his son's routine and personality, interspersed with loving anecdotes.

At last, she stood up. "That's all I can think of for now. I'm fast getting too sleepy to think at all. I want to begin getting to know Bruce in the morning, and from what you've told me, he gets up with the birds. I'd better get to bed."

He got up, too, standing close beside her in the warm darkness. His breath smelled pleasantly of wine and smoke. At first, his hand only grazed her shoulder, guiding her to the door. Then it encircled her soft upper arm before sliding down and releasing her.

"Good night." His voice followed her up the stairs, and she opened the door to her room before letting out the breath she'd been holding since he touched her. Control, she reminded herself. How did one control a pounding heart, and bones that seemed to melt just from a touch?

Somewhere across the lake, an owl hooted. Her room overlooked the porch. She could hear the creak of his rocking chair. Undressing in the dark, she imagined she could smell the smoke from another cigarette, floating up, drifting in her window.

Settling herself for sleep, she was conscious of Bluejay around her, its isolation, its beauty, its people—Bruce asleep with Tad undoubtedly nearby, Jenny in her room down the hall, Tom off in his cabin. Most of all, the compelling man still rocking quietly below who in one day had enraged, amused, confused her. Randall Evans, the boss.

It was going to be a very different sort of summer.

CHAPTER FOUR

THE SOUND OF THE TRUCK crunching over the gravel driveway awakened her the next morning. Her clock read six-thirty. Refreshed from a deep and surprisingly dreamless sleep, Alana stretched and swung her legs to the floor, shivering at the unexpected chill. Mountain country, she reminded herself, walking to the window.

The turquoise lake lay bathed in golden sunlight, and everywhere was a glistening mantle of dew, coating each leaf on the birch trees with shiny silver. The sun cleared the mountain tops and each droplet caught the light, sending tiny rainbows shooting into the morning. Entranced, Alana stood trembling with the briskness of the breeze washing over her and the exquisite beauty of sunrise in the valley.

Wrapping her burgundy robe around her she padded to the bathroom. The smell of coffee and bacon wafting up from downstairs assured her the household was awake even at this early hour. Mastering the secrets of the ancient plumbing, she showered and was just back in her bedroom towelling her hair when a gentle knock sounded at the door.

"Come in."

"Morning, teacher." Jenny's beaming smile greeted her. "I heard you up. You like coffee?" She bore a steaming blue enamel pot and freshly buttered rolls on a white napkin. A very shy and hesitant Bruce peered around the door frame, eyeing the rug and obviously thinking of the previous evening. Precariously he balanced a large jug of cream. His yellow flannelette pajamas had horses printed on them, and right behind him was Tad, tail wagging joyously. As he approached her, Alana bent to pat the glistening black fur—at least the dog had fully accepted her presence.

"Boss left for the mine half an hour ago." Motioning to Bruce, Jenny coaxed him in and he carefully set the cream down.

"Stay, and have coffee with me," Alana invited. Jenny showed Bruce the single cup, and held out two fingers. Yanking up his pajamas, he pattered off down the stairs. Soon, he was back carrying two more mugs.

"He understands numbers?" Alana helped balance the tray on the chair, drawing another close for Jenny. Tad flopped at their feet.

"Sure, maybe up to four." Jenny's hand rested fondly on Bruce's tousled head, and the smile they exchanged was one of deep mutual love. With a mug of milky coffee, Bruce squatted down beside the dog. Alana curled her feet under her, warming her hands around the cup Jenny handed her. How had Jenny come here to Bluejay, raising first Rand and then his son? And where was Bruce's mother?

Bluntly, she asked exactly that. "Jenny, Bruce's mother—does she come here often?" *Or do she and Rand stay in Vancouver for their tête-à-têtes?* It was the worst sort of prying, but she had to know.

Jenny's face became guarded. "Never, not since he was born. Bad woman, that Lindsay." Alana felt dreadful for having asked. Obviously, the subject of Rand's ex-wife made Jenny uncomfortable—and Alana wanted Jenny's support, needed it, if her efforts were to be successful with Bruce. But the moment's strain passed, and Jenny asked, "How you going to make Bruce learn, teacher?" A worried frown creased her forehead. "He never stays still, just run, run, all day long. How can you make him sit and learn?"

Obviously, her concern for the child she adored had prompted this coffee party. She wanted to know what was in store for Bruce. Again, Alana glimpsed the astute and very protective part of Jenny hidden behind the smiling bland exterior.

"First, all I'm going to do is make friends with him," Alana reassured her. "I'll follow him around—if he'll let me. Then, I'll start telling him the names of things he's interested in. I'd never try to make such a little boy sit still. Learning will be part of his ordinary routine, Jenny."

A relieved nod met her words. Then Jenny's face screwed itself into another puzzled knot. "You will teach him to talk with his hands like I saw you do yesterday?"

"Sign language, yes. But speech, too, when he's ready. And together we'll try to get him to wear his hearing aid when it comes. He'll have to learn to listen." Alana remembered the charts she'd studied about Bruce. "He has a small amount of what we call residual hearing. Very few people are totally deaf, Jenny. Most of them, like Bruce, have some hearing, which may be usable with the help of a hearing aid." She sipped her coffee, letting Jenny digest all this.

"But I will never know what he says," Jenny wailed, tears welling in her narrow eyes. "He will talk with his fingers," she waved her hand in the air, and Bruce, watching them closely, immediately copied her, setting the mug down with a clunk. If this was how coffee parties were conducted, he was eager to help. Alana grinned at him. "Bright monkey," she murmured. He was proving to be more shy than seriously withdrawn.

"You'll learn to sign with him, Jenny."

But Jenny looked alarmed more than convinced. "I'll have to learn? Boy, I don't know if I can. I guess Tom and the boss will have to learn as well?"

Alana nodded emphatically. "Everyone around Bruce will learn to sign. That way, Bruce will learn language twice as fast." She accepted a bun, savoring the first yeasty mouthful. It was light and airy, freshly baked. Her own disastrous efforts at baking sprang to mind. Poor Gram. She'd tried so hard, but Alana was too impatient to spend much time in the kitchen.

"Alana, you'll have trouble teaching me. Old dogs, new tricks, you know? Maybe I'm just too old," Jenny said doubtfully, munching her own bun.

The uncertain look on Jenny's face and the delicious bun sparked an idea.

"Trade you," Alana suggested. "I'll teach you sign if you teach me how to bake buns like these." Jenny's face lit up with delight. "I warn you, Jenny, I can't cook worth a darn. You'll have a lot of trouble with me."

"It's a deal," Jenny confirmed, and finished her coffee as Bruce tugged impatiently on her arm.

"Time to go, he wants dressed now," she explained.

"Can he dress himself?" It was necessary to find out how many skills Bruce had. Each would be an opportunity for language development.

"Easier for me to do it," Jenny said, following the child out the door.

Tomorrow morning, Bruce my boy, we'll start you do-

ing it yourself. Relaxing back on the stacked pillows with the last swallow of coffee, she planned the beginning of what seemed to her an adventure; the complicated journey necessary to teach words and their meanings to a child without hearing.

Then she leapt up, pulled on faded Levi's that clung comfortably to her legs, and a madras print shirt in tones of pink and yellow and orange. A happy shirt. Wonderful work clothes. No more panty hose and narrow skirts, slips and high heels. Carelessly, she brushed out her mop of still-damp hair. Pulling on old leather sandals, she headed down to enjoy her first work day with the miniature dynamo who was Bruce Evans.

By ten o'clock that morning, Alana was certain they'd covered at least twenty miles. She was beginning to understand the chaotic condition of the house and ruefully agreed with Jenny's claim that Bruce ran all day. Like all children—especially deaf children, he learned by doing, and at Bluejay it was obvious no one challenged most things he chose to do. He and Tad galloped along, enjoying whatever suited them with either Jenny or Tom Saunders carefully keeping the pair out of serious trouble.

This morning, their guardian was Alana. As soon as his miniature blue jeans and cowboy boots were in place, Bruce burst out the back door, with Alana in hot pursuit. After one surprised stare, he ignored her, heading for the barn at a dead run. It lay at the far end of the pole corral, and Bruce simply climbed over fences rather than struggle with heavy gates. Alana copied him, grateful for the hours she'd spent jogging. She vaulted over the rails, exhilarated by the sunny morning, the heady freedom of not being shut up in a stuffy office.

There were three horses in the enclosure, one a shaggy

and absolutely lovable Shetland pony. It headed for Bruce expectantly, who chortled, grabbing it around the neck as it snuffled at his jeans. He dragged out several dirty lumps of sugar, and the pony took them softly in his lips. Bruce's face split in a wide grin, his eyes covertly watching Alana's reaction.

Quickly, she bent to his level, and signed the name for horse, both thumbs on her temples, palms forward, first two digits making an up and down motion, miming the action of horse's ears. Saying the word clearly, she touched the pony's flank with her hand and repeated the exercise several times while Bruce's curious eyes remained on her. He watched closely but made no effort to copy. She made the sign again and his forehead creased. He stared, studying her actions, flicking his intense gaze to the horse, then back to her. Then he seemed to dismiss this strange behavior, heading for the two-story wooden barn with Tad yelping close behind.

They burst into the hay-scented dimness, blinded for an instant by the cool contrast to the blazing sun outside.

"Slow down there, young feller," Tom's deep voice warned from where he was cleaning the horse stalls, managing to deftly use a shovel and still clutch the ever-present crutch under one arm.

"Mornin', teacher." He mopped the sweat from his forehead with a handkerchief, shoving it back carelessly into his denim overalls. Bruce went busily to work beside Tom, finding and using a small shovel whose cut-down handle made it easy for him to manipulate.

"I saw the two of ya' up there sayin' hello to Minnie. Bruce's pony." The friendly dark eyes met Alana's easily today. "Figured my right-hand man would be along to help with the chores." Tom shoved his battered hat to the back of his head and went on with his work, balancing now and then on his crutch to proudly watch the little boy finish his job, carefully clean the shovel with a handful of straw and then hang it in its place on a low nail Tom had obviously supplied.

"Gotta keep this feller busy all the time or he finds mischief. Plumb wears Jenny out some days. Gonna be lots easier for her now with you here, Miss Alana."

Silently, Alana blessed the patient hours her father had spent teaching her to fish. Obviously, that accidental talent had won her a friend.

Bruce yanked urgently on her hand, the first sign of acceptance he'd shown. She resisted gently, squatting down on the clean-smelling hay and making the sign for "go," index fingers pointing away, palms closed and facing out, flicking both wrists forward as if moving away from the body. Both Tom and Bruce studied her actions. Making the sign again, she asked Bruce clearly, "Shall we go? Do you want to go?" Bruce simply turned his back and ran off. But at the wide doors, when she swung around to call goodbye, she saw Tom furtively copying her actions, frowning down at his hands in concentration. At least someone was learning! She hurried after Bruce and Tad.

The next two hours took Alana on an exhaustive and unique tour of Bluejay, giving her a glimpse into the life of the solitary small boy she'd come to teach and some idea, too, of the workings of the ranch.

After leaving the barn, Bruce clambered up a short ladder to a loft in the toolshed. His blue-jeaned bottom disappeared with a wriggle, leaving Alana to follow hurriedly. The dusty space she entered was hot, with shafts of sunlight dripping through cracks in the roof. Bruce lay on his stomach, close under the eaves where a trusting mother cat lay stretched in a low box, three mottled babies nursing, their tiny paws rhythmically flexing her fur. Thrilled, Alana touched Bruce's shoulder to draw his attention. Then she made the sign for "cat," showing a cat's whiskers by stroking her fingers outwards on her cheeks. This time Bruce giggled, using a gentle finger to stroke the tiny balls of fur, raising his fly-away eyebrows, so much like his father's, to express amazement when he felt the rumblings of the mother cat's purr.

Tad whined anxiously at the bottom of the ladder when they appeared, and soon they were off again, this time visiting a cow and her calf in a fenced-in enclosure in the grassy meadow.

With each new activity, Alana knelt at Bruce's level and carefully gave him the graphic hand sign and the spoken word to illustrate actions or animals. He simply watched her impassively, never once miming her gestures as he had done so freely with Jenny that morning. Feeling a bit disappointed, Alana cautioned patience to herself. Miracles didn't happen in an hour or two.

The day grew warmer. By the time noon hour came, Alana's forehead was beaded with sweat, and her small companion's face was flushed. His legs, however, still operated on full speed, although Alana's were protesting. Surely it was time for lunch and a nap for him?

He was heading in the direction of the lake. Ten more minutes, Alana vowed, panting after him, and she'd carry him bodily back to the house. Did he never run out of energy? Smoothing back her own damp hair, she trailed him wearily down a narrow path, through the birch trees, then seemingly in an aimless fashion off into the forest. Several yards behind Bruce, she stooped to admire the dainty bluebells underfoot.

When she glanced up, he was gone. Instantly a cold knot of fear twisted her stomach. "Bruce," she hollered insanely, knowing he couldn't hear her. Then, from almost directly over her head she heard his soft giggle.

The tree house was only seven feet off the ground, but it was old and the branches had grown to form a protective net around it, effectively weaving it into the patterns of the forest. A crude wooden platform with a sheet of corrugated tin forming its roof, it reminded her of efforts she and Johnny had struggled to build when they were little. The ancient evergreen supporting the structure held it in huge limbs, and a small rope ladder hung down the trunk. She struggled up, scratching her arm on a sharp branch, finally joining Bruce where he sat cross-legged and beaming, a miniature king regally allowing her access to his kingdom.

"You little imp," she told him affectionately, miming her confusion and fear to reassure him his disappearing trick had succeeded. He beamed at her with mischievous delight.

The surrounding trees allowed glimpses of the lake only a hundred yards beyond, and bird song filled the hot noon stillness. Gingerly testing the sturdiness of the platform, Alana laughed back into the sparkling sky-blue eyes demanding her approval.

"Who's going to learn the most this summer, rascal, you... or me?" she whispered.

Three crudely boarded up sides produced a small room, and the floor was cushioned by a tattered old rag rug. A tiny mirror hung on one wall, and in a corner was a small, weathered wooden trunk, its cover hinged and secured by a padlock. Bruce watched her intently for several minutes, obviously debating whether or not she was to be trusted. Then, he seemed to make up his mind, for he scrabbled under the edge of the rug, located a large rusty key and struggled valiantly for long seconds until at last he had the trunk open. He'd decided to trust her. Alana felt a warm surge of pleasure, and a glow of accomplishment. One small step, she gloated as Bruce unearthed his treasures one by one and handed them to her to admire.

There was a perfectly round black rock the size of a baseball, several huge yellow animal teeth, the whitened skull of a rodent, which Alana gave back rapidly, a half-full box of oatmeal cookies from which Bruce extracted two samples and gave her one. Munching, he delved back into his treasure trove and came up with a round key ring containing two suspiciously shiny keys, a bushy and musky-smelling gopher's tail, a large box of kitchen matches—which Alana eyed worriedly, remembering last night's fiasco—and last of all, a small stained book with "Daily Journal" stamped in faded gilt on its soft leather cover.

Still uneasy about the matches and wondering whether she should confiscate them and risk spoiling Bruce's new-found trust, Alana accepted the book and flipped it open absently.

Spidery, faded purple ink spelled out "August 11, 1959. For dear Randall, on the occasion of your eleventh birthday, all my love, Auntie Kate." The book had belonged to Rand. All of a sudden Alana realized that this tree house, too, might have been Rand's. Might, in fact, have been built by him when he was a boy. The structure was far too sturdy and weathered to have been built by or for Bruce. A tiny flicker of excitement spiralled down her nerves as her eyes fell once more to the inscription. She really shouldn't read anything so private. Her fingers flipped the pages. The handwriting was large, unformed, probably much like the long-ago boy who'd written here. She shouldn't look. But the temptation to know that long-lost boy—and consequently, the man he'd become, was overwhelming. Bruce had lost interest in her preoccupation with the book, and was munching crumbled cookies from his bag. Her fingers turned hesitantly to the first page.

"This is the secret diary of me, Randall Evans. I will keep my book where nobody will find it, in my Tarzan house in the tree."

Glancing up, the crooked nails, the determined clumsy construction, assumed new meaning for her. The tree house suddenly became endearing as she visualized the earnest child struggling with it so long ago.

"From my dad I got a Swiss army knife that I wanted for my birthday. My mother in England sent me clothes, scratchy shirts and shorts. Dad says they wear those over there. She don't even know how big I got this year. I wish she'd come home and see. Jenny made me a *real* Indian vest and it's got beads and fringe. I could show my mother if she came."

The wistful words evoked the child so poignantly, Alana's throat tightened. What kind of mother had deserted him? The face of the cool determined woman in the picture Rand had removed from her wall flashed in her memory. How fortunate he'd had Jenny. A rush of affection for the cheerful, loving Jenny warmed Alana. Hurriedly, she turned another page, skimming with a smile over an account of a botched attempt to build a canoe. Then came words printed crookedly in black ink.

"Just six days before I have to go back to school. I *hate*

the city. I *hate* school. I want to be a miner for my dad's coal mine. Lots of miners never went to school. But dad says bosses have to, to be a boss I have to study and be a mining engineer. But it will take years and years. Jenny says if I do she'll call me boss then instead of Randy. That's a baby name for sure."

Alana's lips quirked mischievously. Oh, for the courage to innocently call him Randy. She still shuddered when John called her "Red."

Bruce was lying on his stomach, dropping pine cones down on Tad who whined pathetically from the tree's bottom. It was time to go. Then one more entry caught her eye.

"Dad's coming on the train when I go to Vancouver on Friday. Then he will go on a boat to England to see my mother. Jenny cried today so I made her tea. She had a headache. She will be lonely when me and my father are gone."

Feeling guilty and not a little ashamed of snooping, Alana snapped the book shut and touched Bruce, handing him the diary to replace among his other treasures. Bruce looked sleepy, and Alana heard Jenny's voice float through the still hot air.

"Teacher, Brucy, lunchtime now. Teacher?"

"Coming," Alana called. But all during the delicious soup and chicken salad lunch, Alana found her mind returning to the little book. How innocently a child had recaptured the essence of a long-ago summer.

That afternoon, Bruce slept and Alana slumped on the shaded veranda, filling her daybook with the morning's activities, scribbling notes to discuss with Rand, detailing words and expressions she hoped Bruce would come to understand. Bees buzzed lazily around her, and from the kitchen Jenny giggled as she shared a cup of tea with Tom. High overhead a jet left its white trail across a sky so blue it seemed artificial.

Time expanded here, so that Alana felt she'd been in this valley far longer than just a day. Maybe the place was enchanted, and time stood still. She grinned at her own romantic fancy. But the city seemed distant and unimportant, despite the life she'd made there for herself, her challenging job, the very glitter of a big metropolis. Often, lately, she'd felt an uneasy impatience with her life, as though she were putting in time until a more meaningful era would begin. Had that been only her psyche's defense system, keeping her from utter despair after the aborted love affair with Glen? Was it just a way to keep on going, promising herself a reward for functioning during the unspeakably horrible six months after she'd called off the wedding, after her father had died believing she blamed him?

She shook her head impatiently, closing her eyes and leaning back so the sun felt glowing hot on her lids, ignoring the freckles she knew would pop from the soothing heat. It had become habit, pushing away thoughts of that awful time in her life. It was then she'd started jogging. Sure she couldn't get through even one more day with the pain, and worse, the shame inside her, she'd happened to read an article on the benefits of jogging, including emotional relaxation.

A rueful smile touched her lips now remembering the agony of those first clumsy runs, the aching certainty that she'd done herself permanent damage, the pain in her calf and her thighs. The determination to go still farther and farther. Finally, the day had come when she found herself running five miles without a single twinge—even better, without thinking once of the hurt inside. She'd started sleeping through the night. She'd taught herself to bury the memories, so why was she resurrecting them now?

Jumping up, she headed for the kitchen. Tom was back at work and Jenny was chopping meat and browning it in a huge iron frying pan. The smell of sizzling onions and braising beef filled the spacious room. Jenny had said Rand was responsible for the remodelling of the kitchen, and Alana noted how he'd managed to blend modern efficiency with antique charm. Of all the many rooms in the house, this one alone seemed to know exactly what its purpose was, and whom it belonged to. This was Jenny's domain.

When the round face turned smilingly from the counter to greet her, Alana announced, "I've decided to go for a run, Jenny."

Jenny stared at her uncertainly. "Go for a run?" she repeated, puzzled.

Probably people around here didn't jog much, Alana concluded. She nodded, and added, "I'll be back in an hour. I'll just follow the path out to the highway, where we came in yesterday."

Now Jenny looked concerned as well as confused.

"Teacher, maybe better if you wait till Boss comes home. Always, he's here by three. Maybe you should wait and check with him," she suggested, glancing at the large wall clock attached to a cupboard.

Alana's ready temper flared at the idea that everything she might want to do while at Bluejay would first have to be approved of by Rand. Did anybody here take a deep breath without his consent, she fumed mutinously? And probably his entire staff at the Evans Mine treated him the same way. Talk about a power complex! Well, she hadn't asked anyone's permission as to what she should or should not do in Vancouver, and certainly she wasn't about to begin here.

"I'll be back in an hour," she told Jenny firmly, and raced up the stairs to change into her running gear.

Slipping out, she turned up the gravel driveway, enjoying the earthy smell from Tom's plowed meadow. Her feet soon found and maintained the rhythm of her pace. Up the incline to where the forest began, into the softly whispering trees. The air was cooler here. Her breathing became regular and even. The half dreamlike state induced by running overcame her. Random thoughts came and went. Several miles passed and the woods on either side deepened. Thinking became more an absorption and appreciation of the deep tranquility around her. The little wooden bridge sounded hollow when her legs carried her smoothly over its rise and fall. She opened the gate and left it swinging wide behind her. The good sweat of exertion trickled down her forehead, catching in the navy-blue headband.

When the gravel stopped and the paved highway lay at right angles to her more primitive path, she was unaware of how long or far she'd been running. The paved road stretched hypnotically on either side, bracketed at either end by the ever-present mountains. Hardly hesitating, she turned right. Just a few more minutes, and she'd head back. The road was empty. It was the first time she could remember being the sole occupant of a highway. This was a heady sensation. Drunk with freedom, she gave in to the urge to run criss-cross, back and forth.

When she heard the truck behind her, she was in the road's exact center. The blast of the horn jolted through her. Leaping for the shoulder, she jerked her head around. The truck was a crew cab, used to transport workers. Eight or ten men, faces grimy from dust, sat behind the grinning driver who held a firm hand down on the horn. Alana kept running, but now her feet were in rough gravel at the very edge of the drop-off to the ditch. What was wrong with this stupid driver? The vehicle pulled alongside, slowed to a crawl, keeping pace with her. Windows rolled down and rough looking men poked their heads out, whistling, calling, "Hey, honey, run over here," and, "If we catch you, can we keep you?" as well as more explicit comments about her shorts, her legs, her bottom.

The isolation of the road became a danger suddenly. She'd parried wisecracks in the city, but there had always been people nearby. Here, there was no one. The green truck slowed still more, and Alana's breath caught in terror as a bearded blond giant in dirty blue coveralls jumped out and began to trot clumsily beside her. His huge work boots crunched just behind her, and she caught a whiff of sweaty male body odor.

"Slow down, Wonder Woman," he grunted. "Ain'tcha scared of bears around here, huh?" Guffaws and catcalls from the truck encouraged him.

"Don'cha worry, slim! Max'll save ya. Nothin's gonna hurt a nice piece like you, long as Max is around."

"Nothin' but Max," the audience chorused. To her horror, his hand patted her backside.

Fear made her heart bang her ribs so hard she was certain the man behind her must have heard. Her knees quivered as though they might quit supporting her. Media accounts of rape and murder in deserted areas like this ran across her brain like microfilm. Why had she been so thoughtless?

Her pursuer panted along, and it would only be a matter of time till he took further action. Far ahead until it disappeared among the trees, the road was empty. To turn and dash for Bluejay's turnoff was folly—its even deeper isolation held greater danger. She shuddered with terror.

Max again reached out. She darted as fast as she could past him, behind the truck and across the road, then swiftly reversed direction so she was running away from the vehicle.

Max swore loudly, lumbering after her. The truck driver simply did a U-turn. The hoots and suggestions of the men echoed in the empty afternoon.

Fear accelerated to near panic. Her feet seemed to fly along, but as if in a nightmare, it seemed she was glued in place. The men and the truck pulled effortlessly alongside.

"Please," she heard herself murmuring. "Please, please, please..."

Max's voice intruded. "Slow down there. How... about... a ride... now? That's enough of this racing... you... hear?" Once more, the tentaclelike arms reached for her. Striking out blindly with a clenched fist, she walloped his forearm, deflecting the grasping hand. Now there was a new note in his voice. He was angry. "Stupid god-damned—"

The men in the truck seemed to be tiring of the game. "Forget it," they were calling. The driver hollered, "C'mon, Max, game's over, get in. We want a beer sometime tonight."

But Max pounded behind her, cursing in a steady stream. Sickened, she felt him grab a handful of her jersey top, and then one paw closed around her upper arm sinking into the soft flesh. He hauled her around like a weightless top, off balance and staggering. His foul breath made her choke as he dragged her to his chest. She tried to kick, to bring her knee up as Johnny had taught her long ago, but his grasp was too firm around her lower body. His blurred and grotesquely large face descended toward her own.

Then, a horn blared angrily.

"What the hell's going on here?" It was Rand's voice, and in one confused instant, Max released her. Rand burst from his truck, and in two strides was beside Alana. He gathered a fistful of Max's shirt in one hand, drawing the other fist back menacingly. Max stammered, "Hey, hey, guy, it was just a joke." He held up both hands in a placating gesture, appealing to his companions who were now watching the scene warily. "Tell him, you guys, we never meant no harm, we were just teasing..."

Alana forced her shaking legs to move to Rand's side, all too aware of the burly men in the crew cab, uncertain what they would do if Rand—

"He didn't—I was just frightened, Rand," she stammered, her breath coming in gulps, her voice unnaturally high.

"Did he touch you? Did he hurt you in any way?" The knuckles holding Max's shirt were white, and Rand's voice had a steely edge.

Alana shook her head, desperate for the episode to end without violence, without Rand getting hurt because of her.

"I was scared, that's all," she assured him breathlessly.

With a powerful, sudden shove, Rand sent Max sprawling backward, clumsily staggering to keep from falling.

"Get out of here," Rand snarled. "If I ever catch you near her again, I'll—" His words were lost in the noise of a third vehicle screeching to a stop behind them. With an ugly curse and a threat hollered only after he was safely in the crew cab, Max and his friends drove away.

Rand and Alana turned towards the woman hurrying from the fire-engine-red Toyota parked at an angle behind Rand's truck. The young woman had left the car door swinging open with the haste of her exit. Arms akimbo, she demanded, "What was all that about, Rand? Are you both okay?" Her attention centered on Alana, who tried to answer, and found her voice simply wouldn't work. The shaking in her legs spread over her entire body. Feeling a complete fool, she stood in the road and trembled violently.

Quickly, the other girl was at her side, wrapping a warm and sympathetic arm closely around Alana as Rand, eyes still smoldering with anger, explained rapidly what had happened, then hurried over to his truck for a jacket to wrap around Alana's shivering form.

"I'm Katy Sinclair. Those stupid baboons—try to relax. Want to sit in my car till you feel better?" She tucked Alana into the little red car, then kept up a reassuring patter, standing beside the open car door, addressing her remarks to both Rand and Alana.

"I've seen those apes before. They drink at Black Jack's. The tavern where I work," she explained to Alana. To Rand, she added, "Did you know they hired me to sing four nights a week? The pay's not bad, and it lets me be home with Lissa during the day—my four-year-old daughter," she added to Alana. "Why don't you two—hey, you are together, aren't you? I mean, I just assumed..." Her voice trailed off, and her heavily fringed turquoise eyes seemed to query Rand. He didn't immediately respond. Alana found her voice worked again. Slowly, she was regaining control, willing the quivering in her limbs to stop.

"I'm Alana Campbell," she explained, noticing how Katy's blue-black hair waved gently down to her shoulders, how the vibrant young woman seemed to emanate sensuality from every pore. "I teach deaf children, and Rand hired me to tutor his son. For the summer," she amended, wondering suddenly what Katy's relationship might be or have been with Rand, despite the wide gold band Alana noted on Katy's left hand.

Katy's face softened, and her eyes were teary when she said, "Rand, I heard your little guy was deaf. I'm—I feel bad for you and for him. I know how hard it was when Lindsay left..." Her response, clumsy as it was, was obviously sincere, but Rand's entire body stiffened at her words.

His face became impassive and cold, and he extended a hand to Alana, saying "If you're able, we should drive home." He helped her out of Katy's car and into his truck, thanking Katy formally for her help, but not inviting her to accompany them to Bluejay as Alana thought he might.

"Bring Alana down to the tavern some evening," Katy suggested, ignoring his remote attitude. "You're such a recluse, Rand, an evening out would do you good, and Alana should meet some of the eligible bachelors around town. Besides you, of course." She waved a cheery hand, seemingly oblivious to Rand's silence, and climbed into her car, calling goodbye as she accelerated away.

It was very still as the sound of her engine faded. Rand got in the cab beside Alana, but made no move to start the vehicle. He stared at her instead, the grooves beside his mouth and in his forehead deepening as he frowned.

Alana shifted uncomfortably.

"You are all right?" he demanded roughly. "You wouldn't say you were just to avoid the violence you're so opposed to?"

"Of course not," she denied vehemently. "I told you, I just had a bad scare."

He turned the ignition key, and the truck roared to life. His words were low and scathing. "You deserve to be scared. It's plain stupid to go trotting around alone in a strange place, dressed—or undressed—like that." His hot eyes raked her body, and she burned with anger, with awareness of him, with resentment at his accusation.

"I'm dressed for running, Rand. If that's unique here, it's certainly not my fault, and I don't intend to stop either running or wearing shorts because of what happened, or because you disapprove." She tilted her chin up and glared at him, even as a sense of desolation and exhaustion washed over her. Katy's mention of his ex-wife had obviously upset him. It seemed that no one else knew that he and Lindsay were seeing each other again—or still....

"I suppose this latest fiasco means you'll be on the next plane to Vancouver," he growled unexpectedly.

"Why would I do that?"

He shrugged belligerently, making no move to drive away, still idling the engine.

"Since the moment you arrived, every damn thing possible has gone wrong." He sounded so enraged, so much the innocent victim of injustice, Alana had to smother a smile. This huge man, with his blue work shirt rolled above his elbows, powerful forearms matted with hair over smooth muscle, this giant who had come so gallantly to her rescue was actually shaking his fist impotently at circumstance. It was an emotion she understood, one she had experienced herself.

"Isn't there some law that says if anything can go wrong it will, and if possible, will then get worse?" She met his eyes. "I'm no quitter, Rand. I'd rather fight than quit."

"Wouldn't you think I'd have learned that about you by now, Alana Campbell?" Her spine tingled with the affection in his voice. She had a sudden mad urge to fling herself into his arms, hide there. There seemed such security, such safety, in those arms—but he looked abruptly away, shifted into gear and drove off.

"Starting tomorrow, we both get up an hour earlier," he said.

"Why's that?" *And when are you and Lindsay going to make your reconciliation official?*

"If you must run, you run with me. God help my nicotined lungs," he added ruefully, stubbing out the cigarette he'd just lit, fingers inches from her bare leg.

Every nerve ending signalled her proximity to denim-covered male thighs, the softness of his worn jeans outlining every masculine contour. Alana shifted restlessly on the seat, and blurted, "Is Katy Sinclair married?"

Rand shook his head. "Katy's husband left her when the baby was small. I'm sure she's divorced by now."

Why did she feel so relieved at his impersonal answer, Alana wondered? It shouldn't matter to her what his relationship was with Katy, or any other woman. Even his ex-wife. Even Lindsay.

"Why in hell can't I accept it?" The outburst seemed wrung from him, confusing Alana, linking as it did to her own thoughts.

"Accept what?" she asked, half fearful of his answer.

"Bruce's deafness," he said despondently. "People, even friends like Katy, expressing sympathy, for God's sake. I can't stand pity, damn it."

If only she could believe that was the sole reason behind his aloofness. Regardless, Alana wanted to soothe him. A warm rush of compassion and understanding made her touch his corded arm with her hand. "It's not pity, Rand. People don't know how to react, what to say. They want you to know they care. And often they say exactly the wrong thing."

He didn't answer, but he flashed her a grateful glance, and the harsh lines in his face relaxed. He made no comment about the open gate, just stopped and shut it firmly behind them. And when Bruce threw himself boisterously into his father's arms the moment they arrived home, Alana saw Rand close his eyes tightly, a look of tender anguish on his features, as he held the child fiercely against his chest. And Alana couldn't help but wonder, as she climbed the stairs heading for a hot bath, whether Rand's pain wasn't partly for the separation from Lindsay. An unmistakable pang of jealousy ripped through her. To have shared his life and his love, to be the mother of his son; how wonderfully fortunate Lindsay had been... how fortunate she still was.

CHAPTER FIVE

HER FRAGRANT SOAK in the claw-footed tub revived her and gave her time to assimilate the day's events. She'd learned a great deal about the place and the people here. A sting of guilty color washed up her cheeks as she remembered the diary; nevertheless, the day had been mostly rewarding. Her work with Bruce thrilled her. She would explore the furthest reaches of her imagination to stimulate him.

Rand? She squirmed uneasily in the soothing water. Rand presented far more complex problems. Alana couldn't deny the immense physical attraction between them, and she knew instinctively that Rand felt it, too. But the barriers between them went much further than the ethical problem of her tutoring Bruce, as she'd first thought. There was the matter of his marriage, his wife. If he were still involved with Lindsay, why on earth wasn't she here in Bluejay with Rand and Bruce? Unless she was somehow unfit to be a mother.

At that point, Alana curbed her imagination. Making a mountain from a molehill, Gramma would have called it. Besides, it really wasn't her business.

The last thing she wanted was any involvement with Rand personally. It wasn't nearly long enough since Glen had left her emotionally bankrupt and she'd vowed never to get hurt again. But that was before

Rand's kiss in the park. It had cleansed her, cured her, left her open and vulnerable. Too vulnerable. A flood of warmth spilled through her, sending a fullness and an ache into her lower abdomen. Damn, damn the man. Glen's lovemaking had been clinical, had left her unprepared for the amazing and exquisite response she'd felt to Rand's single kiss.

Hormones, she decided. Physical hunger, perhaps to be briefly indulged as most of the people she knew in the city seemed to, with casual, frequent affairs mutually enjoyed and lightly ended.

But she also knew she was too old-fashioned for that. Her upbringing, even though her mother had died before the time Alana could discuss such things with her, had still left her with an idealized, romantic dream of love, commitment, marriage; of sexual fulfillment with only one man.

Steam fogged the bathroom, and when she stepped out onto a thick brown mat, all she could see in the wood-framed mirror was a blurred image of a tall, slender girl whose slanted gray gaze stared back at her questioningly.

"Dinner's ready." Jenny's shrill and cheery call sounded, and Alana hurriedly towelled, dusted on lemon talc, and scurried to her room to dress.

As she pulled out lacy underwear from her drawer, she noticed the square box on her dresser. Curiously, fastening her bra, she eyed the box, then cautiously lifted the lid. Her mouth opened in a soundless "Oh." Inside was an elegant makeup case of smooth burgundy leather, which when unzipped, revealed an entire array of pink and bronze lipsticks, gloss, matching jewel-toned polish bottles, her favorite shades of understated gray and green eyeshadows plus endless, tiny pots and pencils. It was a professional makeup kit, the type any model would covet. There were sharpeners, translucent powder, small jeweled hand mirrors, tweezers, even a tiny vial of her special musky cologne and—heavens—a matching vial of outrageously expensive perfume. Her hand extracted a plain card, tucked inside, showing the adroitly sketched round face of a repentant small boy with riotous curls, and a dog's head beside him wearing an identical "hang-dog" expression. The hand-lettered message read, The devil made us do it...please excuse? It was signed with a smudgy hand print, and the mark of a dog's dirty paw. The makeup shades and even the brand names were identical to the ones she'd had to discard the night before.

Rand must have taken time from his work day to drive into town and carefully choose this. For her. A thrill shot through her. How had he even known what to buy? And his artwork was perfect. She couldn't look at the card without grinning. Rand. Tender warmth enveloped her at his thoughtfulness.

Pleasure welled inside her as she pulled on her navy V-necked jersey top, adding a casual denim wrap skirt, which she swiftly knotted around her waist. Flat leather sandals with tiny straps and then light, almost hesitant wisps from her new makeup case completed her preparations. Nervously, she headed down to thank the complex and very disturbing man who'd supplied the gift.

He sat on the wide porch, Bruce lolling comfortably on his knees. A bit embarrassed, he waved away Alana's shy and sincere thank-you's with the explanation that he'd simply phoned Jenny, who'd sifted through the wastebasket in Alana's room for necessary evidence. But Alana could see that her own delight in his gift had pleased Rand.

"Bruce dragged me down to see the horses," Rand announced, an undertone of excitement in his voice. "Then, he made motions with his fingers, over and over." Self-consciously, Rand imitated the sign Alana had tried to teach Bruce that morning. Bruce's alert gaze followed his father's fingers, and he nodded vigorously, copying the motions with his own chubby fingers.

He *had* understood. He'd remembered, and even repeated the word for horse. Alana's eyes filled with tears. Elated, she crouched at Rand's knee, thumbs on her temples, bending her fingers up and down exuberantly, trying to convey by repeating the "horse" word, and by her immense and shaky smile, how proud she was of Bruce.

Starry-eyed, she beamed at Rand from where she knelt, almost at his feet.

"If he's learned this one word, he'll learn a million more," she whispered softly. "He's a brilliant boy, to learn so quickly and so well."

Rand nodded, then said, "Maybe he simply has a brilliant teacher." The intensity and open longing on his face almost frightened her, and she sprang up self-consciously, aware of being far too close to an inferno.

Dinner turned into a merry celebration. Bruce took full advantage of the admiration lavished on him. Jenny, Tom, Rand and even poor Tad were all prompted by Bruce to make the now-famous "horse" sign repeatedly.

"We've created a monster," Rand groaned as Bruce imperiously demanded a third bowl of chocolate ice cream. "You'll go too far, my boy," he growled mock-threateningly at his son. There was a closeness tonight, a family feeling about the little dinner party, that Alana treasured. The dining room seemed bathed in happiness and sunshine, in tender loving voices and unified pride in this one small child's achievement. The hour sparked an idea for Alana. Each evening over dinner, she could introduce new signs, words and eventually phrases, turning the learning of sign into a dinner game. Excitement made her flush happily, and to her confusion, Rand reached out a gentle finger to touch her nose.

"Looks as though you were kissed by the sun today," he mused. His eyes lingered on her lips, hinting at kisses of quite another sort, and she was grateful that Jenny was in the kitchen, and Tom absorbed in lifting Bruce to his lap. Never before had freckles sounded appealing.

Finally, Jenny carried off a sleepy child, Tom went off to evening chores, and Alana remembered the list she'd made that afternoon of equipment and supplies. She found her notebook. When she returned to the dining room, Rand motioned toward a door at the far end of the room.

"We'll have coffee in my study. Care for a brandy?" At her nod, he filled two snifters from the sideboard, and led the way.

Like the kitchen, this room had a specific personality, but here the flavor was totally Rand. Lined in rough cedar, boards were nailed to the walls at angles rather than straight up and down. A Franklin fireplace in the corner increased Alana's first impression that she'd walked into a log cabin. Book shelves lined one far wall. A coarse white wool rug, almost like an animal skin, covered the floor. Soft old leather armchairs and an immense oak desk with brass corners were grouped near the only window—more a glass wall than simply a window. The grove of silver birch she'd admired from outside that day seemed to be incorporated into the room's decor. Soft early-evening twilight sifted through the branches and the glass. All at once, Alana imagined the room as it must look in winter, when the open doors of the stove crackled red and golden with burning logs, when the trees hung heavy with snow. Perhaps deer or a raccoon would silently cross the clearing. An intimate scene, where lovers curled together in one roomy armchair and long dark evenings wrapped them in peace...Nostalgia flooded over her. She would be gone by winter.

Rand was watching her curiously, a goblet of amber brandy extended to her.

"Thanks. I—I was admiring this marvelous room." Her interest now was caught by a wall covered in both old and new photographs. Savoring the fiery burn of the liquor on her tongue she moved to study the display, some strange radar signaling when he moved silently to stand behind her.

Obviously, Rand had taken most of the photos. Many were of Bruce, as a tiny baby, yawning widely, as a toddler with drooping diapers and a toothy grin, the subtle transformation of baby to boy. Rand had obviously spent hours waiting and watching for just the right moment, the precisely apt expression. Both surprisingly professional and intimate, they revealed still another side of Rand, artistic and sensitive. There were photos of Bluejay, house and mountains shrouded with fog, emerging like shimmering ghosts from the mist. Another photo, black and white, was of crumbling timbers surrounding what must have been a mine shaft, poignant in its suggestion of a forgotten place and time.

Half turning to him, Alana caught a vulnerable and naked appeal on his tanned male features. It was as though he'd exposed a hidden side of himself for her approval, like a little boy shyly revealing a dream. The glowing words of praise died on her lips, and instead she said softly, "I like them, Rand. Very, very much."

Deliberately then, he drew her attention to older, faded photos of burly-looking men standing beside the raw beginnings of a log house, axes posed over their shoulders.

"My grandfather and my dad," he explained, pointing to a young giant with a handlebar mustache.

"They were building Bluejay. Dad must have been about twenty. I wasn't even a gleam in his eye as yet. He hadn't met mother."

"How did they meet?" Alana's curiosity was fueled by the words she'd read in the old diary, but she was also wildly aware of his nearness and needed the distraction. His breath felt warm on her neck, making the tiny hairs quiver. She took a quick gulp of brandy. It made a burning path down to her stomach. The resonant voice just behind her ear rumbled pleasantly.

"The Second World War came, and dad enlisted. He was in the air force, posted to London. Mother, Martha Jane Whitby, was the only child of a widowed businessman. It was a wartime romance. They married in haste, only to repent at leisure as the saying goes. Dad painted a glowing and probably inaccurate portrait of this valley for her as being gracious and beautiful. He was homesick, remember. He forgot to mention that in those days, this was the frontier."

Remembering the terror she'd felt that afternoon, Alana couldn't help but speculate that perhaps the valley was still a frontier of sorts. Rand's voice went on, hard now and full of bitterness.

"When the war ended, he brought mother here to Bluejay. My grandfather was still alive, and he and mother didn't get on. She was used to London. Concerts, civilized society. She'd learned her father's business, and when he became ill, she went back. She did wait till I was born, and she hired Jenny to care for me. But she never did come back here to stay, even after her father died."

The words Rand had scribbled long ago came back to Alana. *She don't even know how big I got this year. I wish she'd come home and see.* The child had been hurt by his mother's desertion, and the man still resented that hurt.

"What about your father, Rand? Did he ever consider moving to be with her?"

Rand moved to the swivel desk chair, sinking into it. He tilted back, turning toward the view of trees and darkening sky.

"I told you once that mining's in my blood. Well, I guess I inherited that from my father. The Evans Mine and this valley were his career—his life—just as they're mine. Mother came back for dad's funeral. I haven't seen her since."

He set his glass on the gleaming desk top and clasped his hands comfortably behind his head. The long, lean legs sprawled across the furry rug.

"I've wondered why they didn't divorce. Mother was financially independent, so it wasn't the money—in fact, she invested in the Evans Mine when dad needed capital. Maybe it was just convenient, having a husband in the background."

"It—it must have been very hard for your father to raise you alone." How ironic that Rand too should be a single parent, as his own father had been.

Rand was silent, then laughed sardonically. "The situation has its...compensations for a man alone." There was no mistaking his meaning. Women would fall over themselves to comfort a father left pathetically alone with a child, even in this generation of single parents. Alana's cheeks flushed scarlet as she silently acknowledged that she herself had been emotionally affected by her first meeting with Rand and Bruce. And of course, any man would be insane not to take full advantage of the opportunity his poignant situation presented.

And wasn't she still achingly aware of Rand's potent male attraction? Anger at herself boiled slowly. At least his offhand remark had served as a warning. For the remainder of the summer, she would guarantee their relationship would remain strictly professional.

"It's your turn, Alana. Now you know all my family skeletons, what about your own parents, your childhood?" Rand was still wrapped in the web of intimacy that had enveloped both of them a moment before. But now Alana had her own reasons to withdraw. She reached out and switched on the overhead light, bathing the room in a sudden glare.

"My parents are both dead. Now, could we go over these notes? It's been a long day, and I'd like to get to bed." She spread her daybook open on the desk. "These are the toys and games I'll need for teaching. And here is a tentative timetable of our work week. I'd also like to study the assessments of Bruce that were made at the clinic. They'll help me decide where to begin."

If this rapid change in mood puzzled him, he didn't say

so. She carefully avoided his eyes for the next half hour, willing herself not to respond when his arm brushed hers over the papers, or when she caught a whiff of his particular scent. From here on, Rand Evans was strictly employer, and temporary at that. To emphasize the point, she made him a concise list of other teachers of the deaf who he might contact over the summer, to work with Bruce in the fall.

When they'd covered everything, she tossed a snappy "Good night" over her shoulder and headed for her room. She thought he called her when she was halfway up the stairs, but she didn't turn.

In her room, the first thing she saw was the makeup case, the cleverly drawn funny card propped on her dresser. Of all the confusing men she'd ever met, he was the ultimate. How could he be so many conflicting things all at the same time? *Forget him, Alana,* she told herself. *Lindsay can have him!*

Stripping off skirt, jersey, sandals, she carelessly belted a white cotton eyelet "happy coat" around her middle and barged into the hall, heading for the bathroom. Rand was two steps from the top of the stairs when she burst from her room. His dark eyes traveled slowly, heavily, up her length, tracing bare feet, long smoothly muscled calves, rounded thighs bared nearly to where her scanty underwear began. Her hand moved nervously on the flimsy robe's cross-over front, the sleeve falling away from her tanned arm. If they were going to live in the same house, meetings like this one were inevitable, and she refused to turn and run like some frightened spinster, she decided angrily. She glared defiantly at him.

His burning eyes met her own full on, and a powerful shaft of raw, hot desire passed between them. He reached out a hand, and for an instant, she imagined he would draw her toward him. Instead, he handed her an envelope, a small box, and a file folder.

"This came today, apparently. I just noticed it in the hall. In the box is Bruce's hearing aid. The folder is his assessment." He remained standing on the stairs, two steps below her. His soft curls were level with her chin. If she stretched her hand, she could touch his hair, run her fingers through its beckoning mass, trace his ear. She snatched the items from his grasp and bolted for the bathroom. If he thought she was going to be one of his "compensations," he was sadly mistaken!

"Alana?"

She swung around at the door to face him.

"Take it easy. You're glaring at me as if I were a depraved, sex-mad maniac, and that only happens when there's a full moon. Besides, Jenny sleeps just down the hall." He gave her a broad grin and a deliberately lewd wink before she slammed the door.

It wasn't at all reassuring to catch a glimpse of herself in the tilting mirror and find that besides flushed cheeks and partly open lips, she could clearly discern her underwear in all its briefness through the thin eyelet wrap. And why did that incredibly infuriating man always manage to have the final word?

Back safely in bed, she scanned the envelope Rand had given her. It was from Johnny, sent to her Vancouver apartment, readdressed here by Grace. Damn. He obviously hadn't received the message she'd left at headquarters about her change of summer plans. Ripping the letter open, she scanned it avidly, then went back to read impatiently. Her brother could ramble on without revealing a single important fact about himself.

Weather's hot and muggy here, but the women aren't. What's your friend Grace's phone number? I'll call her when I'm back on the coast—

Alana checked the postmark. Toronto, over a week ago.

Tried to phone you the other night. You were out. Won't be in touch again for a while—

Grace must have been out. Little did Johnny know he already had Grace's phone number. Alana had told her friend to fill Johnny in on the sudden change of plans. Well, maybe he'd call again. This undercover intrigue made Alana uneasy. In a sudden rush of homesickness, she scurried to her bag and got the picture of Johnny she always carried, propping it on her bedside table. It had been taken when he graduated from the RCMP Academy, and he looked young and handsome, ramrod straight in his formal red uniform, the stiff brown Stetson half covering the rich chestnut hair, gloved hands held at attention at his sides. How bursting proud their father had been that day, she remembered wistfully. But Alan Campbell had been inordinately proud of both his children. He'd positively glowed at Alana's graduation from university as a teacher of the deaf.

The next thought rose before she was able to smother it. Why should Alan Campbell have had to die believing his own daughter was ashamed of him, believing he'd ruined her chances at happiness?

Nausea thrust into her stomach with the force of a blow. She drew a deep, slow breath and with incredible effort, pulled her thoughts back to the present as she'd scrupulously taught herself to do. She reread Johnny's letter until it again made sense, but sleep was still a long way off.

She reached for the file folder, deciding to skim its contents, flipping it open on her propped up knees beneath the quilt.

Rand had given her the wrong folder. Alana stared dumbfounded at the neatly filed clippings from newspapers and magazines, all detailing reports of a jewelry-smuggling ring operating between North America—B.C. particularly—and the Orient. The dates ranged over the past two years. Bewildered, she skimmed the reports, noting that certain phrases had been underlined. "Authorities speculate that airline personnel—" "An RCMP investigation is underway—" And then she saw something that made her gasp. "Police have charged a Mrs. Lindsay Evans with conspiring to act as accomplice—"

Alana searched for more news, but found nothing and closed the folder. Lindsay—a criminal. Or at least involved in crime. An accomplice...to whom? The possibility that sprang to mind was too bizarre to contemplate, and most likely a result of having a brother who was a Mountie. Rand simply couldn't be involved in smuggling. Could he? The one real fact that Johnny's job had illustrated for her was that anything was possible in the realm of human folly. Not this, though. Not Rand.

She snapped off the light and arranged her pillows. But the moon had inched its way across the window and disappeared before she slid into restless slumber. Rand's obvious interest in the case bothered her, especially since he had never mentioned it. Of course, if he were still in love with Lindsay, he'd want to protect her, but just how far did that go? Her thoughts went round in circles, until finally she slept. But her dreams echoed her turmoil. They were about gates, all locked securely, which she struggled hopelessly to open.

PERSISTENTLY, THE GENTLE TAPPING dragged her from sleep. Her clock read 5:00 A.M., and the world outside was barely gray. Puzzled, groggy, she knotted her robe against the shivery morning air and staggered to the door.

Rand grinned down at her, wide awake, cheerful, breathtakingly virile in ragged blue cutoffs and a threadbare white T-shirt. "Wake up, sleepyhead. Exercise time," he announced, handing her a peeled and segmented orange.

He was sipping coffee in the kitchen ten minutes later when she hurried down. Her face felt shiny from cold water, her hair curled wildly around a striped headband. He ran a speculative eye down her, noting the cheery matching yellow shorts and top, the Adidas runners.

"Mind slumming?" he queried, indicating his own haphazard garb.

He led the way across the meadow, over a footbridge, onto a hidden forest path where dew wet their shoes and a million tiny prisms shattered as the sun broke through the evergreens. Bird song was all around, and she could hear Rand's steady breathing as he ran beside her.

"Haven't run...since...college," he panted after a mile or two. The high altitude was playing havoc with Alana's breathing, too, so they slowed to a walk.

"Time to stop smoking," Rand admitted as they followed the path up a steep incline to a grassy meadow ringed with poplars. They jogged home in companionable silence. Rand left for work before she could ask him about Bruce's assessment folder—and return the other one.

The rest of the day blurred past. Alana worked hard with Bruce, pouring out signs for everything, endlessly repeating the names of the objects and people in his world. She introduced the hearing aid, securing the custom-made molds in his delicate ears, resting the small instrument behind his earlobe. First, she introduced only gross sounds using a toy drum, making a game of having him cover his ears and listen, rewarding him when he responded.

While he napped that afternoon, she slipped into Rand's study and found the folder containing Bruce's assessment, replacing the other on his desk. Without thinking and so, she told herself, without guilt, she opened his desk drawers, searching for... she didn't know. She only knew of her need to find out more about the extent of his involvement with his wife—his criminal wife. In the left-hand bottom drawer she dug out a journal, and flipped open to the most recent entries. Two months ago—"Lindsay 2 P.M. airport." A few days after that, "Pick up—George—airport." Every few weeks there was something about Lindsay or the airport or names she'd never heard.

Guilt and confused panic flooded her mind, and she quickly stuffed the book back. She would simply ask Rand, that's all. There had to be a simple explanation.

Outside in the sunshine, she opened the file on Bruce and became engrossed in his records. They indicated what she suspected; his deafness was profound, so even if he learned to use every scrap of his residual hearing, his ears could never be the main source of communication.

Over the next few days, Alana worked to help Bruce with that communication. Hungry blue eyes devoured every movement Alana's hands made, her signs matching the spoken word for lip-reading purposes. He mastered two more signs, then four, then ten. His legs and Alana's ran marathons through the days, and each morning began with Rand's gentle tap on her door. When had she last felt so truly fulfilled?

Apprehensive at first with Rand on their runs, she had soon relaxed, grateful to him for making the effort to jog with her. She'd pushed his unsavory activities to the back of her mind, vowing to find out the truth—but not yet. Morning followed perfect morning. Rand soon conditioned to their long, slow runs, his huge frame lean and naturally athletic. He chose numerous woodland paths for them to follow. They often saw squirrels or rabbits, and once, a waddling fat porcupine with glimmering silvery quills hastily crossed their path. One day, a group of six gray-brown animals with shaggy coats and the beginnings of antlers tore away into the woods, startling Alana.

"Elk," Rand explained. "The second-largest member of the deer family, whose huge herds gave this valley its name." He showed her how he had posted No Hunting signs everywhere on his land, in an effort to protect the valley's wildlife. Often, they came upon several fragile-looking, long-legged deer, feeding in the meadow at the top of the slope.

One morning, Rand stopped her abruptly, motioning toward a low shrub. She gasped with delight as she noticed the tiny, perfectly camouflaged spotted fawn, suspended on legs that seemed too delicate to hold its weight. Its coloring blended exactly with the foliage. It had an innocent mouse face with limpid trusting eyes, and huge ears Alana ached to stroke. Rand cautioned her about touching it, because the mother would reject it should she return and smell human odor on her baby.

Tears of appreciation and wonder sprang to Alana's eyes. She turned, and Rand was watching her instead of the fawn, a peculiar, haunted expression on his face. He gently reached a finger and traced the path her tears made.

"Bagpipe music and parades make me cry as well," she gulped.

He cradled her chin in his rough palm for a fleeting moment, and said wistfully, "You're very lovely, teacher. So damned healthy, so—normal."

"I'm also sweaty, and starting to shiver," she said lightly, shying away from his intensity, determined to maintain the casual friendship they shared on these runs.

Healthy, and normal. How very dull! She called over her shoulder, "Race you down the hill," and stretched her legs into a gallop. Might as well demonstrate how really healthy she was!

Panting and laughing, they arrived at the ranch, detouring to the kitchen door. Alana remembered something she'd been meaning to ask.

"Are there nets for the tennis courts?" She'd discovered the cement enclosures behind the house, near the meadow, unused and naked looking.

"Who built them?" she added, before she noticed the guarded look that crept over Rand's features.

"Mother had them built. They've not been used for several years. Tom stored the equipment."

Probably his wife had used them. Alana forced herself to confront the issue she'd been deathly afraid of, and took a deep breath. Enough! She had to know about this woman from his past... and present?

"Did Lindsay play tennis?" Alana nearly choked on the query.

Anger and pain were in his terse reply, and he closed the kitchen door behind them unnecessarily hard. "Yes, she did. We both did."

The implied camaraderie, his bitter, almost wistful tone, told Alana much more than his words. He had loved—still loved—Lindsay passionately. Why else did his mood change when he spoke of her, of an activity they'd enjoyed together?

Alana's heart hammered wildly. Overwhelming suspicion, jealousy and longing burgeoned within her, yet some demon made her continue.

"Do you—do you see Lindsay often, Rand?"

His eyes were cold and intimidating; his face a stiff, unyielding mask. The intimacy their runs had encouraged might never have been. "Stay out of it, Alana. My life with Lindsay has nothing to do with you. Nothing." And with that he left her standing just inside the kitchen door, shock and hurt crumpling her face.

Under the shower's pulsing hot spray, Alana was finally able to think rationally again, rather than succumb to the agony of the emotions Rand had stirred. The encounter had been painful, forcing her to admit that a powerful bond still existed between Rand and his ex-wife. Alana wasn't ready to analyze her reactions to him, and what she now knew about him. She had allowed herself to be seduced by the beauty and solitude of Bluejay, and she had become reliant on Rand for companionship. Mistake, she berated herself viciously, using the soap and washcloth until her skin stung. But since her arrival, there had been no visitors to Bluejay. Rand bought groceries and supplies from Jenny's lists and the mail from the box at the road. Fresh milk, eggs and vegetables came from Bluejay's own produce. Rand might be a recluse, just as Katy Sinclair had said, but such solitude for Alana was unhealthy. Bruce, too, needed contact with other children, with a world not bounded by Bluejay. And by his father. What was Rand locking out, or locking in? She brushed aside her tumultuous thoughts.

But not before her traitorous imagination whispered, what if? What if Rand and his former wife *were* part of a smuggling ring? But that was preposterous. He *was* hiding *something*, that much was definite...beyond that, Alana stopped guessing.

THE NEXT AFTERNOON, Jenny's piercing call reached Alana where she and Bruce were sharing a picnic lunch with Tom, in a shady corner of the sun-drenched meadow. Bruce was lying flat on his back in the grass, squinting up at two noisy jays, flitting from branch to branch. Their spectacular colors had caught his eye, and his fingers were practising the newly learned sign for bird, his palm forward in front of his face, repeatedly opening and closing the thumb and index finger of one hand, imitating the way a bird's beak chirps or eats. Giggling, he insisted Tom try. During the past week, Tom and Jenny had learned signs almost as fast as Bruce and used them in simple conversations. Rand, though, was self conscious and reticent at signing. His large fingers seemed to freeze when the others insisted he try, and usually he refused.

"Telephone, teacher," Jenny called again. Alana

sprinted to the house and breathlessly retrieved the receiver from the shiny yellow counter. Maybe it was Johnny, or Grace.

"Hel—hello?" she panted, heart hammering.

"Alana? Hi there. It's Katy—Katy Sinclair. Is somebody chasing you again? You sound out of breath."

Alana recovered her breath enough to laugh. "Hi, Katy. Just running for the phone this time." Suddenly she was delighted to hear the other girl's distinctive musical tones. She'd rather liked Katy Sinclair. It would be fun to get to know her better.

"I phoned for two reasons. First, to find out if you'd recovered, and second to give you a chance to meet the true and charming Katy. So how about lunch tomorrow here at my trailer? You can meet my mother that way—she's like me, but she talks more." Alana hesitated, and Katy went on, "Rand can't keep you a prisoner up there forever. Oh, and bring Bruce with you. He can play with Lissa. I'm sure they'll get along fine. What do you say, Alana? About twelve-thirty?"

"Why—" Alana wanted to go. This was just what she needed, and Bruce, too. But Rand had been adamant about Bruce staying here at Bluejay. Alana had a suspicious feeling Rand would object to her taking him, even to Katy's.

Then an idea came. He'd never said a word about children coming here to visit Bruce. Alana grinned wickedly. If Mohammed couldn't go to the mountain, she reasoned...

"Katy, I'd love to see you. But I...I have no car. At least, not one I'm used to driving. So how about you and Lissa coming here tomorrow for lunch, say about one?" She was certain Jenny wouldn't mind, and she'd offer to help with preparations.

Katy agreed at once. "Love to," she said enthusiastically. "Lissa would love to see the farm—she's horse crazy right now. You and Bruce can come to my place next time." With a cheery "See you tomorrow," she hung up.

Now to check with Jenny. Banging the screen door behind her and blinking at the sun's brightness, she located Jenny kneeling in the dirt of the flourishing garden Tom had created. Neat, colorful rows of lettuce, cabbage and onions were sprouting. Jenny was putting up sticks for the tomatoes to climb. She raised a placid, beaming face to Alana.

"Damn nice day, huh, teacher?" she sing-songed. She wore bibbed blue overalls, pant legs rolled to her knees above red knee socks and dirty tennis shoes. On top, a lime-green shirt and an immense straw hat made her look like a color-blind oriental elf, round and bright and smiling.

Jenny had a gentle inner radiance and peace, a dignity that seemed to come with her contentment with life. She worked hard, all day, every day. Alana knew after spending several days with Bruce exactly how difficult it must have been for Jenny to care for the active child, keep house, cook and do the myriad other tasks needed in a house the size of Bluejay. Already, order had been restored just in the short time since Alana's arrival. Though Jenny never complained about her workload, it was obvious she should have help. Tom, too, was aware of this. He did as many chores as possible for Jenny. There was a shy but obvious affection between the brusque man with his crutch and this round little woman.

Hesitantly, Alana told Jenny of her impetuous invitation to Katy. To her delight, Jenny said, "Good idea, teacher. Bruce needs kids to play with. I told Boss that before—" Her words were interrupted by a wild cry cutting the afternoon peace.

"Jenny! Teacher! Come, come quick!" The obvious panic in Tom's voice galvanized both women. They raced to where Tom balanced in agitated fear beside the high pine tree. He was peering anxiously into its branches.

"I went to let the horses out, gone for not five minutes, and Bruce climbed—"

High in the tree above their heads, the child clung precariously to a branch, reached a small arm out to grasp the next, and collectively their breath stopped as he slipped, cried out in fear, jerked as his shirt twisted around a branch. He was at least thirty feet above their heads.

"He's gonna fall. Damn this crutch, damn it..." Impotently, Tom cursed, his hoarse voice cracking with frustration and fear.

"I'll go after him." Sounding far more confident than she felt, Alana reached up, dragged herself to the first branch, clumsily began to clamber up the tree. Bruce twisted to look down at her, and she smiled up at his tear-stained face reassuringly, praying the cotton shirt would stay firmly hooked on the branch until she could reach him. She hadn't climbed a tree in ten years. If only she could get to him before he panicked and slipped again. She grasped the thick branches desperately, feeling the sticky sap oozing onto her fingers, glancing down just once and gulping as she saw how high she already was from the ground. Now she could see the huge bird's nest above Bruce, probably what he'd decided to explore.

Her heart thumped with fear. Hurrying as much as she dared, she scraped the soft skin on her palms painfully on the rough bark. Her shirt caught and tore. Her knee slipped on a branch and she lunged for the next in a rush of panic.

Below, Tom and Jenny frantically called instructions, each contradicting the other.

"Hurry, Alana, hurry."

"Go slow, teacher, take your time."

"He's going to fall—hang on, Brucie." The last was a hopeless, desperate cry from both bystanders, repeated over and over.

Almost, almost...one more limb. It whipped across her face painfully, bringing tears to her eyes and blinding her for a moment. Through her haze, she saw Bruce give one last frantic twist immediately above her, squirming to reach her. His shirt tore free. He came hurtling down, bumping his forehead hard on a branch. In a desperate lunge she grabbed his arm. With superhuman effort, she gathered him to her, clinging for dear life to the tree with both legs. Bruce was husky for his age, and it felt as though her arm had been wrenched from its socket. Red hot needles of pain shot into her chest. She hung on grimly, as he locked arms and legs around her neck and body in a death grip. He was roaring out his fear so loudly into her left ear it hurt, but it was absolutely wonderful to have the sweaty, howling child close against her. Taking a deep breath, she began the infinitely slow, painful descent.

She was trembling and weak by the time she finally reached the place where Tom and Jenny's eager hands could help, but by then, Bruce wouldn't let go. He clung to her, soaking her neck and blouse with tears, loud wails still ringing in her ears, nose running and an ugly purple lump rising like fast yeast on his forehead.

Her knees simply wouldn't work. She dropped the last foot to the ground, clutching Bruce protectively.

"Easy, tiger. You're okay now," she murmured as much to herself as anything. Jenny attempted to peel him away, and a trickle of blood from his head was mixing with his tears into a pink-tinged mess. His face was pasty white. Jenny cradled him, and suddenly he was sick, retching violently while Tom helplessly patted and wiped his face. Jenny met Alana's eyes and they nodded in unison.

"He has to see a doctor," Alana agreed.

"I'll call Rand home to take him," Tom said. He smacked the crutch in frustration. "Can't drive with this, and Jenny never learned."

"But it will take an hour or more for Rand to get here," Alana said. "I could drive him if there were a car—"

Tom was already hurrying toward the double garage.

"There's a car you can take. I'll start it up, and you get ready," Tom called over his shoulder.

Hurriedly, Alana washed, yanked on fresh jeans and T-shirt, hardly noticing the pitch blackening her cheek and palms. The scrapes were starting to sting and burn, and her arm and shoulder were aching, pains shooting down her side. In a few moments, she was carefully backing a silver-blue Fiat out of the garage with Tom's direction, and Jenny tucked a freshly bathed Bruce into the seat beside her, complete with pillow and blanket.

"You think I should come with you?" Jenny had demanded anxiously, but Alana thought a moment and shook her head. She knew Jenny had bread dough set and food half-prepared in the kitchen. The car was small. With Bruce strapped securely in a safety seat, his favorite blanket already clutched against his cheek and his thumb comfortingly in his mouth, he was certain to go to sleep.

"Just please phone Rand and ask him to meet us at the clinic," she directed. The way her arm was feeling, it might be necessary for him to drive back.

Before they reached the turn to the highway, Bruce was asleep. The powerful little car handled easily, and Alana blessed her brother's insistence that she learn to use a stick shift. Fleetingly, she wondered whether the car had belonged to Lindsay. Certainly, she'd never seen Rand use it the past weeks. And thankfully, it was her left arm and shoulder she'd wrenched. Hardly noticing the tunnels of trees falling away into grassy meadows, Alana concentrated on following the route she vaguely remembered from her first trip with Rand, and on the white-blond curly head resting close beside her. Soon, she was slowing carefully, entering the small town of Elkford.

She couldn't help but notice the newness of the town. All the buildings looked freshly constructed and slightly raw. Piles of lumber and busy workmen everywhere illustrated that building was still going on at a great pace. Pulling over, Alana asked a friendly man in a hard hat to direct her to the medical clinic Jenny had described. The man glanced at the sleeping child with the immense lump on his head and hurriedly and concisely pointed the way.

Moments later, a groggy Bruce lolling on her shoulder, she entered the low gray brick building whose large windows announced Elkford Diagnostic Centre.

The middle-aged nurse behind the desk gave her a friendly smile, and immediately bustled away to bring a white-coated figure from the back. Alana glanced at him, and then her eyes widened in glad recognition. It was the friendly young doctor she'd met that very first day at the airport.

"This is Dr. Williams—" the nurse began, but David was already hurrying to Alana, his friendly light-blue eyes shining a welcome to her even through his glasses.

"I told you we'd meet again," he greeted her, as his professional eye ran over the child she held.

"Come along here," he ordered, leading her into an examining room, gently helping her lay Bruce on a white-sheeted table.

David looked different here, older than the boyish young man who'd flirted with her at the airport. Very much in control, despite the unruly sandy hair still falling over his forehead as he bent to look at Bruce.

The strange surroundings and now this white-coated stranger brought first a quivering downturned mouth and then tears of rage and fear from the boy. Struggling frantically, he was soon back in Alana's arms, hands locked behind her neck, legs clamped viselike around her middle. His roars echoed through the tiny room.

"What happened?" David was forced to shout over Bruce's healthy lungs.

Alana called out the story, and the doctor did his best to examine the lump on Bruce's head, trying to look into the boy's eyes. Alana could feel the small body shaking with fear. She slid into an available chair and tried gently to calm and soothe Bruce, stroking his head and patting his back. Slowly, he grew calmer and quieter.

David waited patiently. He lounged against the wall, and his scrutiny made Alana suddenly shy as she realized how she must look, covered in pitch, hair even more tousled than usual, face bare even of lipgloss. Yet the doctor's friendliness and admiration were every bit as evident today as they had been that first day in Cranbrook.

"I've been planning to find you since the day I arrived, but Dr. Monroe caught the flu and I've been on call every minute since I got here." His ingenuous smile flashed, and he added, "Of course, that's exactly why I came. I love my work, although it certainly curbs any social life. Anyway, Dr. Monroe is due back tomorrow, and he's promised me the weekend free. Could I talk you into a sight-seeing tour with me? So far, all I've seen of this magnificent valley is my apartment and this clinic."

A day spent away from Bluejay was appealing. Perhaps going out with this nice young man would help Alana put her reactions to Rand back into perspective. She smiled gratefully at the stocky figure.

"I'd like that, David," she agreed. Bruce was quiet now, watching David out of the corner of one suspicious eye, long lashes matted with tears and his lump turning a rich purple. Alana pointed at the doctor, making a "D" on her left wrist where a doctor would feel a pulse. She made the sign Bruce knew for "look" several times as well, hoping Bruce would understand she was telling him David wanted only to look at him. Bruce's eyes widened when David again slowly approached him, but he didn't howl. David bent very close to Alana, explaining, "I should just get a look in his eyes with this." He indicated a small instrument, giving it to Bruce to look over before he tried to use it. Finally, the little boy handed it back to the doctor, huddling even closer against Alana.

"We won't upset him again by putting him on the table," David decided, leaning intimately near Alana, but intent on his work as he braced himself with one hand on her chair back, his thigh pressing against hers, trying to follow the light beam's reflection in Bruce's elusive eyes. Bruce squirmed back and forth. David's soft clean hair was so near it tickled Alana's cheek. She could smell his faintly medicinal odor, and his breath fanned gently over her.

At that moment, the door of the tiny room burst open, and Rand filled the opening, the clucking gray-haired nurse at his elbow. He took in the scene with one glance and strode in, towering over David like some avenging God.

"What the hell's going on here?" he demanded, smoldering eyes narrowed on Alana, the doctor, his son. His well-muscled arms were bare, and the green work shirt looked too tight for the bulk it contained. From where he stood, it must look as though David was embracing her, and Alana felt a rush of angry heat flood up and over her face as Rand's eyes flicked from her to David and back again. Bruce immediately began to cry when he saw his father, reaching out his arms to him pathetically, and to Alana's absolute horror, tears welled up in her own eyes and began to run down her cheeks. The afternoon's events, and this ridiculous finale were too much. She, who hardly ever cried, began to sob helplessly.

CHAPTER SIX

THE LONG RIDE BACK TO BLUEJAY that evening was quiet. Alana wearily cradled a sleeping Bruce with her right arm. He snored gently, blessedly unaware of the tension vibrating between the two adults.

Hours before, only David's professional calm had averted what threatened to become a disastrous scene. David had ignored Rand's rude entrance, calmly waving away the agitated nurse and extending a friendly hand in Rand's direction, giving Alana a chance to recover.

"You must be Bruce's father. I'm David Williams—*Doctor* David Williams." The gentle emphasis had been unmistakable. "I'm relieving for Dr. Monroe. How do you do?" David had stubbornly left his hand hanging between them, and finally, reluctantly, Rand grasped it. A second later, he'd gently lifted his son into his arms, and Alana had felt the awful tension in his body, seen the tendons in his throat constrict as he'd touched the purple lump with a light forefinger. There might also have been remorse in his quick glance at her tear streaked face, but by then Alana was too angry with him to care. She had understood his concern for his son, but his rudeness to David had infuriated her. She'd refused to meet his eyes, feeling the scarlet flags of her anger burn on her cheeks.

David had then quietly reassured them about Bruce.

He suggested they should wake the boy several times in the night to be certain there was no danger of concussion, insisting it was only a precaution—he was certain Bruce had survived the bump with no side effects. Then he'd turned his perspective gaze on Alana.

"You've injured your shoulder," he stated. "Let's just have a look at it." Ushering Rand to the waiting room, David had quickly and professionally probed and assessed the damage, his touch gentle but remote.

"Some torn ligaments and muscle strain," he'd pronounced, confirming what she suspected. He fashioned a temporary sling, to reduce swelling and make her more comfortable. When she'd entered the reception area where Rand was waiting with Bruce, his eyes had widened at the supported arm, and he'd quizzed David thoroughly about the extent of the injury.

David had given Alana a bottle of strong painkillers, emphasizing the need of rest for her shoulder. Then he added pointedly, "We'll take a week's rain check on our sight-seeing date, Alana. You won't feel much like it this Sunday." He had quietly but firmly let Rand know their plans. Alana felt a growing respect for the bespectacled doctor. He'd refused to be intimidated by the glowering Rand, who had stalked from the room without so much as a good-night. David had winked eloquently as he caught Alana's eye as she'd followed Rand more slowly, and blandly called a cheery "Good night, now," as Rand had practically lifted her into his sports car. Accelerating out of town with far more energy than necessary, Rand had hardly spoken between then and now.

At last, he reached between them, his hand very near her leg, to switch the radio on. In the light from the dash, she could see the weary lines of strain etched around his mouth and eyes, and it annoyed her to feel a pang of sympathy for him.

They had reached the Bluejay turnoff before he broke the silence.

"Jenny told me on the phone how you raced up that tree to rescue Bruce. I want you to know I appreciate it. I'm very grateful." His gruff tones could barely be heard over the blare of the radio. "I'll make it up to you, I promise."

Alana drew a deep breath, trying to accept his thanks graciously, subdue the anger she felt with him, be cool, remote, controlled...and as usual, she lost the battle with her tongue.

"You have to be the most bad-tempered, ungrateful, tactless, insufferable man I've ever met! Furthermore, you owe Dr. Williams a big, fat apology. You acted like—like a cave man, for heaven's sake!"

Her narrowed gray stare caught the enigmatic half smile twisting the corners of his mouth under the mustache. Surely her hair was on end with the furious current of anger raging through her!

"I don't find anything funny about it, either," she snapped.

His powerful hands maneuvered the car over the little wooden bridge.

"I'm smiling at your ability to always assess my character. Also because you're quite beautiful when you get this furious, in spite of the pitch all over your cheek."

Her hand flew to the sticky patch she'd forgotten about, and the motion brought a sudden stabbing pain from her shoulder. She gasped, and Rand growled a vivid curse under his breath, pulling into Bluejay's graveled driveway with a flourish and braking to an abrupt stop. In one fluid motion, he was out of the car and had opened the door on her side.

"Jenny," he bellowed at the top of his lungs. Every light was on in every room of the house. The front door slammed and Jenny hurried toward them, with Tom following a short distance behind.

Smoothly and tenderly, Rand handed the sleeping bundle of his son into Jenny's welcoming arms, and then Alana found herself out of the car and swept into Rand's arms. The world tilted giddily.

"Put me down," she ordered, twisting, but her shoulder jostled when she moved, and another small cry of pain escaped. She stopped struggling. There was something so very comforting about Rand's arms. Profoundly disturbing as well. Her head sank weakly onto his shoulder, and she held very still. Any motion caused waves of pain, but partly she wanted to savor the feeling of being helpless, and cradled by these arms. His special odor enveloped her, a tantalizing tobacco-male smell, and the iron firmness of his body, his very bulk, made her own slenderness seem nearly fragile—a rare sensation for a tall woman. Their bodies were so very right together, she thought dreamily, almost hypnotized with exhaustion and the unreality of the scene.

"I'm very heavy," she muttered, but Rand's breathing hardly seemed affected, even as he mounted the stairs to the veranda. Tom opened the house door.

"Stay right there," Rand ordered in a no-nonsense tone as he lowered her to the sofa, hurrying off down the hall to check Bruce and relay the doctor's orders to Jenny. Tom awkwardly pulled an afghan up to cover

Alana, and the look of concern on his face reminded her how worried he must be about Bruce. Forcing herself to sound calm, reassuring and wide awake, she reviewed for him everything the doctor had said and done for Bruce, repeating his assurance that the child was fine.

The worry lines in Tom's weathered face eased, but he kept repeating bitterly, "No thanks to me, he didn't fall. Godblasted leg, anyhow."

Then Rand was back with a mug of hot chocolate, propping a cushion behind her so clumsily she had a wild urge to giggle at his male ineptness. Sipping the chocolate instead, she closed her eyes for a blissful moment. She felt so sleepy, so warm...the room blurred, and slipped away.

Someone had tucked a soft pillow under her head, covered her warmly. Waking, she was first aware of the amber glow of a small lamp, a circle of light by the darkness of the window. The living-room window, she realized after a second.

"You don't even snore when you sleep." A low chuckle accompanied the statement, and Alana turned her head to where Rand sat in a deep wing-back chair, an arm's length away.

Too relaxed to even be startled, she murmured, "I should hope not." Then, coming more fully awake, she asked, "Why are you still up? It must be very late." Another concern came. "Is—is Bruce all right? Where's Jenny?"

"I sent Jenny to bed, and as the doctor recommended, I'm waking Bruce every hour to be sure he's fine. So far, so good—he's raving mad with me for spoiling his sleep."

Then she remembered how she'd come to be on the

sofa. Struggling up, her shoulder screamed a protest. Rand was instantly out of his chair and at her side. His arm slid behind her, supporting her back and relieving the strain of her position. His body blocked out the light from the lamp, and there was only a profile of strong male features close to her own. His free arm encircled her front, cradling and imprisoning her in his embrace. Her sleepy languor still dulled her brain, the shadowed darkness making everything dreamlike. Her slow pulse accelerated at his nearness, its hot throbbing singing in her relaxed body. She snuggled closer, and her breath quickened as his arms closed around her. Then, with a muffled groan, his warm lips closed over hers. Greedily, she tasted the spicy tang of tobacco, savored the rough-smooth texture of lips and mustache. At first, the kiss was one of discovery, retracing the memory of the kiss weeks ago in the park. Gently, he explored the moist, smooth contours of her mouth. Gently, too, his arms drew her nearer his chest, pressing the firm round breasts tighter against his half-unbuttoned shirt. She felt his heartbeat against her nipples, and its rapid pace echoed her own. His lips nibbled, teasing. The tip of his tongue probed, seeking entry. Still drugged in the aftermath of deep sleep, it seemed so natural to open for him, admit the hot, wet tongue that made her body's length arch in search of his.

Without releasing her lips, he slipped an arm beneath her, lifting and rearranging so now he rested on the couch with her on his knees, her buttocks pressing hard, corded thighs, his need for her tangibly apparent as his hands cupped her hips, drawing her lower body tight against his maleness. Her own fingers crept beneath the shirt, wandering into the soft mat of chest hair, aching shoulder cushioned by his body.

Tasting, stroking, licking, his mouth feasted on hers. He ran his tongue into the corners of her mouth, sought the soft inner tissue, flicked in mimicry of another, more intimate exploration. Cradling her head, ever mindful of her injury, he kissed her nose, and eyes and forehead. One hand set out on a path of discovery down her body, skimming its shape as though molding it, slowly tugging the bottom of her T-shirt from under her jeans waistband, sliding it up, finding and releasing the catch on the front of her skimpy lace bra.

His hand seemed to scald the fragile skin of her breast as he cupped it in one calloused palm, thumb flicking the rising nipple, circling and stroking till her breath caught and held in a gasp of aroused delight. His mouth traced a path, hot, fast, across her cheekbone to her ear, flicking the moist tongue tip into that opening, too, sending shivers of agonized need into the depths of her stomach. He nibbled down the tickling cord in her neck across the hollow where her pulse hammered. At last, tantalizing, erotically slow, his tongue reached its destination and his burning lips closed over her throbbing nipple, tugging at the swollen coral tip connected magically to the throbbing ache between her thighs.

His own arousal excited her, making her press closer in primitive, instinctual response. His shuddering breath and her own rasped loudly in the silence of the room, and half-formed words of need and delight bubbled and faded. For Alana, there was no hesitation, no cautious holding back. She wanted only to explore, to further the unexpected and engulfing hunger Rand had created. She clumsily tried to get closer to him. Her lips bravely trailed kisses down his face, loving the roughness of his unshaven cheeks. A part of her she'd kept protected and unexplored now uncurled and offered itself to him.

"Rand," she breathed. "Will you love me now, please?"

Without any warning, he swore sharply and twisted up and away from her body, as though he needed to put distance between them as quickly as possible. Groping in his shirt pocket, he found the crushed cigarette package. Extracting one, he found a wooden match and snapped it alight with his thumbnail. The flame lit his features, throwing the downcast eyes and firmly etched nostrils into sharp relief. Large hands cupped the flame, and he dipped his head to draw the smoke deep into his lungs. His retreat had come so swiftly Alana still lay frozen where he'd abandoned her. Finally, breathless and confused, she sat up.

"Rand?" Her voice sounded hesitant, and inside humiliation threatened.

The small red tip of his cigarette glowed, and he released the smoke in a slow thin stream before he answered. His glance raked over her crumpled T-shirt, her gaping bra. She struggled to fasten it, feeling the hated flush of embarrassment rise from her neck and creep over her face.

"I didn't bring you here to Bluejay to have an affair with you—although the offer's tempting." The huskiness of desire was still in his voice, and she couldn't believe she was hearing the correct words.

"Offer?" The word squeaked past the lump in her throat, and an awful feeling of disgrace built as he went on.

"For liberated women, I know sex is totally casual." The tone was now ever-so-slightly contemptuous. "I'm a normal man, and I find you damned attractive, Alana—almost too attractive to resist. But I think we agreed that some passionate summer affair isn't part of our contract. It would end badly. Bruce would suffer." His profile was outlined in the dim light as he turned half away. "So would you and I. All my relationships with women seem to end in disaster," he added bitterly.

Hardly able to assimilate what she was hearing, Alana sat stunned. Wasn't he making it sound as if *she'd* done her best to seduce *him*? "But how...how can you think—" Her voice quivered with shame and outrage, and frustration.

His own frustration showed plainly when he turned on her. "How could I what? Refuse your body? So warm and sleepy and welcoming? No red-blooded man could resist you like that."

"You...you disgusting, conceited oaf." Fury made her voice hiss and quiver in the silent room.

"Are you going to pretend now that you weren't enjoying it as much as I was? There wasn't a trace of ice in those lovely exotic eyes of yours a moment ago, Alana."

His anger matched hers in intensity, and he raked his fingers through already tumbled hair. A tremor in his voice revealed his emotion. "How the hell I've let myself become obsessed with you, I'll never know. You'd think I'd have learned my lesson." His mouth was a bitter line beneath the mustache, grooves etched deeply on either side of his mouth. "You don't need my scalp to add to your collection, Alana. I'm sure you could have *Doctor* David Williams hanging there, and—who knows how many other trophies in Vancouver?"

"One, Rand. There's been exactly one man in my life.

Oh, why am I bothering?" Whatever she said, he'd probably believe what he wanted. But at least she had the right to set the record straight. Her lips pressed down so hard her jaw ached. He'd done her quite enough emotional damage for one night. And, she promised herself, he wouldn't get another opportunity. Tears burned treacherously just behind her eyes. It was becoming an effort to hold them back. Why should he be so vicious with her?

Maybe he sensed how close she was to breaking, because his voice gentled just a little. He rubbed wearily at his eyes with his fingers. When he dropped his hand, he shot her a rueful look.

"I'm tired. We both are. God knows, simple animal attraction is nothing to fight about." His words made her feel infinitely worse.

"I—I take it you don't believe in 'love'?" Her attempt at sarcasm came out wrong, more like a question. She struggled up from the low couch, favoring her throbbing shoulder awkwardly as she bent to retrieve her shoes from the rug. Stubbing out his cigarette, he impatiently snatched her shoes, wrapped a supportive and still-disturbing arm around her waist.

"You just let go of me—I don't want your help." Furiously, she pushed his arm away.

"Well, you're getting it whether you want it or not," he snapped. "And my opinions as well, seeing you've asked." He easily resisted her efforts to dislodge his grip. "Love," he spat in disgust. "'Love,' just a sentimental, woman's word for sexual desire. 'I love you,' just a catch-all phrase for emotional blackmail." His contemptuous tone contrasted sharply with the gentleness he used to guide her to the stairs, but he obviously believed every word he was saying. A chill shot through Alana. Rand was inadvertently telling her of his marriage, his relationship with his ex-wife. And underneath the contempt was pain.

His comments punctuated their slow ascent, step by careful step. Alana tried to avoid jarring, but her strained muscles sent shards of pain all the way down to her bare toes—just as his cynical monologue jarred painfully the half-formed dreams of the past hour.

"Between parents and children, sure there's love—sometimes." He swung her runners by their laces. "But between consenting adults?" He shook his head. "If they're honest, they'll call it what it is. Passion. Sex. Animal attraction. Body need—like hunger and thirst."

He hoisted her to the landing, his arm a steel band of muscle around her. He maneuvered them down the passage.

"My marriage taught me one thing well. No woman will ever hear me tell her I love her, ever again. It doesn't exist. Does that answer your questions?"

They were at the door to her room. She tried one last time to escape his grip, but he swung in, still holding her firmly. In another moment he had the bedclothes flipped back, and had deposited her on the sweet-smelling cotton sheets.

"But surely you loved other women, before you married? Women aren't all the same." She felt foolish, but she *had* to get through to him, even though her words probably fell on deaf ears. It seemed communication with Rand was far more difficult than with Bruce!

"Only Lindsay. Most of my childhood was spent at boarding school and Lawrence Ross, my English teacher, became my counselor and friend. A boy needs a man to pattern himself upon. My own father and I were—well, we weren't close. Lindsay is Lawrence Ross's daughter." Rand stood beside the bed, fists low on his narrow hips and eyes on Alana, but not seeing her. She lay still, listening intently.

"He was a widower, and Lindsay was his only child. She was away at school most of the time, but when I did see her, she was like a creature from another planet to me. Beautiful. Lawrence spoiled her hopelessly, but of course I didn't realize that." Rand's mouth twisted sardonically. "She became a stewardess, and I graduated, took over the mine. Sure, there were women. Just none I cared about . . . the way I cared for her." He half turned away.

"How did you—" Every word, every phrase, hurt, but Alana had to know.

"Marry her?" He shrugged. "Lawrence had a stroke, made me executor of his estate and Lindsay's legal guardian." Rand laughed shortly, bitterly. "Some guardian. She was nineteen, and aeons older than I in experience. Sex was already a commodity to her, to trade for the things she wanted. Clothes, jewelry—she was frightened because Lawrence was no longer able to pick up the pieces of her problems and solve them. I represented security, I was guilt ridden for having seduced her. We married, and Lawrence was overjoyed. Unfortunately, we couldn't live together. However, I did learn a great deal in a short time."

"You learned to lock yourself up and throw away the key," Alana accused.

He looked surprised rather than angry. He reached down to draw the cover up, then eyed her fully clothed form a bit uncertainly. Was he about to undress her as casually and efficiently as she'd seen him strip Bruce at bedtime?

Panic suddenly choked her, and she shrieked, "Would you leave me *alone* now, *please*?"

He left without another word, closing the door softly behind him. From where she lay, she listened to his footsteps going down the hall toward Bruce's room. Trembling, she struggled out of her jeans and shirt, giving up on the lacy pink panties when her shoulder objected violently. She'd sleep in them, and forget about her nightshirt. She collapsed on the pillows, praying for sleep, but it eluded her. Rand's rejection of her, his cynicism and the reasons for it consumed her thoughts. Over and over, she heard his caustic remark. *No woman will ever hear me tell her I love her. It doesn't exist.*

Alana believed in love. Her own limited and very painful experience should have soured her, but still she believed. She'd seen love between a man and woman—her parents. She'd grown like a flower basking in the reflected sunshine of that love, she mused, aching physically and emotionally from both her shoulder and Rand's rejection.

Her mother, Liandra Campbell, was little more than a memory of warmth and laughter to Alana, but remembering her mother was remembering love. Liandra had totally loved her husband, Alana's father, just as he'd loved her—worshiped her, in fact. Her father's loyalty to that love had lasted after her mother's death when Alana was ten, and on to the end of his life. From that nucleus, love had spilled over her and John, illustrating by silent example why she could never settle for less in her own life.

Rand was wrong. Knowing he was wrong was no comfort, though. It left her desolate. Between him and Lindsay a bond still existed—and it wasn't a common interest in Bruce. Alana feared it had much less honorable motives. Alana tugged the covers up over her nearly naked body, uneasily longing for sleep, for oblivion. The mad laughter of a loon far out on the lake seemed fitting counterpoint to the mad conjectures racing through her mind. Slowly, the sound became part of the ironic confusion of her dreams.

IT WAS LATE when she woke. She felt groggy and unbelievably stiff and sore. She staggered to the bathroom and back. Jenny must have heard, because Alana had just returned to her room when she appeared with a tray.

"Back into bed." Jenny's sharp eyes took in Alana's pale cheeks, the evidence of strain from a badly aching arm.

"Boss ordered you to stay in bed all morning. Bruce is fine, only a big lump on his head, but he's tired, too. He's with Tom, and soon he will nap. Boss said that sore arm made you groan half the night." Alana's face flamed as Jenny tucked the covers around her, settling the tray across her legs. There was a disquieting memory of being half-awakened some time in the pale dawn, and made to swallow the tablets David had suggested. Uncomfortably, Alana remembered Rand's soothing whisper, like part of a dream, and him straightening the twisted bed covers, tucking them firmly around her naked shoulders. Rand, who last night had... She sipped her rich hot coffee, and Jenny hurried away.

Whole-wheat toast from Jenny's good bread, a delicate fruit salad, and Alana reluctantly decided a few hours in bed were definitely what she needed. Despite a second cup of coffee from the antique silver carafe Jenny had brought, she was nearly asleep again.

WHEN SHE AWAKENED NEXT, it was to the spicy aroma of cinnamon and nutmeg. Cookies baking. Stretching lethargically, she realized she felt much better. Even the confusions of the night's events seemed easier to push to the back of her mind. She glanced at the bedside clock. Heavens, already past noon. A nagging feeling that she'd forgotten something—Katy! Katy was coming for lunch, and soon!

Alana showered and dressed in record time. In the sunny kitchen, Jenny was drawing a tray of delicious-smelling oatmeal cookies from the oven. At Alana's apologies, she waved a hand and ordered, "Relax. I made salads, there's fresh fruit, cheese, cookies. Try one." The crisp, nutty texture was irresistible.

"Jenny, how I need you to keep order in my life," Alana breathed. "How'd you ever learn to cook like this?"

In odd moments, Jenny was doing her best to teach Alana the intricacies of cooking and baking, but as predicted, Alana was a slow learner. Jenny seemed to know so many things just by instinct. Also, they'd both found Bruce's "help" was anything but beneficial to the lessons.

Jenny poured them each a steaming cup of coffee from the ever-full blue enamel pot.

"My parents came from China when I was small, opened a café in the old towns in the Valley, named Natal and Michel. Those towns are gone now, the big mining companies came and relocated the people to Sparwood and destroyed all the old buildings."

Jenny added a generous dollop of fresh cream to her coffee and Alana's.

"Working in that café, I learned to cook. Chinese-

Canadian cuisine, you know?" Her eyes twinkled and Alana smiled fondly, thinking of all the little restaurants all over Canada run by families like Jenny's, people who worked hard and still managed to bring up happy, productive children while serving endless meals to the public.

"We were a big family, six children in all. Too many for one small business to support. So when I was seventeen, Amanda Evans needed a nurse for her baby. Boss was very small, and sickly, and she had to go to England where her father was dying. Anyhow, I came here and I stayed."

"Do you see any of your family?" Alana was curious. Jenny didn't seem to have any friends or relatives who visited.

"Not much, most moved away to Vancouver's Chinatown. My mother and father are dead now, but they always were angry with me because I didn't marry a man they'd picked for me." Jenny laughed good naturedly, as though it were all one of life's practical jokes.

Hadn't she ever yearned for a life of her own, a man's love, children, perhaps? "Didn't you ever want to marry, Jenny?"

A guarded expression flickered across the tranquil, plump face. But she simply said, "This is my home, here at Bluejay. All my life is here." Setting down the coffee cup, she gathered the baking pans to wash, adding casually, "Here, I am needed, you see, teacher."

Thoughtfully, Alana sipped from her mug. For Jenny, being needed was obviously enough. Was it unrealistic, a childish dream, to demand love, marriage, children from life—in that order? Rand spoke of "animal attraction." Jenny had built a lifetime around "need." Maybe everyone compromised as they went along. What compromise would she settle for as the years of her life went by? Maybe disillusionment would replace her dreams...

The vibrant arrival of Katy Sinclair and her daughter in their red Toyota, just then, drove all depressing matters from her mind. Tad did his usual mad-dog act, barking and baring his teeth as the car pulled to a stop in a shower of gravel. Alana hurried out.

"You old phony, Tad," she accused. "Talk about all bark and no bite." When the car door opened hesitantly, the dog almost knocked Katy down in exuberant and friendly greetings. Bruce had just gotten up, and his arms crept like tight rubber bands around Alana's thighs when he saw the blue-jeaned Melissa bound from the car, pat the wriggling Tad and dash his way. Despite his impressive goose egg, Bruce seemed less affected by yesterday's adventure than Alana—her arm still ached painfully. His shyness, however, confirmed Alana's belief that he needed to get to know other children.

Four-year-old Melissa, almost exactly his size, stared at him from huge violet eyes, the replica of her mother's.

"Hiya!" she carolled, getting as close to Bruce as she could. Her long, straight blond hair hung in a beribboned single plait down her back, and her delicate hand reached out to touch Bruce's face. Matchstick thin, Lissa's being seemed to exude sparks of pure energy. Her elfin face pressed still closer to Bruce, and she grabbed a convenient post—Alana's leg—to draw still nearer. A look of apprehension crossed Katy's features.

"Lissa," Katy warned in a stern voice—but her ebulliant child paid no attention.

"His ears don't look broken, mama. See, his ears look same as mine."

Katy reddened, clapping a hand to her forehead in frustration.

"This kid! I tried to explain about deafness. Look, Alana, I apologize...."

"There's absolutely no need to," Alana assured her warmly. She peeled the children's fingers from her legs and knelt, swiftly explaining to Lissa that Bruce's ears were indeed broken, but that he talked a "magic" language with his hands.

Lissa's rosebud of a mouth formed an impressed "Oh." Then she said, "His head sure got broken, too. Boy, he gots an egg on his head!"

Alana, seeing a way to further promote Bruce's stock with Lissa, told the little girl how Bruce had climbed up the tree, and had to be rescued because he went so high. She translated simultaneously for Bruce, but he only half watched, staring at the girl instead.

By now round-eyed and very impressed, Lissa asked breathlessly, "Can my fingers talk like that, too? Could he show me, maybe?"

Within an hour, with the aid of Jenny's cookies and much encouragement, the children were fast friends.

Katy and Alana relaxed on the sunny veranda with tall glasses of iced tea, watching the two take turns on Bruce's tricycle up and down the gravel lane. Already, Lissa had learned to sign "my turn," "your turn," "stop" and "go."

"That's all I need!" Katy sighed. "That kid talks nonstop as it is, and now she'll carry on two conversations at once."

Jenny joined them, pulling up a white wicker chair.

"How is your mother?" she asked Katy shyly.

Katy's unusual turquoise eyes shone with affection.

"Mum's always great. Why don't you come and visit sometime soon, Jenny? She'd love to see you. It must be years since you two got together."

"Since Bruce was born. No time, after that." A wistful expression crossed Jenny's face. "And of course, I can't drive, and neither can she, so..."

An idea made Alana sit erect, and run excited fingers through her hair.

"You *must* learn how to drive, Jenny. I'm going to start teaching you how tomorrow."

Katy enthusiastically agreed, drowning Jenny's protests.

"It's dangerous *not* to know how to drive," Alana declared firmly, remembering the previous day. "Besides," she added, "we've got lots of time for you to learn before the summer's over and I have to leave."

Katy shot her a glance. "Do you have another job in the city, come September?"

Alana shook her head, watching the children follow Tom over to the pasture where he'd saddled Minnie for them to ride. "No job yet."

"Then why don't you apply at the school in Elkford? I work there part-time as a playground attendant, and I happen to know they're looking for a special-ed teacher. Bruce will start kindergarten there, won't he? So it would work perfectly." When Alana didn't answer, Katy added a bit apprehensively, "You do like it here in the Valley, don't you?"

The lake twinkled under the sun's warmth, and the trees and birds made happy sounds. 'Like' was a dishwater word for the way Alana felt about Bluejay.

"I love it here," she said emphatically, and the two women watching her beamed. "It's just that—" she glanced up into two pairs of expectant female eyes. It was just that being close to Rand, living anywhere near him, would never work for her. She felt again the humiliation and hurt of the night before. How could she feel this way about a man she hardly knew...about a man who, it seemed, was somehow involved in smuggling jewels, for heaven's sake? How was she even to get through the rest of this summer around him? She longed to feel totally neutral and cool toward him. If she even could hate him successfully. But her damned body, her emotions, betrayed her every time she tried.

Weakly, she cleared her throat.

"It's just that my home is in the city."

"Home is where the heart is," Jenny unexpectedly quoted. So Jenny sensed something. Alana felt her heart thump a warning. She'd have to learn to hide her feelings better than she had.

The sound of Rand's truck approaching affected each woman in a different way. But each of them was aware of Rand's temper when he banged the truck door viciously. Without a glance their way, he headed in a long legged stride toward the enclosure where Tom was supervising rides on Minnie. Lissa and Bruce's excited squeals echoed through the peaceful afternoon.

Jenny leapt up, and with a guilty look at Alana, headed for the safety of the kitchen. Katy simply stared openmouthed after Rand.

"What's biting him?"

Feeling an ominous sinking inside, Alana reviewed what Rand had said about Bruce and other children. What if he made a scene? She'd better warn Katy, she decided.

"Rand's...sensitive about Bruce's deafness," she

tried to explain. "He's afraid other children won't understand, and Bruce will suffer."

"Single parents," Katy snorted. "We're all paranoid one way or another. I was petrified Lissa would get teased about not having a father around." She glanced Alana's way ruefully. "Truth is, I still am."

Before Alana could answer, Rand was climbing the steps to the porch. He had a wildly excited Bruce riding high on his shoulders, and Lissa, jabbering earnestly, clung to his hand. She skipped along, and he shortened his stride for her. He wore the inevitable tight faded jeans and light-blue faded shirt, and his hair was still damp from the shower he took at the mine. Lines of fatigue around his eyes made him appear years older than he was.

Although he welcomed Katy politely, Alana felt the greeting was somewhat forced, and when he turned to confront her own brave stare, he looked both guarded and accusing. It took immense effort not to look away, hide from the intense look he gave her.

Why, oh why couldn't she sort out her feelings about this man once and for all? How did he always stir up so many conflicting emotions? Even now, she felt angry, defensive...and flooded with warmth, every traitorous pore aware of his maleness. Katy rose to leave.

"Sit back down a minute, Katy."

It was more an order than a request. He moved to the kitchen door, still carrying Bruce on his shoulders.

"Jenny," he called imperiously. "Is there any cold beer around?" His brows lifted questioningly at the women. "Join me?" he invited. They refused, and he lowered himself like some great cat into a chair, stretching the incredible length of his legs out before him, closing his eyes wearily for a moment. Then Jenny appeared with an icy bottle and a frosted glass, and he thanked her with a smile and a wink. Watching, Alana could only marvel at his appeal. He really did charm every woman around him, she mused, including the already adoring Lissa, perched on his knee. His patience with Bruce always amazed her. Even now, the boy's dirty sneakers were drumming an incessant rhythm on Rand's shirtfront, bumping the glass he was raising to his lips and slopping amber liquid over him. He just laughed and grabbed the boy's feet in one of his powerful fists, forcing the shoes to be still. When Bruce objected, he reached high, muscles bulging in his arms as he lifted his son down to join Lissa on his other knee, cradling the children, giving first Bruce and then Lissa tiny sips from his glass. He should have had a dozen children, Alana thought desolately.

Offhandedly, he addressed his words to Katy.

"Any chance you're free a week from this Sunday, Katy?"

Flicking a confused glance from Rand to Alana, Katy said hesitantly, "I'd have to check my busy calendar, but I have a feeling I might be free. Why?"

Damn, damn him. Pulsing anger and hurt washed over Alana. Here he was, asking Katy out right in front of her, flaunting the fact that his relationship with Alana was strictly business. But wasn't this what she'd wanted?

Nonetheless, how could he? Of all the insensitive, thoughtless... She half rose to her feet, face set in what she prayed was indifference. She wanted more than anything just to be somewhere else. Rand shot out a restraining hand, however, grasping her wrist in steely fingers, forcing her back into her chair while awareness of his touch flickered up her faithless arm. He held on, the pressure of his fingers steady. She'd be bruised from this in more ways than one.

"There's a new doctor in Elkford who was very helpful yesterday when Bruce needed him. I thought it would be a nice gesture if the locals—like you and I, Katy—took a day to show him and Alana our area. Sort of a guided tour, with subtitles. What do you say?"

He studiously avoided Alana's amazed eyes, still gripping her wrist so hard it was starting to ache. Katy looked astonished but also pleased as she enthusiastically agreed. "Want me to write a script?" she teased.

"I've already spoken to Dave Williams."

Dave? After the way Rand had acted the evening before with good old Dave? The sudden familiarity astounded Alana. And his arrogance at inviting himself and Katy along on what she now figured out had been *her* date left her speechless.

"Dave doesn't have a car, or know where to go, so he was delighted when I suggested we make up a foursome," Rand continued blandly, still carefully avoiding Alana's now-venomous glare.

I'll just bet he was delighted, Alana seethed. *You probably twisted his arm, you...you brute.* What special perversity had prompted this? Surely last night Rand had made it abundantly clear he wanted no involvement with her. His too-innocent gaze finally collided with her own accusing, stormy eyes, registering her mop of electric bright curls and the honey-tanned skin with its dusting of golden freckles. She could almost see her own reflection in his pupils, as well as the carefully controlled amusement hiding there.

Katy collected a reluctant Lissa, and Rand courteously settled them in the car, making arrangements for the "tour." Alana heard him instructing Katy to bring a bathing suit as Katy pulled away, tooting her horn cheerily at them while Lissa waved madly.

Then, except for Bruce, they were alone. The jays filled in where Katy's car noises faded. Dozens of hot accusations rose in Alana's throat and were choked back before they spilled from her mouth. Let him do the explaining.

"I thought you'd be pleased to hear I apologized to your doctor friend, like a civilized cave man," he began, "just as you ordered me to." He tipped the remaining beer into his glass. He was challenging her, daring her to answer, to admit his sneaky manipulation of her. His tired features looked mutinous, as though he'd welcome the chance for a full-fledged quarrel, something to clear the ominous tension so palpable between them, now Katy was gone.

Determined not to satisfy him, she purred sarcastically, "It's nice you always do as you're told," and her surprise showed when he dissolved into hearty chuckles.

"You're feeling better, you silver-tongued wench. So I assume you must have done as *you* were told and stayed in bed this morning. You weren't quite so talkative at 4:00 A.M. when I brought you your pill." His laugh boomed again, and she colored, aware of her lack of conversation, and of clothing, in those dawn hours. How tactless, to mention that!

Springing up, she turned stiffly on her heel and headed in, the echo of his laughter following all the way.

His good humor lasted all through dinner, and he even conceded that Lissa's visit had been good for Bruce. Jenny caught Alana's eye at that and winked conspiratorially as she served a meat pie encased in tender golden pastry.

"Was there any mail?" Alana was expecting letters from both Grace and Johnny.

Rand snapped his fingers and hurried out to the truck. "Forgot," he apologized, handing her a letter in Grace's handwriting. He also had a large blue paper parcel under one arm.

"This one's addressed to Bruce." His voice was puzzled. "Postmarked Vancouver, but no return address."

Shrugging, he handed it to Bruce, who tore it open in ten seconds flat, and lifted out a huge brown teddy bear, dressed ludicrously in a replica of a red RCMP uniform. He even wore a tiny Stetson. It was the type of expensive toy usually seen in exclusive shops.

Bruce turned the ornate bear over several times, removed the hat and the miniature holster, and abandoned the toy on the rug.

"Was there a card with it?" Rand inquired curiously. "Who sent it?"

Jenny rescued the bear, propping it on a corner of the couch.

"Whoever did doesn't know our Bruce very good," she remarked fondly. "Ever since he was a baby, he never played with stuffed toys."

Glancing at the unopened letter in her hand, Alana suddenly said, "Why, that's from Grace, of course. She's forever giving the kids toys." The RCMP uniform was the clue, although Alana didn't say so to Rand and Jenny. Grace had hinted broadly to Alana about her policeman brother. This was probably her not-so-subtle way of reminding Alana of her interest. Grace really was quite impossible at times. That bear must have cost nearly a week's wages, for heaven's sake. And in typical fashion, she avoided any mention of it in Alana's letter, although she did promise to phone Alana soon.

Later that evening, when the phone rang Alana leapt up.

"I'll get it," she called to Jenny. It was probably Grace.

"Hello?" she carolled eagerly. There was a long, humming pause. Then a cool, pleasant voice said, "Lindsay Evans here. I must speak to Rand."

Alana's heart began to beat in heavy, sick cadence. "Of course," she managed. "I'll get him." Carefully, one step at a time, she walked to the door of the study. "The telephone's for you, Rand."

He was studying brochures, and he glanced up impatiently. "Who is it?"

"It's your—she says her name is Lindsay Evans."

His face became an impassive mask as he picked up the desk phone beside him. "I'll take it here," he said. Alana hurried out, and as she hung up the kitchen extension, she could hear the intensity of Rand's tone coming through the receiver. She'd closed the study door conscientiously behind her. Several long minutes later, Rand swung it open impatiently, bellowing, "Jenny? Jenny."

Jenny appeared, and looked expectantly at him.

"I'm leaving for Calgary early tomorrow morning. Is there anything you need urgently?"

Jenny shook her head, her face a mask of concern. "Is it Mr. Ross again?" she queried.

Rand wearily rubbed the back of his neck. "Partly, but she's there as well."

There was no need to ask who "she" was. All at once, Alana felt like an eavesdropper in the intimate scene. She rose, heading for the stairwell.

But Rand was beside her before she'd taken more than two steps.

"Come for a walk beside the lake with me," he asked quietly, adding, "It's important I talk with you, Alana."

They walked in silence along the shore. Rand absently draped the soft old sweater he'd been wearing around her shoulders, warding off the sudden chill of the high mountain air. The garment was still warm from his body, and carried his own special odor—tobacco, aftershave, Rand. The night was clear, cool, full of stars. Crickets and frogs filled the silence. The lake waters lapped softly against the wooden dock.

When Rand finally spoke, it wasn't about Lindsay at all.

"I was a bloody fool last night, Alana," he said roughly, tossing a half-smoked cigarette viciously into the water. "I've cursed myself all day, for hurting you the way I did."

A confused avalanche of emotion washed over her. Why did he have to bring it up again? Anger, hurt, misery, puzzlement, all mixed with the need to understand. Why was he like this, warm and wonderfully open one minute, cold, withdrawn, hurtful the next? Even now, he didn't explain any further. Instead, what he said next seemed totally unrelated at first.

"There's a standard line in a divorce document," he began. "It says, 'Irreconcilable differences having arisen' and then goes on to list them, with the divorce as a solution. But it's only half a solution." His voice rose, questioningly. "Have you ever been married, Alana? No, of course you haven't. Sorry."

"What makes you so certain?" She sounded belligerent, and typically, he laughed gently down into her mobile face, tracing a work-roughened finger softly down her set jawline.

"No man in his right mind would give you up once you were his, Alana. If you'd married, you'd still be married. You're that kind of girl. Besides," he teased, "your friend Grace told me you'd never been married the morning I came to the school."

Absurd pleasure at the first part of his explanation overcame her annoyance with Grace. Rand went on, "People marry for all the wrong reasons. I certainly did. I desperately wanted children." He made a derisive noise in his throat. "I had some romantic vision of Bluejay teeming with kids, rooms all used the way they ought to be, boys and girls swimming and playing ball. My own childhood was lonely. Father was gone a lot, and he didn't care much for children anyway. Mother was in England."

The straightforward words, in such a calm, accepting tone of voice, hurt Alana like a physical blow. Tenderness and aching sorrow for him made her shudder violently.

"Cold?" He wrapped the sweater more securely around her, the feel of his hands on her arms and shoulders making her long to step into his embrace. As though he knew, he pulled her urgently to his side, molding her body tight to his own warmth, rubbing his hands absently up and down her arms. But he was careful not to go further. Instead, he moved slightly away, holding her but staring out over the night blackness of the lake where a half moon floated in the water. Alana sensed the deliberate restraint he imposed, and she cursed the involuntary heat rising in her own center. *Animal attraction,* she reminded herself. *Pull away. Alana.* Instead, she pressed closer to the warmth flowing from his body. *He'd be wonderful to sleep beside,* she thought dreamily. Like a built-in electric blanket. She harnessed her thoughts, glad that the darkness hid the flush that stole up her face. It wasn't sleeping beside Rand she was fantasizing about now.

He seemed unconscious of her wayward dreams. Harshly, he stated, "Divorce severs the legal ties in a marriage, but you can never get rid of the emotional ones." As though revealing something he'd thought long and hard about, he said passionately, "I've made serious mistakes in judgment, Alana. Now I have to accept the consequences."

Fear twisted her stomach. Were the mistakes emotional? What sort of consequences, she wanted to ask—but his deep voice had softened, assumed a gentle, proud cadence. "I was lucky enough to have Bruce, and he's worth everything, all the problems—anything."

Alana felt as confused as ever. All she knew was that he was rushing off to Calgary at a moment's notice when Lindsay beckoned.

"Does—is Lindsay working in Calgary?" It seemed an innocent enough question, but he instantly removed his arm from her shoulder, and walked several symbolic steps away, out onto the dock. Lake water slapped the boards, as agitated as his voice.

"I told you! She's a stewardess—works out of Vancouver on overseas runs."

Authorities speculate that airline personnel... Police

have charged a Mrs. Lindsay Evans... The words seemed entrenched in her brain. It was absurd to suspect Rand of being involved in any way. Almost as absurd as every unlikely crime Johnny had ever related.

"It must be hard for her to see Bruce, with a job that takes her away so much—"

His response was icy. "Lindsay hasn't seen Bruce since he was one week old. I doubt she looked closely at him even then." Now there was a deep, tired sadness in his words.

"She could hardly wait to leave after Bruce was born. In fact, I had a hard time keeping her from aborting him." He seemed to grapple for control, then went on. "Right after his birth, she took off with a pilot, a guy she'd worked with on transatlantic flights. I didn't fly high enough for Lindsay in any respect. She always wanted—needed—much more in the way of luxury than I could supply." He was searching his pockets for the ever-present cigarette package.

"Bruce has no mother, in any but the strictest clinical sense. There are women to whom children are repugnant, women with no motherly instincts. Lindsay was one of those women. So was my mother. You'd think I'd have recognized the type." He cupped and lighted his cigarette, keeping his face and eyes hidden with his hands. He drew smoke in deeply, expelled it.

"It's painful to know your wife despises being pregnant with your child, hates you for making her have your son. So painful, it convinced me not to marry again, or ever have more children."

Alana's heart ached for him. "How fortunate the majority of people have more courage than you, Rand," she choked out. "Think of the numbers of people who are brave enough to try again and end up wonderfully happy.'' The effort to sound dispassionate drained her. "I'd like to go in now."

He conducted her formally up the walk. "I'll be back sometime next week. Jenny will know where to reach me if you should need me, Alana."

Need you? Don't flatter yourself, Mister hot-cold Rand. I'll practise until I don't need you at all. Your mysterious wife may need you, but Alana Campbell won't.

Liar, her heart taunted her. *Liar, liar, liar.*

He was gone before she awakened in the morning.

CHAPTER SEVEN

WITH RAND GONE, the days were peaceful and easy, but the nights were filled with vague doubts, suspicions, fears, which Alana could neither ignore nor confirm. Knowing Lindsay was a stewardess on an overseas route intensified the nagging suspicions dredged up by the file folder Alana now wished passionately she'd never seen. One sleepless night, she had even crept stealthily down to Rand's study, determined to read the clippings more carefully. But the desk top was empty, and when she tried the file drawer it was locked. Feeling dreadfully like a criminal herself, she scurried back to bed and another sleepless eternity of "what if's."

Mornings found her groggily unable to get up at her usual early hour, and Bruce would creep into her room, mischievously landing like a projectile on her comotose form, reveling in the tickling punishment she meted out. He was now warmly affectionate with her, and it tugged at her heart to watch the way his eyes widened exactly like hers at some point in a story, how he lifted one brow quizzically, how he'd copied her own encouraging wink. Best of all was the speed with which he was learning.

His growing attachment both thrilled and worried her. It was natural, though, for a child to love his first teacher. He would make the adaptation necessary when a new teacher arrived. She refused to explore her own ever-increasing love for Bruce, or how she would cope at summer's end without him.

"Remember the family album you once mentioned, Jenny?" Alana asked one morning. "Do you think I might borrow it to teach Bruce about relatives?"

The concept of family was difficult for deaf children to grasp without visual help. Jenny hurried off, returning with a thick red leather album. Tom moved his coffee cup, together they cleared the table, and all of them grouped curiously around to peer at the yellowed photos. Bruce was mesmerized, especially with photos of Rand as a child, riding a pony much like Minnie.

"Who took these, Jenny?" Rand, about ten, balanced a new bike.

"Me," Jenny answered, turning a page and exclaiming as a slender young Jenny stared back at her.

Alana was amazed at the girl's young beauty, the half-shy, half-proud tilt of the gleaming black head. Most revealing of all was the unabashed expression of love on the delicate Oriental features glowing at whoever held the camera.

"Who took this one of you, Jenny?"

"Andrew." She glanced at Alana's still-puzzled expression. "Rand's father, Andrew Evans." She said no more, but Tom gave a grunt. An expression of disgust and near-hatred flashed across his usually agreeable features. Hoping to erase the tension, Alana blurted, "You look absolutely beautiful in that picture, Jenny."

"And she's no different now," Tom boomed, his face a terra-cotta shade. He rammed his hat farther down his forehead, grabbed his crutch and stomped out, slamming the screen door nearly off its hinges.

Jenny stared after him in amazement. "Damn, now what's got into him?"

"My guess is he's jealous, Jenny." But why? Alana knew Tom loved the joyful, vibrant little woman at her side, but why fly off the handle at an old photo?

Jenny wasn't coy. She just nodded, her dark eyes troubled. "Tom loves me, long time now. Once, I thought maybe—" She didn't finish the sentence, sighing heavily instead. "After the mine accident, Tom changed. Now, he feels only half a man. Doesn't matter to me, I've told him." She shook her head sadly. "But for him, it makes a difference." Jenny understood and accepted the situation. What could Alana say? She pondered, idly turning the pages of the album. A loose photo tumbled out, and there was Rand, smiling down at a lovely, doll-faced blonde hanging on his arm.

Here, the silvery hair hung loose, blowing in the breeze, and the dress was white and less sophisticated than the black jump suit. This was the elegant creature Rand had taken to dinner at Pelican Bay the night Alana had been there with Johnny. And this was also the woman he'd hurried off to rescue now, in Calgary. She was simply exquisite, and an icy chill squeezed Alana's heart. How could any man resist beauty and appeal like this? How could another woman hope to compete?

It was several moments before Jenny's voice registered. The phone had rung, and Jenny's puzzled voice was repeating, "Teacher? It's for you."

Grace's welcome familiar voice bubbled out over the miles.

"How's life in the boondocks of B.C.?"

Overjoyed to hear her friend's voice, Alana felt marginally better by the conversation's end. Just as she hung up, she remembered that she hadn't asked Grace about the teddy bear. It sat, forlorn and neglected, in the corner of the sofa.

When Alana returned to the kitchen, Jenny was waiting impatiently for her driving lesson. Previous attempts had turned out to be nothing less than hair raising, and this one was no exception. Jenny had both a heavy foot on the gas, and no mechanical ability whatsoever. From a safe distance, Bruce and Tom watched the small blue Fiat career down the driveway, until Jenny at last braked to an abrupt halt.

"Damn, teacher, I *love* to drive." Alana burst into helpless giggles. That night, Tom invited them to dinner at his cabin—probably, Alana suspected, to avoid another of her cooking experiments.

Tom's cabin was enchanting. Constructed of hand-hewn logs, it consisted of one huge airy room, a smaller bedroom and bath at the back, and was scrupulously clean. Only the lack of any plants or curtains made it seem a bit austere. Dinner was delicious, and afterward they sat outside while Tom played the mouth organ, his haunting old melodies floating off and echoing back down the darkening valley.

When Rand had been gone a week, Alana went for a jog one afternoon. The day was bright enough, but windy, and the creaking and sighing of the forest was eerie, like voices talking in muffled tones all around. She glanced nervously over her shoulder from time to time, aware of Rand's order not to jog alone. She reached the gate, and in a fit of exuberance climbed over the top. Just as she was about to leap for the ground on the far side, she spotted a slight movement in the forest to her right.

There was a man there, standing quietly watching her. Every nerve in her body stiffened, and she understood why hair was described as standing on end.

He wore a green jacket and dark trousers, and his face was shaded by a broad-brimmed hat. When he knew she'd seen him, he turned away, sunlight flashing on the brilliance of a ring, sending its reflection into Alana's eyes and blinding her. When she could see again, he was gone.

Absolutely panicked, wondering whether he'd been following her, she leapt to the ground and ran as fast as she could back to Bluejay. Tom was tinkering with machinery by the garage, and his comforting familiarity calmed her somewhat. He listened quietly as she blurted out her story, his forehead crinkled with concern, wiping greasy fingers on an old towel.

"Prob'ly just some poacher, teacher. Hunting season's open. I'll phone the game warden and maybe take a walk back up there."

Alana sighed with relief. She was getting paranoid. Bruce came charging over, begging her to take him swimming in the lake. As he and Alana floated in old inner tubes he giggled delightedly, and just then it occurred to her that the man in the forest hadn't had a gun. So much for the hunter theory.

Later that evening, Rand came home. He was strained and tired. Alana didn't mention the man in the woods.

Sunday. She scanned her limited wardrobe impatiently. What to wear for the picnic? She finally chose a sunny yellow T-shirt dress with a jaunty navy tie belt, and strappy navy sandals. A dash of makeup, a swift brush through bouncy curls, and she was ready for the day Rand had craftily arranged for her and David and Katy and himself.

She stuffed a shiny brown bikini in her large leather handbag. Would she have been just as eager for the day's outing if only she and David Williams were going? But David was her escort, she reminded herself firmly. Rand had asked Katy. Since his return, Rand had seemed almost morose, and even the saintly Jenny had snapped at him the day before when his irritability had become too much for everyone. Today, he seemed determinedly cheerful, and if his smile didn't extend to his eyes, well, at least he was trying. He hadn't said a word about his trip, and with him home again, Alana's suspicions suddenly seemed melodramatic. One day soon, she would simply ask him to explain the clippings. But not today.

Jenny drove confidently off in the sports car, taking Tom and Bruce on a fishing trip. Tom had reassured Alana that they would follow deserted back roads, and Jenny's driving had improved enormously.

Rand watched them leave. "Strange," he mused. "Jenny would never try to learn to drive before. I tried to convince her several times, but she always insisted she didn't want to leave Bluejay." He flashed a warm, knowing smile at Alana. "I detect some subtle persuasion here."

"Jenny's so outgoing, it's unusual she doesn't have a large social circle, go out for lunch, that sort of thing. Why, do you think?"

Rand shot her a quick glance. "There used to be a lot of gossip about Jenny, living here with my father."

It took Alana a shocked moment to assimilate his meaning. Then, things that had puzzled her became all too clear. Andrew Evans and Jenny had been lovers.

Alana thought about it while Rand helped her into the

truck, and they bounced off down the road. Jenny's devotion to Bluejay, Tom's reaction to the photos.

"Jenny loved my father," Rand confirmed. "Being Jenny, she gave her love wholeheartedly. I think—I know—my father cared for her, too. It simply wasn't to his advantage to get a divorce and marry her." The words were caustic, condemning. "My mother controlled the capital for the Evans Mine. Coal mining's risky, and several times the mine would have gone bankrupt without her money. She's still a major shareholder. Divorce wasn't a good business move for father, unless mother insisted, and she never did. Jenny lived with dad, and the local gossips had a field day. Jenny suffered. Her own family turned against her, ostracized her."

"But it was your mother who hired Jenny."

Rand nodded, one strong hand on the steering wheel, the other slung as usual, out the open window. They were turning from Bluejay's road onto the Elkford highway, and he waited until the truck was again speeding along before he answered.

"Ironic, that. I don't think Martha Jane ever saw Jenny as a person. Jenny was a servant to her, you see. An inferior species."

"Why didn't she divorce your father when she found out?" The story was both tragic and enlightening to Alana. What a profound effect it must have had on Rand, this confusion of emotion and loyalty. And love.

"Martha's reasoning is beyond me, and we're not exactly on intimate terms, so I've never asked her. You can bet it wasn't family feeling that stopped her. She's a totally egocentric woman."

Covertly studying the hard, rugged features of the

man at her side, Alana could better understand his deep cynicism about relationships and about love. His mother, his father, Jenny—and then his own tragic attempt at marriage. Yet the situation that had made Rand bitter and distrustful had created a Jenny whose tranquility and loving nature had won Alana's respect and deep affection.

As though he read her mind, Rand added, "Jenny's free now. The scandal's ancient history. Dad left her shares in the mine and a trust fund and she's financially secure. There's too much work for her at Bluejay, and I've hired several girls to help her, but it never worked out. She's emotionally tied to all of us, just as we are to her, and in her way I guess she's jealous of our affections. But you won her heart, Alana. You charmed old Tom as well, and he's a hard man to get to know." He turned his head toward her, but all she could see was her own face, mirrored in his glasses.

"It's a gift you have, teacher. You're irresistible," he teased, slowing the truck as they entered Elkford.

Her response was out before she could stop it.

"Except to you." Her heart began to pound.

"*Especially* to me," he answered.

Then they were pulling up in front of Katy's double wide trailer. David arrived, was introduced, and the foursome was on its way.

In the back seat—Rand had manipulated the seating, to Alana's surprise—Katy and David seemed to have formed an instant camaraderie. Their comments and laughter effectively shattered the spell of mystery created by the scenery—a narrow gorge and its towering mountains, the invisible ghosts of little towns that were no more. Conversation flowed easily, and soon they were comparing backgrounds. Rand explained that he and Alana had attended UBC, although at different times. It was amusing to find that David, too, had studied medicine there. Joking about their alma mater, Alana swiftly changed the subject when she caught a glimpse of Katy's face. Obviously, Katy was uncomfortable, and Alana remembered her mentioning being a high-school dropout. Rand, too, sensed Katy's unease and diverted the conversation. His sensitivity pleased Alana, and she flashed him a conspiratorial smile.

Diamonds of sunshine caught the windshield as they drove east up the narrow valleys, toward the Crows Nest Pass and Alberta, just a few short miles away.

Rand entertained them with a lively and fascinating review of the territory, its history and myths, but it was Katy who made that history come alive.

"I grew up here, in a town called Michel, and dad was a miner. We lived in a red company duplex, one of four rows of identical houses." She went on to draw a charming, loving word-portrait of life in a tiny mining hamlet, and Alana twisted around, her attention drawn by the throbbing warmth of Katy's unusual low voice. David, too, was mesmerized, his gentle features intent on the girl beside him. Rand was relaxed, smiling now and then at Alana as he drove and listened.

Rand was expertly guiding the truck around hairpin curves and rocky cliffs, and Alana stole sidelong glances at his profile. He wore gleaming white chinos with a dramatic wine-red knit shirt, arms bare, both tan and physique evident.

Once, studying him appreciatively, she intercepted his own perusal of her. His eyes stroked along the length of leg exposed by the clinging dress, along the bared expanse of knee and thigh. Twice now, his hand had brushed against her as he reached for the ashtray, and the minutely prolonged action made her breath catch. But this physical response that she couldn't control served only to reinforce her mental determination to resist him. He was still tied—irrevocably, it seemed—to his wife. Why and how did he perversely insist on ignoring that?

They passed through grimy small towns nestled protectively into the mountains, and then, without warning, the friendly landscape abruptly changed. Rand slowed. Alana caught her breath in amazement. They had entered a moon vista of immense gray boulders, miles of rock that stretched all the way to the foot of a lowering mountain in the near distance.

"Turtle Mountain," Katy said quietly, "and Frank Slide."

Rand stopped by a sign. They climbed out, and Alana felt the intense silence overcome her. They were standing on what had once been a bustling village, where now the rocks formed gigantic tombstones, witness to nature's power and whim.

According to the sign, the mountain looming in the distance had, at 4:10 A.M. in 1903, slid or exploded, destroying the sleeping mining village of Frank. Seventeen miners had been working the night shift inside the mountain when their entrance was blocked off by the upheaval. They had dug for ten hours, with their oxygen supply diminishing rapidly before they finally hit sunshine and fresh air.

"How must they have felt, digging and digging, never knowing what lay beyond the next five feet of rock?" Alana asked softly.

"The only way to come close to appreciating how they felt is to visit an underground mine," Rand said.

David immediately asked, "Any chance of visiting the Evans Mine, Rand? I'd like firsthand knowledge of the underground injuries we treat in the clinic. And I'd like to get some training in mine rescue."

"I'll arrange it," Rand promised. Today, he seemed to be developing a growing respect for the doctor and his avid desire to learn about the area he'd chosen to work in. Suspiciously, Alana also thought Rand was more than pleased at the obvious and surprisingly sudden ambiance between David and Katy Sinclair. He looked just a touch too smug as the two wandered off toward another information board, and Alana found herself alone with Rand.

She stared out at the jungle of rock and a shudder convulsed her. The sign had said it would take 100 gravel trucks 66 years to remove what nature had deposited in 100 seconds.

"The safe patterns of life can drastically change in an instant," she mused to Rand. "I wonder what happened to the survivors, how they dealt with this tragedy?"

"I guess the same way we all deal with tragedy," he answered. "By doing the best we can with what we're given."

His sadness made her shudder. An icy wind seemed to encompass the two of them for an instant. She had a momentary flash of foreboding, as though nature itself was warning. Then, Rand's arm came protectively around her shoulders, his bare forearm making the sensitive flesh on the back of her neck tingle, his hand cupping her shoulder gently.

"Cold?"

She shook her head and moved away from the disquieting contact.

"It's this place," she admitted haltingly. "That mountain is sinister, threatening somehow."

Instead of scoffing, he agreed readily.

"That's exactly how I always feel here. The Indians who hunted this area long ago would never camp by that mountain. They said it was moving slowly, like a turtle. That's how it got its name, Turtle Mountain."

Haltingly, Alana strove to put her feelings into words, needing to share them with him. "This country you love is so rugged, Rand, so...untamed despite the industry. It's totally removed from city life. There, society seems in control of nature to a degree." She stared up into his face. "There's so much here that's primitive and...frightening. The mining itself, wresting coal from the bowels of these formidable giants, it's—it's a far cry from—" her eyes rested on David, head bent to catch something Katy was saying "—from being a doctor in a city hospital, or...or working as a stockbroker or accountant." She struggled for words. "It molds the people who live here, who were born here—you, Katy, Tom, and Jenny. There's a kind of power about all of you, a fatalistic acceptance of nature's strength. You seem to...wrestle the elements like pioneers."

"Unsophisticated barbarians," Rand agreed, his eyes twinkling, the sensuous mouth beneath the mustache quirking with amusement. But he was serious again when he demanded, "Those doctors, stockbrokers, accountants; are they the type you prefer, Alana?" He touched her arm lightly. "Men in business suits with no coal dust under their fingernails?"

There was something insulting in his tone, and she pulled away from his hand.

"I don't see any coal dust under yours," she retorted, temper flaring. "Why do you always assume I'm such a connoisseur of men, Rand? And anyway, why do you care? You're the one who demanded we keep this relationship strictly business." Then realizing what she'd just revealed, she blushed furiously.

Whirling around, she began to flounce toward the truck. What on earth was taking Katy and David so long? The limestone rocks underfoot shifted ever so slightly, and her right foot slipped roughly off the sole of its flimsy sandal. She lost her balance, but Rand was quick to support her, drawing her reflexively against his chest, lighting sparks of awareness down her entire length before she pulled away and bent to examine the sandal dangling from her foot.

"Damn." The strap was broken, and the shoe slithered from her foot. Rand surveyed the useless bit of leather. A wicked expression crossed his features.

"Either you go barefoot on these stones, or..." In an instant, she was slung over his shoulder like a sack of meal, her cries of protest smothered by his laughter. "Never let it be said I deserted a damsel in distress," he said.

Her yellow dress was hiked shockingly high on her thighs, and his steely arm encircled her intimately. She pounded her fists against the expanse of wine shirt pressing into her nose, shrieking "Put me down, you—you *cave man*!"

She could hear Katy and David laughing, feel the thundering of her madly racing heart as she flailed wildly at her captor. It was like pounding on a stone; the muscles in his back were rock hard. Rand reached the paved parking area, but he still didn't set her down. For a paralyzing instant, his head turned into her side, and his searing breath blew through the cotton covering her hip. His teeth nipped the skin of her hipbone in a series of wildly unlikely caresses. Shivers of delicious sensation shot into her stomach and her pelvis. His rapid burning breath scalded her skin where it connected with her flesh, marking her as surely as a hot iron would. Then she was slipping, inch by inch, toward the earth with Rand totally controlling her descent, his hand traveling up the naked back of her thighs insolently, sensually, under her dress as he lowered her. Breasts, stomach, bare legs pressed close to him as he prolonged the action. His mischievous grin belied the fevered heat she felt from his body, the male arousal he couldn't conceal. Calmly, however, he surveyed her scarlet cheeks and silver sparking eyes. He'd been careful to approach the vehicle on the other side from Katy and David, effectively blocking their view. Now they came walking up, teasingly complimenting Rand on his fireman's carry.

Short of making an all out scene and ruining the outing, there was little Alana could do except smile and accept the fact that she couldn't accuse Rand in front of the others of biting her on the hip. Breathing unsteadily, she wrenched open the door. Behind her he murmured in mock annoyance, "Now I'll have to pack you around all day, seeing you wrecked your shoes."

Alana regained her composure by the time they'd left the limestone valley far behind—at least, on the surface. Inside, her feelings were so confused she gave up even trying to sort them out. For a man not interested in her except as a tutor for his son, Rand's actions today were puzzling. No doubt, he desired her—the slithering, intimate descent down his body had proven the hard extent of that desire. Animal attraction, for Rand. And for her? She wasn't prepared to explore that area now, but one fact was apparent. No matter what Rand said, Alana was not naive enough to believe such intense attraction could be ignored or avoided for the remainder of the summer. Not when he insisted on staging such scenes as this. Not when her traitorous body glowed and pulsed and ached with need of him.

Why couldn't she feel the same electricity for David as she felt for Rand? It would make life less complicated. But when Alana turned to the back seat to determinedly join in the banter, Katy's hand was firmly held in David's, and the deep flush on the lovely girl's full cheeks hinted that she very much liked things that way. So, falling for David now wouldn't be the smartest move in the world anyway, Alana decided.

Rand found them a picnic spot with almost everything. A waterfall tumbled down a rocky gorge into a little pool, and several willow trees shaded the spot where they arranged the food on a tablecloth ringed by blankets.

David eyed it hungrily. "This is a feast," he exclaimed

"You can't eat till after the blessing," Katy teased him.

Alana's fingers nimbly signed her father's favorite grace seconds before her slower lips could repeat it aloud.

"Good wine, good food and absent friends," she murmured, caught in a private moment of nostalgia.

Then she glanced at her companions self-consciously. They were watching her. She blurted out, "It's a saying my father had. Not very formal, I'm afraid."

Bluntly, Katy demanded, "Why did you use sign language?"

"Habit, I guess. My mother and father were both deaf. We always spoke in sign. My brother and I learned to sign before we ever learned to speak."

Amazed silence greeted her words. It was a reaction Alana had learned to anticipate, a drawing away from her, as though suddenly she had changed into a different person. Always, she tried not to mind—and never quite managed. Always, she did her best to help her listeners understand a bit more about the world of silence.

"We spoke English as a second language, after Ameslan."

Her audience, attention frozen on her, looked confused.

"American Sign Language," she translated. "The language of movement that I'm teaching Bruce, the hand language of the deaf." Still, they expected more of her, watching, not eating the picnic spread before them. When she was a young child, and even as a teenager, this reaction had upset her. Time had taught her to handle it better, but she still became very protective of the unique parents who had supplied, through their love, all any child could need or want. They hadn't needed hearing to know about compassion and honor, mutual respect, understanding.

She shifted uncomfortably, stretching her bare feet and curling them back beneath her, unaware of Rand's intense awareness and empathy for the emotions her vibrant and animated features transmitted as naturally as her flying fingers spoke.

She was only aware that with the finesse of the true diplomat, he rescued her. Only Alana realized what an effort it took for him to reveal his own sensitivity, overcome his deep protective instincts for privacy when he said, "Unfortunately, Bruce has a father whose fingers are almost arthritic when it comes to learning to sign." He poured the bottle of sparkling white wine David had brought into the plastic glasses. "I wasn't fortunate enough to learn it as a child the way Alana has. So my deaf son will have to be patient with me."

Only Alana knew what effort it took for him to refer so casually to Bruce in respect to his deafness. It was the first time she'd heard him matter-of-factly discuss it. She could only look meaningfully at him with her gratitude shining in her eyes. He'd subtly aligned himself with her, so she needn't feel alone or different.

He ate his way appreciatively through lunch, arms resting on his bent knees. If he'd been wearing a suit of armor, he couldn't have seemed more a knight to her than he did at this moment. A crumb clung to the well-trimmed mustache. She had an irresistible urge to lean over and brush it away, trace the hard masculine lips softly with her fingertips, her lips—Katy and David sat just a few feet away, curbing her impetuous desire. Rand's eyes and hers connected, though, and he slowly lowered one eyelid in a wink that locked them together in delightful conspiracy.

The rest of the picnic passed pleasurably and uneventfully. The day had grown hot and muggy by the time they once again drove off, and Alana tousled her glowing copper head absently with her fingertips, delighting in the cool breeze coming in the window. She felt relaxed, and ridiculously happy.

And when David asked a tentative question about deafness, Alana was pleased to supply all the information she could. Rand and his support made all the difference in her ability to talk freely about the circumstance that had determined her choice of career, had such a lasting impact on her childhood and her life.

"After treating Bruce the other day," David began hesitantly, "I felt the most overwhelming frustration at not being able to communicate with him. Doctors may learn the technical aspects of deafness, but we certainly aren't well prepared when it comes to the practical. I felt such admiration for you, Alana." His earnest, sincere praise touched Alana, and she laughed gleefully when he added, "And of course, when I met this tyrant you work for, my admiration for you knew no bounds." Rand, too, laughed heartily at himself as David audaciously related a comic version of the scene in his office the first time he'd met Rand. Any remaining tension from that outrageous encounter was gone, and an easy intimacy enveloped the foursome.

"Is sign language difficult to learn?" David asked. "Is it a formal language, or just a system of translating English by hand movements?"

It was a question Alana had often been asked.

"Ameslan, American Sign Language, doesn't have any written form, but it's definitely a language, not a visual representation of English. It's *not* English, you see," she explained to her fascinated listeners. "Each sign represents a word or concept, something like the ideograms of Chinese or Japanese. There, the ideas are static, however. In Ameslan, the signs move." Raising her hands, she illustrated. David and Katy sat forward to catch every movement. The highway was empty of traffic, and Alana occasionally felt Rand's eyes on her as well.

Making the signs as she went, she described, "Rabbit wriggles his ears, 'baby' gets rocked, 'girl' has sunbonnet strings down the side of her face, 'bear' scratches his chest, 'dog' is a pat on the leg to get his attention. It's a living language, Ameslan. It can be signed faster than words can be spoken. The way a sign is moved changes its meaning. It's a subtle language, a language of feelings. Emotion shows in Ameslan, visible as intense or minimal." She pondered a moment, seeking an example, a small frown creasing her forehead, hands quiet in her lap.

"The sign for 'together,'" she illustrated, making the circle with fists held together, palms facing, a picture word for two things moving in unison.

"Held close to the heart, together means an intense, loving relationship. Held farther out, it becomes more casual. It can change meaning instantly. It can have depths of meaning it would take many English words to convey."

"Is that, teacher," Rand's deep-timbered voice queried, "the reason you once told me sign language was the language of love?"

"That's beautiful," Katy sighed. "How romantic! Lovers could say all sorts of things to each other, and if no one else around understood Ameslan, their words would be completely private."

Alana didn't answer Rand. She remembered all too clearly his opinions on love, and the memory caused a sharp pang in her. What good was a language of love, if one didn't believe in love itself?

"If signs are that romantic, I intend to learn them," David stated firmly. "Unless it's too difficult for us poor hearing guys to master?"

Alana shook her head. "Signing isn't difficult. Heavens, Katy's daughter picked up several signs in just a few hours, and both Jenny and Tom are learning very fast. Bruce, of course, is my star pupil—but he has the advantage of deafness, you see."

She didn't mention that Rand refused to try to sign, and the others didn't comment or notice. It was a problem that concerned her as Bruce's teacher.

While the others were engrossed in conversation, Rand had turned off the highway onto a narrow side road surrounded by heavy brush, snaking a way tortuously along the side of a heavily wooded mountain. They were bounced and tossed around, but finally there was a bone-jarring jolt as Rand pulled into a clearing. There, in a natural depression, steamed a small hot spring, clear aquamarine.

"Sulphur Springs," Rand announced.

The smell was overwhelming. It crept up Alana's nostrils as she gingerly approached the swimming hole in her bare feet. Her eyes watered with the odor.

"Once you overcome the smell, the water's wonderful," Rand assured her from very close behind. His hand supported her elbow when a sharp rock bruised the sole of her foot.

"It also has healing powers. Any soreness in that shoulder will be relieved," he added. "But it won't do much for that sharp tongue of yours, teacher. That's incurable." He looked at her lips as though he'd enjoy exploring the texture of her tongue.

Would the healing waters have any effect on him, she

wanted to ask? Could it cure him of his bitterness, release his ties to his wife? Rather sharply, she said, "Where do we change?" Having him so near and yet so unattainable had her badly off balance today. Every nerve ending was sensitized by his attentions, his casual arm across her shoulder, his intimate wink, even the mischievous and overdone leer he now flashed her.

"Right here. I won't look, I promise."

"Thanks, but I'll take my chances with bare feet in the bush. It's safer."

The next hour turned the isolated glade into a laughter-filled playground, reminding Alana of long-ago days of innocence and total joy.

The difference today was her not-so-innocent awareness of Rand. Brief, low-slung black trunks hid little of his lithe body, and dark, curling hair trailed tantalizingly downward from his chest and taut stomach. His shapely, powerful legs were slender, yet muscular, his impressive shoulder development the result of hard physical labor. Biceps bulged when he laughingly tossed her into the air. Once, he encircled her legs underwater with his own in a steely scissor grip, boisterous as a little boy, as beguilingly sensual as the most sophisticated of men. And her emotions went wild....

CHAPTER EIGHT

THEY WOLFED DOWN hamburgers and French fries back in Elkford that evening, relaxed, happy, and hopelessly bedraggled. A picnic table in a small park on the town's outskirts held their Styrofoam coffee cups, and the sleepy evening twitter of birds formed a backdrop for their easy laughter and the camaraderie the day had produced. Alana was almost ready to accept that Sulphur Springs was a magic elixir. The soporific effect of the water lingered even now, hours since they'd driven reluctantly back to town. Her nose wrinkled as the breeze carried the powerful odor of the sulfurous perfume they all wore. The effect of the water lingered in more ways than one.

Katy had taken one look at Alana when they'd left the pool to change back to their clothes, and had burst into chuckles.

"If you look that bad, I don't want to see myself at all," she'd gasped between peals of laughter. Studying her friend, Alana couldn't help giggling with her. Katy's hair, sopping wet from the mineral water, had dried in stiff hanks, its natural luster totally subdued. Their skin had developed mottled purple and white spots as the air reacted with the chemicals in the water. They resembled victims of some sort of tropical disease.

Doing the best they could without showers or mirrors,

they'd combed each other's hair into some semblance of order, applied minimal corrective makeup over the facial splotches, and finally, giddy with helpless mirth over the total hopelessness of their appearances, had given up. In the clearing, they'd surveyed Rand and David. Both men had been covered in purple splotches as well, and at first sight of David, they began to laugh all over again.

"Your hair," Katy had sputtered to the puzzled doctor. "The water's turned it bright green!"

David had held a strand between his fingers, rolling his eyes up to see. His features contorted in mock horror.

"Damn," he'd exclaimed. "Mother told me it was real gold, and here it's gone and turned all green."

Their jouncing ride back to the main road and into Elkford had been accompanied with joking and songs. Katy had started them off, singing old favorites in her rich and powerful voice.

Dinner at a restaurant had been out of the question, so Rand solved the problem by stopping at a take-out hamburger stand, and then driving to the park.

"Is that a ski hill?" Alana was idly sipping her coffee and looking out over the mountains in which the village was cradled.

"Yup. We've got a golf course, and a community center—even a recreation center with a pool. Elkford is definitely moving into the twentieth century," Katy commented proudly.

With a sidelong glance at Rand, Alana said, "Before I came, I was led to believe this town had one tavern—period."

Rand looked a trifle embarrassed.

"I didn't want to mislead you," he mumbled. "After all, it's still not downtown Vancouver."

"Thank God," David said heartily, dipping his last fry into a puddle of ketchup. "If you'd ever worked the emergency room at a downtown Vancouver hospital, you'd appreciate the peace and quiet here."

"Did you grow up in Vancouver, David?" Katy asked. Each of them had revealed parts of their childhood today, except David. Now he nodded.

"Dad is a surgeon there, but I wanted to be a plain old family physician."

Something clicked in Alana's memory. "Is your father Dr. Davis Park-Williams?" He was famous in and out of medical circles in Vancouver for both his innovative surgical skills and his enormous wealth. David Park-Williams had been the only son of one of B.C.'s lumber barons, rejecting the easy playboy-style life he might have led for the rigorous life of a surgeon, using his money to finance research.

David confirmed her guess with a slightly abashed nod, and then adroitly changed the subject, back to the promise Alana had made earlier about teaching him sign language.

"I'd better learn," David said with a roguish glance in Rand's direction. "Just in case Rand decides I'll do as his family physician."

Alana was both surprised and delighted when Rand, after a moment's deliberation, suggested, "Why not come to Bluejay on Wednesday evening, and Alana can begin classes?" How long had it been since Rand had invited visitors to Bluejay? It seemed an indication of the rapport and closeness the whole afternoon had held.

It was dusk. The high mountain air was chilly, and

Katy and David said reluctant goodbyes. Katy gave Alana a sudden impulsive hug, then turned to Rand and announced, "Today's been the most fun I've had in years. Thanks, Rand."

David confidently took Katy's hand in his own. "That goes for me, too. I prescribe another day like it, as soon as possible. C'mon, Katy. I'm walking you home."

Watching them stroll away, Alana felt an intense letdown, a disappointment that the magical hours were ending. She, too, had had fun—and much more. Silently, she and Rand collected the empty food containers, put them in the garbage pails, and climbed back into the truck. A few stars were out. Alana suddenly wished that Rand would reach over and draw her close to his side across the wide seat, but he simply started the engine, and soon they were back on the highway leading to Bluejay.

The truck noise lulled Alana into a doze. She woke with a start, aware they had stopped. They were parked on a grassy knoll, and below lay the moonlit Elk River. Rand was sitting behind the wheel, staring at the silvery landscape, deep in thought.

He turned as she moved. "Awake now?" At her nod, he asked abruptly, "Think your bare feet can manage a path down to the river?"

She hesitated. "Where are we? I don't remember turning off the highway."

"It's about a mile over there. I used to come here often, so I knew of a side road. You were sound asleep—even the bumps didn't bother you."

Still, she hesitated. Her concern wasn't her bare feet. Being alone beside a romantically moonlit river with

Rand could end up hurting in a way no bruised toe would.

He lifted a quizzical eyebrow. "This used to be a special place for me. I'd like to show it to you. I'd also like a chance to talk to you, Alana."

Feeling dazed with sleep, she tried to consider this. Finally, she nodded and slid down to the grass from the high truck, loving the prickly cool wetness against her skin. Misty warm air rose from the water a few hundred feet below. Rand reached into the back for the blanket.

"We'll need it to sit on. The logs down there are damp."

The path he led her carefully along was hard-packed earth, zig-zagging down the cliff to the water's edge, where dirt gave way to a smooth grassy apron in a tiny sheltered cove.

The river lapped and gurgled, and overhead the moon had burst from the shielding edge of the hills. Rand's warm rough hand stayed locked around her own even after she stood safely at the bottom. The world was both dark and light, created and reflected by the water and the sky. Willows grew against the darker stone cliffs, and even the truck was invisible high above them.

"I used to sneak away from Bluejay and come here when I was a boy and needed to think something through," he said at last, his low rumble blending with the sounds of the river. "I used to pretend this was a cave, and I was an Indian brave communing with the spirits." Still holding her hand, his other arm groped for and found her free arm, turning her resistant body slowly until she faced him in the darkness. The thud of her heart filled her chest with an echo like the low throb of his voice. She could just see his stern jaw line, the darker patch of mustache above his mouth. Like a small automatic motor starting inside her, tremors of awareness ran up her legs, down her trunk, culminating in that treacherous electric tingling deep in her stomach. She tried to pull her hands from his grasp, put distance between them so her mind could function, but he easily held her captive.

"I was so wrong about you, wasn't I, Alana?" The urgent plea in his voice stilled her, brought her head up sharply to stare at his outline against the sky.

"Wrong? About me?" She could feel the warmth of his breath on her face.

"I had you pegged as a 'book-taught expert.' Like someone who gets a mining degree without ever going into a coal mine, then tells everyone what to do. I—I figured you'd learned to teach the deaf, that you were expert at it. But I told myself you had no idea what it really meant, what it was like for someone to have a deaf child. What the effect is on a parent's life." Passion seemed to choke him. "Then, today when you explained about your parents, I felt humble. I understood—no, I felt how that must have been for you. Loving them, just as I love Bruce, and always having to explain to friends, to strangers, to everyone, the way you had to do today with Katy and David. The way I must, with Bruce. The protective, defensive, almost angry feeling."

He drew in a slow, shuddering breath, as though he were releasing old, pent-up thoughts, replacing them with new. "That's how it feels for me, that confused mixture of emotion that has nothing to do with loving. It's just knowing suddenly that you're different somehow, that your son is different. Not better, not worse. But not the same, either."

The understanding, the bonding she'd felt that afternoon was instantly between them again. Fate had singled them both out, and they had found each other.

"Alana, why couldn't you have told me sooner?" Hurt and confusion mingled in his voice, even as his hard arms gathered her in. His question spun around in her head, even as he repeated it.

"Why didn't you tell me they were deaf?" It echoed and echoed, drawing her down into a vortex of memory she'd buried painfully far inside. His words dug that memory up like a corpse and tossed it at her feet.

Why hadn't she told Rand? Was it fear of being hurt again, fear of trusting? She'd condemned Rand not so long ago for that very thing. She, too, had to begin, somewhere, to trust again. Perhaps the time and place had arrived. Hesitantly, her throat constricting with the emotions her words resurrected, she began.

"There—there was a man I loved. Or thought I loved."

She'd been barefoot that night, just like now. But ocean sand cushioned her toes then. She'd been aeons younger, strolling beside Glen. Dr. Glen Lewis. Their wedding was a week away, small, elegant, understated, just the way Glen wanted. Alana's father had arrived that afternoon, days before she'd expected him—before she'd perfected the careful explanation she'd been trying to make for weeks, where she explained to Glen about her parents' deafness, where Glen took her tenderly in his arms, understanding, proud, sharing. He was a doctor, wasn't he?

She sketched the scene now for Rand, locked in the custody of his arms—secure enough to keep her voice steady as she spoke.

"Why didn't you tell me sooner your father was deaf and dumb, Alana?" Glen's voice had sounded angry, and it held a tinge of contempt. "Did you plan to surprise me with the news on the day of the wedding, when it would be too late to make any difference? Hell, Alana, what will people think? Is it hereditary, for God's sake? I couldn't stand kids who were deaf and dumb, sounding like—well, face it, your father sounds like a trained seal when he tries to talk." She related the searing words just as Glen had phrased them.

Rand's arms convulsed around her, and she felt the tremor shake his body much as it had shaken her own that long-ago night.

Her feet had grown heavy, and the conviction came over her that lead was slowly filling her body: ankles, legs, thighs, stomach. Finally, it reached her heart. Deaf and dumb. Cruel, archaic words no one she knew would ever use about a hearing handicap. In their childhood, she and Johnny had fought bloody battles with other children over that taunt. "Your mum and dad are deaf and dumb." An ignorant child's taunt—but Glen was no child. He was a newly qualified and ambitious doctor who'd once visited her classroom of small deaf children, had pretended understanding of her chosen profession. "It pays well," he'd commented respectfully, early on in their whirlwind three-month romance.

"Mum and dad were both victims of meningitis," she explained now to Rand. "Their type of deafness isn't hereditary. If it had been, of course, I would have told him in the beginning." Rand made a low, rumbling sound in his throat, of shared pain, of compassion, of complete understanding. It soothed Alana like balm on a tender burn.

Looking back, able to view the debacle for the first time with some degree of dispassion, she knew she should have told Glen earlier. But she had needed to preserve the rosy bubble of perfection in which Glen envisioned her. She'd also needed to solve another area of uncertainty first, an area she wasn't about to discuss now with Rand.

Sex. She'd been a virgin with Glen, and at first she thought she probably just needed time to get used to the strangeness of it all. Glen's lovemaking was clinically right: she'd surreptitiously borrowed books and read them after the first few disappointing episodes. But then she guessed that that was the problem—it was... *clinical*. He seemed to be mentally turning the pages in an instruction manual as he kissed, stroked, touched, all the while testily ordering her to relax. There was none of the burning intensity in Glen's arms she felt at this moment, secure in Rand's embrace.

In that final, wrenching moment on the beach, she'd understood that Glen was cold, that despite his passionate attempts, he remained a scientist to whom the weaknesses and imperfections of mankind were abhorrent. He was a critic, not a healer—which was why he was soon to begin a residency in pathology. Alana had tried hard to be perfect for him, neater, better dressed, less impetuous. Sexually, however, she couldn't pretend. Sexual response meant honesty, total abandonment to the loved one.

The moment of clarity helped. The terrible hurting he'd caused was replaced by rage. Fingers fumbling, she'd wrenched off the tiny—but perfect—diamond he'd given her. She couldn't punch him, the way she'd punched taunting children years earlier. So she raised the ring high overhead and threw it far out into the night ocean. It twinkled once in the fading light, and Glen had cried out in horror. He spent his money as stingily as he gave his compassion, and Alana had felt a wicked rush of satisfaction at the outraged expression on his face as the ring disappeared in the darkness.

And that had been that. Almost. She'd been hurt, disillusioned, angry, ashamed. Desperately lonely. How could she ever have believed she loved him? The next weeks were agony. Unfortunately, her father was there to observe and suffer through his beloved daughter's emotional turmoil, and of course he'd guessed the reason for the breakup. He'd seen the look on Glen's face during their only meeting. He was expert at reading the messages of eyes and facial expression.

"Because of me, because of my deafness," he'd signed. "I read it in his eyes."

Alana denied it vehemently, but her father wasn't fooled. He'd tried to make her talk it out, reveal the hurt, the confusing guilty resentment she had, knowing his handicap could so affect her life. For the first time, she wallowed in self-pity. Why had she been born to deaf parents? Why had fate singled her out? Looking back, it seemed to her that she must have had a temporary mental illness during those days. And of course, her vivid, mobile features, her expressive eyes and face had told her father everything, despite her refusal to discuss it.

He'd had to fly back finally, back to his job as a timber cruiser for a logging camp in northern Ontario. Alana did her best never to remember the sad and utterly helpless way he'd looked at her that final morning.

Two days later, he'd been killed by a falling branch.

She'd never had the chance to tell him that his deafness had added to her life rather than subtracted, that she adored him exactly as he was. That she realized Glen Lewis wasn't worth the tears she'd spent on him.

Why hadn't she told her father all that? Why had she let him leave believing she was ashamed of his deafness?

"Why didn't you tell me sooner...? Alana?"

It was Rand this time, repeating the words again and again, holding her closer and still closer against his body, locking her to him with his arms. Her whole body, her very soul, trembled with the memories his words unleashed. Recognition came just as it had that other time, on that other beach.

But this time, it was the recognition of love. She knew with certainty that she was in love with this man who held her, just as that other time she had known how wrong she'd been. This was right. Her body had recognized it before her head, blazing a response each time Rand was near, from the very first.

Yet it wasn't that overwhelming physical response that made her love him. The arms now encircling her back, the warm sweet strength of the male body pressing hers, made it harder and harder to think rationally. Loving him, she decided, had to do with the kind of man he was. Outwardly, he was tough, physically strong. Inside, he was gentle, vulnerable, full of humor. Who could explain love satisfactorily, she wondered helplessly, pressing even closer to Rand, hearing his stifled moan. She tilted her head back for his kiss, yearning for the feel of his mouth on hers...but with a cold shudder of recognition, she stumbled back, out of his embrace, trying to regain her balance and her reason.

He didn't love her. He didn't believe in love. He was tied still to Lindsay, in some twisted fashion, and there were black moments when Alana had believed he might even be her partner in some smuggling ring. Could she really love him and still have these doubts? *He* had clearly stated his intention of avoiding any relationship other than a business one between them.

"I think we need to talk, Rand." She decided to ask him outright, about all the questions, the doubts, the uncertainties. But each time she was near him—"Without you touching me," she insisted firmly, moving farther back near the sheltering bank where the trail led up to the truck.

"I know we do, damn it. But whenever I'm near you, all I want is to—" He checked the admission, fumbled for and lit the inevitable cigarette, tossing the burnt match into the river.

"Sit down, over here," he suggested, pointing to a log a few feet away, retrieving the gray blanket from where he'd carelessly dropped it.

She hesitated, and he said, "Hands off, honest." His gruff attempt at a laugh fell flat, and he added, "How many times is that? I'll lose my credibility if I'm not careful."

Spreading the blanket, he sank down and stretched the lean length of his legs before him. Reaching for her hand, he tugged her down beside him, careful not to have her body touching his, edging away. The silence stretched until her nerves were taut, and she blurted, "I have to—" At the same instant he said "This is hard to—"

They both stopped, and he began again. "This is hard to admit, but you scare the hell out of me."

It was the last thing she'd expected him to say, and she postponed her own words as he went hurriedly on.

"I think about you all day, at the mine, whenever I'm away from you. At night, knowing you're just down the hall makes sleep impossible. I'm obsessed with you, Alana."

She absorbed the words, drawing them in the same way she yearned to draw in Rand himself, through her very pores. He, too, felt this living pull between them! He wasn't making a declaration of love, but the sincerity of his words affected her deeply. He ground out the next sentence, his voice gravelly with emotion.

"I want you so badly."

The hunger in his tone was underlined by the wildness of the river's song in the darkness. It scraped across her nerve endings the way the day's stubble on his chin had scraped her face as she stood in his arms moments before. It forced awareness of his maleness, making her know and feel his desire.

The questions she'd planned to ask were less important than the demands of her heart, her body. The aromatic smell of tobacco floated over her. He turned to face her, directing the words straight at her, straight into her heart.

"My father, and Jenny. I despised him while I was growing up, for loving a woman and yet not marrying her. But here I am, wanting the same with you."

The brutal words hurt, drawing perimeters around their future, around his feelings for her. Jenny had lived in the shadows of Rand's father's life, settling for scraps here and there, never the wholeness of marriage, children.

Agonized, Alana marveled at how little he still knew

of her, if he thought that was possible. He didn't love her... and now had admitted only wanting her.

He was grinding out his cigarette butt on a stone, and she felt he was grinding on her heart.

"From the moment I met you, I tried to convince myself you were a career woman like my mother—freethinking, liberated, ambitious, but also selfish and totally independent. With a clever knack for teaching the deaf, but a person who left deafness at the office each evening. One of *them*, as opposed to one of us. You've proven me wrong in every way. Just now, when you told me about that doctor—Alana, I wanted to kill him. For hurting you, but also for all the times people like him hurt the innocent, like Bruce, like your mother and father. Your father—if I could only have met him, talked with him about Bruce. You're a strong woman, but you're also vulnerable and very lovely. Absolutely lovely in every way." His hand reached out and gently tousled the curls, which retained a springy stiffness from the sulfur water. Alana was certain she'd never looked worse in her entire life.

"I almost wish I'd been right," he added harshly. "Maybe then I could have ignored the way you make me feel. I could have kept away, forgotten you at summer's end." He shook his head and chuckled ironically. "I sound like some sex-starved teenager. There have been a lot of women in my life..." He didn't have to complete the sentence.

"I'm a man, Alana, with all a man's needs. Till now, all I wanted were—one-night stands, I guess you'd call them."

Alana's throat was so dry she could hardly force the words out.

"Is that all you want from me, Rand? A one-night stand? An affair for the summer, and then..." She nearly choked on the words.

His hands on her forearms were like steel, gripping so hard she felt each finger's imprint.

"That would be easy. I wouldn't have to try to understand or explain. I won't lie to you, Alana. I won't make promises of forever, and then break them. All I have to offer is today, one day at a time. It's become a survival tool for me, living that way." The huskiness in his voice deepened.

"Today, I want you more than I've wanted any woman. I want to talk with you, laugh with you, and I want to love you, but I can't go that far. I know I need you with every breath I take. I admire your intelligence, your humor, your beautiful expressive face. I yearn to hold you in my arms. But I cannot tell you I love you." The intensity of his voice transmitted clearly to her.

Words of protest welled inside her. Before they could tumble out, his lips came crashing down, smothering her own. His long arms pulled her toward him and encircled her body, twisting her awkwardly against him on the log. Her breast was crushed against the solid wall of his chest. His tongue flicked across her lips lightly, then harder, stabbing hot fire, demanding entry. Her own soft mouth opened and welcomed the thrusting rhythm, countering with shy messages of its own. How she needed this man to hold her, to kiss her, how she wanted this.

Careful, counseled her brain. But her mind couldn't control her lips or tongue, or the moan that grew in her throat as her hands stole up and around, restlessly cradling his head, exploring the shape of his skull and savoring the soft texture of the hair at his nape. Her fingers stole down over the knitted shirt and skimmed the bunched muscles she felt tensing in his back. With a low, strangled sound he gathered her to him. With one fluid motion he rescued them both from their precarious seat on the log. He slipped one arm beneath her, lifting her so they stood facing each other in the brightening moonlight. With hands widespread he welded her body to his own, cradling her buttocks, pressing her into his heat.

"I want you. I want to make you part of me." He held her insistently, grinding her lower body against the swelling of his need, making her gasp with the ferocity of his desire.

Still, the cautionary faint voice of reason warned her to pull away, think, resist. But that voice was no match for the wisps of heat and urgency gathering like a volcano low in her body, sweet, yearning, building with each rough urgent thrust of his maleness against her thighs.

Just before his lips claimed her again, driving all coherent thought from her mind with his expert lapping, teasing, pulling, she managed to drop her chin in one final struggle for control—but his mouth followed her blindly, trailing moist kisses across her forehead, down her temple, finding her ear and wetly inserting a tongue tip. She shuddered, and wild flashes traveled down, down.

His mouth tugged at her earlobe, traced the sensitive cord in her neck. He teased along her jaw, nibbled, entreated. Like a magnet, her mouth moved to his, opened hotly for him, welcomed his tongue.

She wanted to explore the inner reaches of his mouth

for herself. Her hands slid shyly up the hard planes of his cheeks, touched his mustache, which had first tickled and now enticed. Inside his mouth her tongue found the texture of his, savored the tobacco tang, the delicious faintly salty male taste of him. Her body met the pulsing motion at his hips with a matching beat of her own. His groan resonated in her throat and he planted his legs still wider apart, urging her narrow hips closer and still closer to the aroused and fevered maleness of his body. He molded her with his hands like some blind sculptor, worshiping her shape, tasting her greedily, murmuring broken love words that she felt more than heard.

His hard mouth roamed over her cheeks, nibbled at her nose, tongue-traced each closed eyelid and she shivered with an ecstasy of feeling new to her. His husky whispering caressed her skin, so she felt his voice penetrate.

"I want to taste every part of you, absorb your perfume until it becomes mine. I want to trap you, naked and shivering below me." The soft catch of passion in his voice thrilled her.

His hand slid around her ribcage, fingers feathering against her breasts with a touch as gentle and tantalizing as moth's wings. Instinctively, she pressed into him, wanting more. His thumb flicked the firm tip of her nipple and she strained against the flimsy covering of her clothing to reach his palm. His mustache teased and tickled the skin on her neck. She heard herself moaning softly as smoldering bits of his warmth made her want more and more.

At last, his hand fully encircled the aching globe of her breast, her nipple hard and throbbing. She should stop him now—but the fleeting impulse was lost in the wonderful controlled trembling she felt in his body that created so easily an answering, less-controlled quivering deep inside her own. His hands no longer needed to pull her close to his thrusting hips. She strained to reach him, pressing and releasing in unconscious cadence.

She was weightless suddenly as he swung her up in his arms, face pressed tight to his shoulder. His bare forearm burned her thighs. He lowered her gently onto the riverbank, spreading the blanket in a soft, moss-covered area formed by the meeting of trees and cliff. The earth was soft beneath her back, through the warm blanket. Above her, the purple sky was pierced by rivets of stars, the moon floating casually, clear and softly glowing.

Beneath her she felt the heartbeat of the river, pulsing as clearly through her as the full strong current of her own heated blood. Was the roaring in her ears the river's song, or only an internal signal of the chaotic, unbearable desire Rand had created? Never before had she felt such primal need, such hot and throbbing urgency within.

"I want to make love to you."

Alana's breath caught and held at his urgent whisper. Kneeling beside her, he yanked his knitted shirt gracefully free from his waistband, tugged it off over his head, then carefully, clumsily, folded it and tucked it under her head for a pillow. It was warm from his body's heat. His face and features were a blur against the lesser darkness of the sky, and she had to strain to catch the throbbing murmur of his voice.

"You know I want you, my darling. But I won't mislead you, either. I can't. For the moment, this has to be all, this physical love. I just can't offer you empty words." His shuddering breath belied the calmness of the words, and he was careful once more not to touch her, crouching instead with his hands on either side of her body. "If that's not enough, tell me now, before we go further. Because after this, I doubt I can stop."

Impatiently, she reached up for him. She wanted him to sweep her mindlessly along on the tide of passion so immense between them. But that wasn't Rand's way, she realized. He cradled her to him once more, but she felt his reserve, the incredible self-control he exerted waiting for her answer. He rubbed his face in her hair, and she had to giggle, realizing how they both still carried the odor of sulfur on their skins. But she sobered quickly as she felt him waiting, watching her, burning his question across the inches between them.

"I refuse to seduce you, Alana. You'll have to tell me, tell me if you want me. It must be right, this, something we both want. Tell me, darling."

She could make out the strain on his features. But still his voice remained quietly controlled, and still he held himself slightly apart, although the hand in her hair trembled.

Her arms locked around his neck, fingers resting on the thick cord of muscle there. The pulse that thundered beneath her fingertips signaled all too clearly the extent of his need. But she knew that if she asked, he would stop in spite of the force making his whole body quiver.

She knew all too well what he was telling her. He desired her, they shared a common bond of understanding and friendship, he liked, admired, hungered for her. Today, right now, he wanted her. But he didn't pretend to love her, and in his ruthlessly honest manner, he would tolerate no misunderstanding. He would make no promises, allow her no dreams beyond this physical act of love. There would be no passionate vows, no visions of a future. Her own love for him would have to be enough. Would it carry her through, would it still be there at summer's end, enough to keep the memory of this night untarnished? And what of all the lonely days and nights of her life after this, without him?

Imprinted on these uncertainties she could see in her mind's eye the smiling, happy, tranquil face of Jenny, lined and growing old, but at peace with herself and her world, Jenny working in her garden, cooking in the kitchen. Jenny had once given herself totally to a man, given her love freely, savored it. Had it been enough? Jenny had *made* it enough, made it her life. Perhaps love such as Alana felt for Rand was only experienced once in a lifetime.

Deliberately, then, Alana made her answer even and emphatic. Rand leaned closer, watching her lips as though reading them, not trusting sound alone to convey what he longed to hear.

"I want you, Rand. I understand, I accept your—your terms." Her voice nearly broke just there, and fiercely, she controlled it again.

"I do want you. I want you to...to love me."

If he recognized that her words had a different, more permanent plea, at least he didn't question it. The tension, the awful control of his body flowed out, and he half slumped beside her.

"Rand, I haven't—I mean, I've not...I—" She finished the sentence in an embarrassed rush. "What I'm trying to say is I doubt I'm very good at this." All her previous failures threatened suddenly to overwhelm her.

He was very still. "Do you mean you haven't done this before?"

Humiliation at her own clumsiness made her voice quiver.

"I'm not a virgin. But—" Words failed her, and she wished fervently she'd said nothing.

"For me," he growled softly, "you're the first, the only woman in the world. Here, by this river, in my valley." He pillowed her head on his arm, interspersing his words with kisses and licks of his tongue across her face and neck. "I'm going to claim you as my own. Now, in this wild place, you'll belong only to me, and I to you."

Deftly, he slipped open the back zipper of her dress, teasing it slowly down her shoulders. Like a singer with the river as his instrument, he crooned to her, fingers stroking her neck, pushing back a stray tendril of bright hair from her ear, lingering on the frantic pulse drumming in the base of her throat.

Languorously, he eased the crumpled cotton dress to her waist, drawing his breath in a slow sigh as she lay before him outlined by moonlight.

"I need to touch every part of you," he said almost apologetically. "I need to look at you."

Devouring her with his eyes, he released the front catch of her wispy satin bra. The roundness of her breasts with their erect nipples appeared slowly as the lace slipped away. As though he had all eternity to explore her, his head bent, and he tasted first her lips, then her throat. He moved agonizingly down, trailing the hot tip of his tongue between the swelling of her breasts, teasingly flicking at their aching tips until at last her hands flew to his head in frustration and she guided his mouth down to enclose her waiting nipple.

An exclamation of surprise and delight escaped her lips as his strong nuzzling sent shivering pangs of awareness into her depths. His lips seemed suddenly connected by a chord of delight to her lower body. She felt his hand glide down, stripping away the dress, and she was grateful to be free.

He relinquished her breast only long enough to slide the yellow fabric down and off her body. She gasped as his lips trailed fire down her hipbone. He traced the edge of filmy lace covering her abdomen where the tiny bikini panties clung. Each moist caress was a separate promise of more to come. He awakened sensations that made her arch instinctively, invitingly up toward him, and his fingers and then his tongue slid under the narrow elastic. She was suddenly shy, moving her hands to his head to stop him, and he tenderly replaced the flimsy barrier, only to allow his mouth and the heat from his breath to wander down over the lace, down to the root of her passion where he lingered, setting her afire. When she sighed with pleasure, he nibbled his way delicately up her sensitive side, discovering places exquisitely tender and unexplored to nuzzle, move away from, return to.

The night air sensuously cooled and dried the damp hot reaches where his mouth touched, and Alana was no longer aware of any slight discomfort her mossy bed might have had. Tentatively, her hands stroked his long and smoothly muscled back, taut beneath her wandering fingers. She slid her palms down his sides, marveling at the hardness and muscular beauty of his body. And she resented the interruption of cloth when she reached his trousers.

Sensing her need, he rolled away for an instant. Then

his fevered skin was naked against her own, wonderfully different and exciting with its harder textures, body hair, rippling muscles just beneath smooth skin.

Over and over, he relentlessly tantalized her breasts with mouth and tongue, lifting her from one sweet level of sensation to the next, higher and higher until she writhed against him in wanton abandon, wanting more, needing him with desperate immediacy.

At first, segments of disconnected thought flickered through her consciousness. She was amazed at the power of the response she felt to this man whose hot breath now fanned her neck, whose soft litany, "Lovely Alana, beautiful girl," sounded like a blessing here under the dark curtain of night sky. Supreme among these fleeting impressions was a shining sense of rightness, a clear and soaring certainty that what was happening was inevitable and good. Different, so blessedly different from anything she'd experienced before: At this moment, he was more than just her lover. He was the individual her soul recognized as the other half of itself. He was her mate.

Tenderly attentive only to what should please her, quivering beneath her stroking hands with his own leashed passion, Rand eased the satin panties down the now eager length of her trembling legs. With tongue and rough-gentle hands he stroked the softness of her lower belly, making her cry out with little choked sounds. Then, gradually, he slowly ventured with his fingertips into her soft down, finding her secret center, pressing tenderly, releasing, making her arch eagerly up to meet him. Her whole being welcomed his touch this time. Here was no intruder, no stranger seeking unwelcome entry to her places. Here was the man she loved.

The burning inside her grew, until she forgot even her earlier concern that at the final moment her own traitorous body might lessen the magic of what was happening between them.

But Rand's relentlessly tender fingers explored, stroked, moistly sensitized the soft folds, his mouth and tongue devoured her, lips, breasts, stomach, thighs, and slowly back again.

She could stand the exquisite torture no longer. Pressing as near to him as she could, her arms encircling his chest so his wildly pounding heart echoed the singing in her own blood, she opened herself to him urgently. Frantically, she moved to his bidding. Still, his control held, waiting for her to voice the final decision. She opened her eyes wide to the night sky, and the moonlight seemed to bathe them both.

"Now, Rand, please love me now. Please..."

The tremor that shook his body indicated the intensity of his desire. With almost desperate haste, he spread her legs gently wider, covering her pulsing limbs with his own. Lifting her arms, she welcomed him as he lowered the rock hard swelling of his maleness slowly, then wildly, gloriously deep into her.

For a long, endless moment, he was still. He groaned against her throat, a sound of joy and utter tenderness. She felt flooded with the pleasure of pure sensation. His stillness lasted only a moment, and then the ancient rhythm of his movements engulfed her, and the instinctive answer to the question his body was asking grew stronger with each pulse, each thrust, retreating like the river water from the bank where they lay, only to return again at a higher level. His love murmurs were wordless and encouraging in her ear, his being one within her. Tension and urgency grew and blossomed beyond anything she might have dreamed. Sensation engulfed her. His skin, his body's texture, his musk odor enveloped her, wrapped her in a warm blanket of pleasure. His relentless thrusts drew her irresistibly onward. The gentle lapping water near them seemed to catch her in its current and send her body swirling soundlessly around and around, faster, faster...harder, deeper.

Her startled eyes flew wide, and pinpoints of stars in the night sky exploded into the water, over, around, through her, infusing her with unimaginable delight.

A pagan, uncontrolled cry of wonder, strange and foreign in her own ears, came pouring out, on and on. Her body convulsed as ecstasy gripped her being. Rand's own cry echoed harshly, a wild and almost lost sound, and together they floated for endless moments, bodiless and dazed.

Then he turned her, so she lay pillowed on him, cradled in his arms. The water's soft murmuring separated itself from the lingering roar in her own blood. Close beside them, a night bird cried once and was still. Rand's low, rumbling voice echoed in her ear, pressed close as she was to his chest.

"My darling, now I would like to wrap you in soft blankets, bring you wine to sip, feed you sweets—and here we are, on the bank of a river, with no room service." His arm tightened around her, one hand circling her skull. He drew her toward his lips and kissed her tenderly.

"Beautiful, wild river sprite. You're glorious. But you deserve a soft bed next time, some of the comforts of home."

Her fingers flew to his mouth, silencing him. Twisting

her head to the side, she looked out toward the untamed magnificence of Rand's valley. A languorous peace filled her, a sense of oneness with the universe. Lying just so with Rand—on Rand—in this spill of moonlight with this lovely new knowledge of herself, the secrets her body had kept from her, the discovery of Rand; this was all she wanted. She wished it might never end.

But the slight cool breeze made her shiver, and reluctantly he disturbed them, rescuing her clothing and his own. Then, clumsily, he dressed her, saying, "Lift your foot," and "Hold up your arms," and with touching masculine gestures, smoothed her dress down over her hips.

In too short a time, they stood once more at the foot of the path leading up the hill. Rand's arm circled her fiercely.

"Now you belong to me, teacher," he whispered. She glanced back at their mossy bed. Already harsh reality was nagging, making her admit how rash, how impetuous, this lovemaking had been.

Halfway up the path, she turned again, staring back down where they'd lain, and was reassured by the trees, the rocks, the river. The enchanted magic of the past hour belonged to her forever. For this space in time, she and Rand did belong to each other, wholly. She squeezed an answer into his hand, holding hers.

The drive to Bluejay was almost silent, intimate at first with shared peace and pleasant exhaustion. Alana dozed on Rand's shoulder, interrupted when he blurted, "I have to tie up the loose ends of my life, Alana. There are complications, so much you should know..." He sounded disquieting, ominous. "But I want you to know I loved being with you, making love to you."

Then he lapsed into silence again. Those "complications" just might destroy them. She yearned desperately to hear the words he didn't say, the words he'd vowed to her no woman would hear him say again. The three silent words filled the cab, creating distance between her and Rand where there had been only contentment. Why did he say anything at all?

Slivers of pain began to shred her happiness. Better silence than half promises. "I loved being with you, making love with you." Past tense. An awful foreboding crept over her.

They pulled into Bluejay's driveway. The sound of the engine died, and Rand reached for her. He was about to continue explaining, apologizing. She couldn't bear it. She slid across the seat and out the door, forgetting her bare feet until they made harsh contact with gravel. She sped stubbornly toward the house, fiercely bruising her toes and welcoming the pain. Physical hurt was easy to deal with. It was the aching void his apologetic words had created in her heart that she couldn't bear. The finality of those stumbling few sentences had escaped her at first, secure as she was in her newfound bubble of happiness. Now, she could only interpret them as his way of telling her she was just another sexual conquest, a one-night stand.

Tying up the loose ends of his life was another way of saying he still had a commitment to Lindsay. Well, she'd been warned.

Her tear-blurred eyes hardly registered the soft small light burning in the living room beside the tall wing-backed chair. Alana burst through the door, intent only on gaining the stairs and her bedroom before Rand should catch up with her. His hurrying steps were close behind her, and the low growl of his voice sounded as he absently greeted Tad. The dog was outside for once, instead of at his usual post beside Bruce's bed.

"Damn it, Alana, wait up!" His order cut through the silence.

Alana's headlong flight was stopped short, as a tall shape rose abruptly from the shadows of the wing chair. Alana's mouth opened, ready to scream. Rand stopped in midstride a few steps behind. He moved quickly and protectively alongside, slipping a hard forearm around Alana's waist, holding her to him.

The woman before them crossed her arms on her chest. She was tall, Alana's height or maybe an inch more, and angular; all sharp planes and corners. Her iron-gray hair formed a nimbus around her face; soft, curly, fluffy. But any illusion of grandmotherly gentleness stopped there. Her features made her look sixty, but her true age was difficult to guess. What was plain was her displeasure with the world, her conviction that she could control its haphazard order.

The blue-gray eyes behind their small round glasses were as hard as marbles, and the lips that might have once been soft and full were compressed into a straight and unpleasant line. She wore a well-cut gray flannel skirt and a lighter gray silk shirt, both expensive, but colorless.

The pressure of Rand's grip on Alana's waist increased. In a precise and very English voice, the woman said accusingly, "Well, Randall. It's about time you've come home, I must say. I'm quite exhausted, and I've been here since early afternoon. I hired a car to bring me, and then there was no one here. Where have you been and who—" the piercing glance she shot Alana took in everything, from the soles of the bruised and bare feet to the top of the rumpled spiky red curls "—is this?"

Alana felt her kiss-swollen lips burn, aware of the tear tracks on her cheeks and the sadly crumpled and stained yellow knit dress she wore.

"Alana Campbell, this is Martha Jane Whitby Evans." Rand's icy coldness made Alana glance up at him in shocked amazement. Then he added, in the same derogatory voice, "My mother."

CHAPTER NINE

IN THEIR WORST ENCOUNTERS, she had never heard Rand sound so harshly cruel as he did now. He made no move to embrace his mother, nor she him. They stood equally planted in aggressive stances. Rand with his arm still encircling Alana's waist, his mother with arms folded defensively across her meager breasts, as though to ward off a blow. The words they threw back and forth across the barrier could only be described as weapons to injure each other.

Alana stood helplessly immobile, trapped between mother and son. The very air seemed to crackle with the animosity the two generated.

"Ms Campbell is here helping out for the summer."

Martha Evans glanced contemptuously up, down, and away from Alana.

"Your domestic... *affairs* don't concern me, Rand."

"You made it plain long ago that my life was no concern of yours," Rand all but spat at her. "But you might be mildly interested to know that your grandson is deaf. Alana is Bruce's tutor. Now, I know how you hate this place, so why the hell are you here?"

There was a fractional pause, and something flickered across the stern face. "Finances, of course," she said. "I have a rather substantial investment in the mine, and that last financial statement was outrageous. One learns a great deal by arriving unannounced." Her stony glance clicked over Alana. "You might have warned me that Bruce was handicapped."

Rand gave an exasperated sigh, releasing Alana but giving her arm a cautionary squeeze before he moved to the cabinet housing his liquor.

"Bruce is deaf, but he's not tragically handicapped." The firmly confident words sent a thrill of pride through Alana as Rand gestured to the bottles before him.

"A drink, Martha? Alana?" Without waiting for an answer, he handed a small glass of sherry to his mother, then he came to Alana's side, holding out a glass, ignoring the small shake of her head.

"Drink it," he ordered, propelling her into a chair farthest from where his mother sat.

Alana realized she'd been shivering when the warming fire of the brandy slid down her throat. She needed to escape this room and the antagonism it contained, yet she had the feeling Rand was desperate that she stay.

Rescue was unexpected. A small, pajama-clad body sidled into the room, giving Martha Evans a wide berth and a foul glare, hurtling into Alana's arms and spilling the rest of the brandy into her lap.

Hugging her desperately, Bruce made urgent signs for "dog" and "bed." His features expressed outrage, and he turned to point an accusing finger at his grandmother, making the sign for "bad."

"He wants Tad," Alana explained to Rand, her arms protectively encircling the warm child. How comforting he felt. Burying her face in his fragrant silvery curls, she caught a strange yearning on Martha's stern features as the older woman stared. But Martha's strident tones followed Rand as he went out for the dog.

"Animals don't belong in the house, Randall. I made that plain to the child earlier. If he had a decent nurse," she stated primly, "he wouldn't be so selfishly strong willed."

Rand glowered at her as Tad streaked in the door.

"Help me get these two in bed, will you teacher?"

With every ounce of grace she could muster, Alana said quietly, "Good night, Mrs. Evans." Martha didn't reply.

Rand mounted the stairs with Alana close behind. He cursed quietly and steadily. Martha seemed to have won the first round. She was here, and she obviously planned to stay. There was not the slightest doubt that the even tenor of life at the ranch would suffer as a result.

THE NEXT TWO DAYS jerked past in a chaos of domestic unrest. Jenny was reduced to tears repeatedly, Tom grew red faced and mutinous, and Bruce went wild. Alana had introduced a new listening game with alarm clocks, and Bruce discovered the ringing drove Martha into a frenzy. He set the bells clanging as often as he could manage, watching Martha curiously when she reacted.

Wednesday was the day that David and Katy were coming over for sign classes, and Alana considered phoning to cancel the invitation. She felt so drained. Perhaps, she decided without much hope, the change would improve the atmosphere in the house.

The evening began badly. Rand was late. He'd all but disappeared since Martha's arrival, blaming breakdowns at the mine, but Alana suspected he was simply hiding. She couldn't really blame him—anyone in their right mind would hide from Martha, she concluded, listening to the high-handed martinet play lady of the manor when Katy and David were introduced.

"Dr. Williams, how delightful," Martha boomed, assessing and dismissing Katy with one glance, despite the fact that David held Katy's hand firmly in his own.

Alana raised teasing eyebrows at her friend, and Katy whispered in horror, "How long is she staying?" as Martha held court, relating to David the details of her business—fund raising—and the statistics as to amounts raised by her company, Whitby and Associates. The company, Alana thought viciously, for which she'd traded her husband and son and now, her grandson.

Where was Rand? Alana glanced out the window. Bluejay had become an armed camp in the last two days, and things weren't going well with Bruce. Martha had decided talking very loudly would solve Bruce's problems, and she grotesquely mimed her innumerable orders. Signs, she stated emphatically, were a waste of time.

If Bruce's training were to continue successfully, Martha would have to be either won over or subdued. The first was unlikely, and the only person who might accomplish the second was Rand.

His truck pulled into the driveway several moments later, and quietly Alana slipped outside. Martha was still talking.

It was a relief to escape for a while into the cool evening, and Alana slowly walked toward the garage, overhearing Tom and Rand deep in conversation as she approached.

"Somebody, prob'ly some goddamn poacher, has been livin' in our fishing cabin," Tom was relating vehemently as Alana waited quietly some feet away.

"There was cans and bottles around. I woulda laid and waited for the sucker, but not with Jenny and the little guy along," Tom continued.

Rand absently lit a cigarette, eyes thoughtfully intent on Tom.

"Did you see anyone?" he queried.

Tom shook his head, adding, "I figger you and I should mosey up there, Boss. That's private property, yours and mine. Besides, it's game reserve."

Rand nodded, his eyes now on Alana, smiling at her. The weariness in his face, the slight unusual slump to his shoulders, convinced her not to lay any more problems at his feet, at least not tonight. Maybe she could outwit Martha, although it seemed unlikely.

Rand looked bone weary, lines deeply etched around eyes and mouth. He looked older, and somehow vulnerable.

"We'll take a trip to the cabin, Tom, maybe this weekend," he promised, and Tom headed off in the direction of his house.

Rand's eyes seemed to drink in Alana's purple silk blouse, tight-fitting jeans, the high-heeled purple sandals she had defiantly strapped on after Martha scathingly called the outfit "inappropriate." Might as well be totally wrong, Alana had decided, and then ruefully had to smile at how successful Martha was at causing rebellion.

The effect of Rand's lovemaking clung to Alana like heady cologne, and the memory must have been just as poignant for Rand, because smoldering passion sprang to life on his face each time he looked at her. The worst part of the past few days was having no opportunity to be alone with Rand. It had rained heavily, so their early run was impractical, and Martha was always present the rest of the day.

His eyes traced a path down her blouse now, lingering

on the suddenly taut nipples beneath the flimsy silk, admiring the slenderness of her waist, stroking the rounded hips in their close fitting denim.

She drew a shaky breath, aware they could be seen by anyone looking out Bluejay's front window.

"Bloody place," Rand swore under his breath. "Like living in Grand Central Station." He took her arm and walked to the house with her, listening to her concerns about his mother.

After that, much to Alana's surprise, most of the evening went well. Rand gave Martha a silencing glare every so often during the lessons, and Martha sniffed haughtily. But she stayed, and she was quiet. Rand, as usual, listened closely but refused to try to use any sign language.

Alana noticed the closeness between Katy and David tonight, the glances they exchanged, Katy's heightened color when he was near. It was a shock, therefore, to have Katy announce that she was planning to move away in September.

"For heaven's sake, Katy, why?" They were in the kitchen, making fresh tea while Jenny checked on Bruce.

Katy shrugged, watching the kettle intently and avoiding Alana's questioning gaze. "I don't want to be a barroom singer all my life. I'd like to go back to school, learn to be a teacher." Her voice trailed off, and she scrubbed angrily at her face as the brilliant blue-green eyes brimmed over. Catching Alana's hand in her own, she burst out, "Oh, David insists he loves me... but my ex-husband walked out because he said I was too uneducated for him, and you know where I grew up. David's world and mine, they couldn't ever mix. His family's filthy rich, he grew up in places like Bermuda, his father's famous." She blew her nose angrily on a tissue. "Better to leave now, while I still can." Her eyes brimmed again. "If I can," she added.

Didn't anyone's life go easily? Alana stretched an arm around Katy's shoulders. "Don't sell yourself short. You're beautiful, smart and talented. Any man would be lucky to have your love. If David says he loves you, believe him." Katy couldn't imagine how much those words would mean to Alana if Rand had said them. An aching sadness crept over Alana as the evening ended.

"Mum wants you and Jenny to bring Bruce to Lissa's birthday party a week from Saturday. There'll be half a dozen four-year-olds, and we need all the help we can get. You'll come, won't you?" Katy asked Alana. Jenny beamed with pleasure, and they accepted.

The door had barely shut after the visitors when Martha announced, "Randall, I'm visiting the mine tomorrow."

"Fine," he said. "But you'll have to get there yourself. I'm far too busy to play chauffeur."

"Quite all right. Miss Cameron will drive me. It will be educational for her." She calmly strolled to the drink cupboard and poured herself the usual small sherry.

It might be a chance to reach some neutral ground with Martha, and Alana was curious about the mine. She wanted to see where Rand spent so much of his time and energy. In a cool voice she said, "If we're to spend the day together, Martha, perhaps you should learn my proper name. It's Campbell, Alana Campbell. And of course, you may call me Alana." Rand smothered a grin, and Martha gave an outraged snort, but there were no more mistakes.

Early the next morning, she and Martha set off for the

mine, and Alana knew everyone else at Bluejay breathed a collective sigh of relief as they drove off.

They followed, at Rand's instructions, a road Alana hadn't traveled before, heading north up a draw between two steep mountain ranges. Martha was talkative, less acerbic than Alana had yet seen her.

"Randall and his father are very much alike," she commented once, "in their thinking. Of course, Randall isn't the armchair executive Andrew was. He preferred to run the mine without getting his hands dirty. Consequently, the entire operation runs much better with Randall in charge."

Amazed, Alana glanced at the woman beside her. If only Martha would say something similar in front of Rand.

Martha used the remainder of the drive for interrogation, and for some reason Alana answered her questions openly.

"So both your parents were deaf," Martha mused as they approached a guard and gate. Slowing the car, Alana steeled herself for the tasteless, unfeeling comments she felt sure were forthcoming.

"My father was blind for the last years of his life," Martha said quietly. "It certainly changed my perception of the world, as I imagine deafness has for you."

Alana nearly went into the ditch, so surprised was she at Martha's understanding.

Rand hurried out to meet them when they approached the parking area. He was cool, brisk, businesslike. He handed them each a white nylon coverall, a pair of knee-high rubber boots, and an orange safety helmet.

"Get these on, and we'll go down," he instructed, indicating a women's locker and shower area. When Martha's back was turned, he smiled at Alana and dropped one eyelid in a wink.

The women struggled into their suits, and stepped out into the sunshine where Rand was waiting.

Alana could hear large motors running as they approached the mine entrance.

"Fans," Rand explained. "Supplying the mine shafts with fresh air and ventilation."

Men in coveralls much dirtier than Alana's waved or called friendly greetings to Rand, staring curiously at the women. Their stares invariably returned to Alana, and several whistles made her face flame. Rand just grinned.

They entered the mine shaft, and all random thoughts were driven from Alana's mind. She had tried to imagine what it would be like to enter a mine. She'd envisioned it as a sort of hole in the side of a mountain, and she found her unsophisticated idea to be surprisingly accurate. But the entrance was quite complex, with stainless steel and pipes. The sunlight and fresh mountain air Alana took for granted in the valley was gone. She was inside a tunnel of rock, supported by huge wooden beams. All around was the sound of water trickling, and the dimly lit walls seemed to ooze muddy slime. The floor was damp beneath her feet, and she was grateful for the cumbersome rubber boots. The air was cool, but it smelled. The best description she could think of was musky, a mushroomy, second-hand smell. The road tilted steadily upward and soon the shaft turned to the right. Glancing over her shoulder, Alana could no longer see open air or sunshine. Instead, light bulbs cast gloomy shadows every ten feet. To the right of their tunnel a conveyor belt loaded with glistening wet coal ran continuously with a tedious rumble. The tunnel was lined with timbers supporting the roof, and she could see weaker areas reinforced by steel pins.

The moldy damp chill soon penetrated Alana's body even through the coverall and jacket, in spite of the brisk pace Rand set just ahead. Martha was in her element, tramping stoutly along, asking questions about technical matters in her piercing voice. But to Alana the scene around her was as eerie as though she'd been transported to a strange planet.

"This is the mine car that will take us to the face, or workings of the tunnel," Rand was explaining. He seated Alana and Martha, and then himself, in the small rubber-tired cart that ran along a cable on the floor. He adjusted the controls and they began to move deeper into the blackness ahead. Alana relaxed a little, but the disconcerting aspect of the light on her safety helmet bothered her. Its tiny beam illuminated only the narrow path in front, and if she turned her head the light moved as well. She had to consciously fight the paranoic certainty that shapes, formless and ugly, were moving in the furry darkness on either side of her. Always, there was the sound of water, echoing everywhere. The bitter cold increased as they moved farther and farther into the mine's depths.

"What's in there?" Alana pointed to a boarded-off area they were passing.

"It's not safe to work in there anymore," Rand explained. "There's gas, or seepage, or falling rock. We board such areas off and begin exploring in another direction."

"Does anyone go in them again?" asked Alana. To her, they resembled tombs.

"Not if they want to stay healthy," Rand said casually. "They're too dangerous to work. There's no reason to go in again."

He added that miners used to use live birds, canaries usually, to detect gas in the tunnels, and that horses called pit ponies had been used to haul the coal in his grandfather's day. Alana had a mental vision of these tunnels, with helpless birds in cages singing despite the dark, and patient horses pulling loads of coal. She shivered violently.

The car had now left the main tunnel and was winding up an incline. In wider areas of the opening, men with shovels loaded waste material into small cars similar to the one she rode in, to be conveyed back outside. Alana could hear the thumping of some heavy machine close ahead, and in another moment their car stopped. A light bulb illuminated a small room in which a machine dislodged a conglomeration of coal, rocks and dust. It looked an ugly, forbidding monster to Alana, but Rand's eyes sparkled with pride as he gestured at the monstrous contraption.

"This beauty is a continuous miner," he hollered above the noise. "She's my pride and joy—does the work of ten men."

Alana wished desperately, urgently, that this tour would end. She was more aware every second of being in the bowels of the earth, surrounded by palpable, blanketing darkness with only a fragile beam of light at her control. She edged closer to Rand. She prayed he would get them back to the surface quickly before she succumbed to the overpowering, mad urge she had to run down the endless tunnels screaming at the top of her lungs. Never had she felt so trapped, so helpless, so frightened. But Rand was relaxed, exhilarated, unaware of her terror.

"This is the face, the end of the tunnel where the coal's removed. Because it's under the most stress, this is usually considered the most dangerous part of the mine. Here, though, there's nothing to worry about. We're ultraconscious of safety procedures at Evans Mine."

Alana's question squeaked out. "Has—has there ever been an accident here?"

"Not for years," Rand said confidently, a confidence that Alana was beginning to think of as a form of mental illness. "That time, no bumping had occurred for too long. A bump is just a readjustment of the earth, caused by the coal shifting to adjust to new stresses in the ground, caused by mining. Gas bumps give off methane, which can explode, but miners are more concerned if no bumping occurs for a long while. That's what happened that time. The pressure built too high." His matter-of-fact voice drawled on, and Alana's hair seemed to stand on end under the confines of the hat she wore.

"When the bump finally came, there was an explosion. The tunnel was sealed off by falling rock. Mine rescue teams managed to tunnel in, so everyone was saved. Only a few injuries." He turned to glance at her, his pencil beam of light illuminating what she knew was stark terror plain on her face. She felt she'd been underground at least three days. She was shivering, and each moment spent here in the bowels of the mine increased her nervousness. They'd passed and greeted men and women among the miners working this shift, people who passed their working hours in this enclosed and haunted place, with tons of rock and earth pressing, pressing on their pitiful little burrows—while she, until today, had never given mining much thought as she went blithely about her sunny life.

How many of her concepts had changed in the short passage of this one summer!

Their little car inched its way back toward the surface, finally, toward light and air, toward a world Alana felt she would never take for granted again, if she reached it. Rand's strong shoulder pressed reassuringly against her own, and she leaned even closer to his side. His warmth, the vitality and life force emanating from him drew her like a magnet in this subterranean place. Just as the mouth of the tunnel appeared, his arm came around her shoulder in a hug. He withdrew the arm, but took her cold hand in his own and gave it a squeeze before he withdrew that, too.

The blessed sunshine burst over her face, blinding her, and she turned up toward it like a flower opening. Never, never again would she enter a mine. She was a child of the sunshine, and here on top she'd stay.

She gazed at Rand, aware and awed at the myriad facets of his personality. He chose to spend his days there. Down there, she shuddered.

"How can you stand it?" She blurted out the question as Martha moved off to greet a smiling older man who'd called to her. "How can you bear to work in darkness, every day?"

The dark-chocolate eyes pierced her, and his mouth quirked. "You," he purred, "who choose to work with silence, asking me such a question?" He patted her arm reassuringly, traced a finger down her cheek where a streak of coal dust was smeared.

Then Martha was back, and they bid Rand goodbye and set off down the mountain.

Alana negotiated the narrow twists and turns with a buoyant awareness of the world around her, until Martha's voice broke into her reverie like a stone tossed through a glass window.

"You're in love with my son. I must tell you I believe he's in serious trouble."

The little car veered recklessly and Martha grabbed the dash. "Perhaps you'd better pull over, and I'll explain." Alana parked in a grassy spot well off the road, bright with purple fireweed, and turned so she faced Martha fully. Her skin felt tight, and her fists knotted into anxious balls. Martha moved restlessly, hands fluttering over her hair. "You must have wondered what brought me to Bluejay, really. I'm not yet in my dotage, I know I'm anything but welcome here. I'd decided to speak with Randall, but it's hopeless. He and I are simply chalk and cheese. I believe he despises me."

The words tore at Alana's heart, and she mumbled, "Oh, I don't think—"

Martha held out a silencing palm. "My dear, he has every reason to. I was a woman who should never have married. I wanted, needed a career. However, despite what Randall believes, I—I'm fond of him." She looked away, and flushed slightly. "I do love him," she added faintly, "although we don't have a very close relationship." She seemed to mentally dust her hands and continued.

"Well, we live our lives as we must. However, a month ago two men appeared at the door of my London flat. They were from Interpol, the International Police Force."

Alana's heartbeat thundered in her ears, and she longed to scream stop, stop, don't tell me—don't make my worst nightmares reality. But Martha's voice went inexorably on.

"That dreadful creature Randall married, that Lindsay Ross. Interpol believes she transports precious gems out of Hong Kong and into North America. Smuggles them. They also believe Randall is involved." Martha suddenly looked old and frightened. "I was going to confront him, demand he explain. But I find I just can't. He would hate me, you see. Even more than he already seems to. But the whole affair is urgent, because the police are closing in on—on this Lindsay woman. They suspected last month she was bringing in a shipment. They were following her, and she must have become suspicious, because she gave them the slip in London. Would you believe, she told the flight crew she was staying with me. She had to leave them an alternate address, you see. Of course, I never saw her. Had never met her, in fact. It was most embarrassing—the authorities wouldn't at first believe me. In the process, they asked detailed questions about the Evans Mine, were there discrepancies in the books, large amounts of money missing, did my son travel a great deal. In other words, they believed Randall was a part of this dreadful horror." Martha seemed to shrink, to grow thinner and more vulnerable.

"I denied that such a thing was possible, of course, but they skeptically insisted he was in touch with her, could be her partner. After all, he was married to her, not so long ago." There was a pathetic appeal in Martha's eyes.

"My dear, obviously you know Randall much better than I. Do you think—I mean, is it possible... you see, he would never confide in me." She drew a deep, shaky breath. "Is Randall involved against his will? It would have to be against his will, because I know my son to be an honorable man," she declared stoutly. "I must know, Alana. I would do anything... anything at all, to help."

Tears trickled unheeded down the angular cheeks. "You see, I have a great deal to regret with Randall. With his father, too, of course. But it's too late with Andrew. One makes mistakes...and then learns to live with them."

Alana could only sit mute, remembering with horror the folder, the call from Lindsay, the realization that Rand had seen his ex-wife in Vancouver, then in Calgary. She half listened to Martha's ramblings, while her brain sped over the irrefutable evidence of Rand's involvement in disaster. And the whole time her mind listed facts, places, clues, her heart refuted every scrap, refusing to accept logic, knowing with a woman's intuition about the man she loves that they were lies. Rand was honest, her heart protested; honest, moral, beyond deceit.

She told Martha that. Rand could never be an instigator of crime. Martha smiled, sadly and gently. "I'm as certain of that as you. But could he be compromised, somehow, by that woman?"

Alana's stomach clenched. If Rand still loved Lindsay, wouldn't he help her, against his better judgment? She suddenly felt nauseated. *"There are complications in my life,"* he'd said. *"A man makes mistakes, and takes the consequences."*

"Do you think he's involved, Alana?" Martha demanded again, insistently.

"I—I just don't know," she heard herself whisper. "Martha, I just don't know." The pain in the blue eyes behind the spectacles was intense, but Martha recovered her stern control.

"Then we'll simply have to wait and see, won't we, my dear? Let's go home."

Shakily, Alana started the engine, began the journey

back, but an idea was forming as she shifted gears, retracing the path to Bluejay. *"If you ever need me, I'll come,"* Johnny had promised her. The time seemed to have arrived when she must ask Johnny for help. Her decision calmed her somewhat. At least Johnny could tell her what the investigation Martha spoke of was really about, and who the suspects were. Definitely, she'd call her brother—soon.

Martha was talking quietly, reminiscing more to herself than to Alana. "Thank goodness Randall divorced her. Divorce can be a good thing. I realize now I should have divorced Andrew, allowed him to remarry. It was pride that stopped me, pride and anger. I threatened to withdraw my money from the mine, and I knew the mine was all he had. He wasn't a very adaptable man, Andrew. Neither was he strong, like Randall." She shook her head. "It was very wrong of me. I tried at the end, after the mine accident." She laughed mirthlessly. "It was too late, of course. He died before I arrived." She seemed to remember Alana, and in a firmer tone, said, "Don't ever wait too long to tell someone you love them. It's a difficult omission to live with."

Martha couldn't know of Alana's father, or of the many nights of agony Alana spent regretting her own behavior on his last visit. How ironic that she and Martha should share a common grief, and share also a paralyzing fear for a man they each loved in different ways—Randall Evans, son, Randall Evans, lover.

CHAPTER TEN

THAT AFTERNOON, Alana scribbled a careful letter to Johnny, including everything Martha had said about Interpol, Lindsay and smuggling. She excluded every suspicion of her own that Rand might be involved, trying to make the matter seem simply curious, a coincidental linking of Johnny's work and her own.

Had he received her first letter? It was probably stacked in some office file, waiting to be forwarded. She desperately wanted him to receive this one. After a moment's thought, she addressed it to him c/o Headquarters, enclosing the envelope in a large one. Then she wrote a hasty note to Grace, apologizing for imposing on her friend's time, but asking if she would personally take the enclosure to Johnny's commanding officer and insist Johnny get it as soon as possible.

Alana put the letter into the wicker basket of outgoing mail for Rand to take to the post office in the morning.

The days slipped by, and if Alana thought her few hours of near intimacy with Martha would result in a change in that lady's behavior, she soon realized how wrong such an idea was. Martha continued to be her irritating, critical self, antagonizing Rand in a way that seemed deliberate. And Alana now recognized this as Martha's inability to convey her feelings for those she cared for.

One stolen afternoon, Rand spirited Alana and Bruce off for an afternoon picnic in the woods, supposedly to inspect a wooden bridge Tom had constructed. Hastily tossing sandwiches and oranges in a bag, they sneaked off through the meadow, Bruce ecstatic at having both his father and Alana alone with him for a time. Rand had slung his camera case over his shoulder, and Alana pretended desperately that the three of them were a family, off for a pleasant jaunt. She simply wouldn't ruin this rare afternoon with the apprehension growing within her.

Rand snapped casual shots of her and Bruce. They found the rustic bridge, devoured their simple lunch and played among the huge trees. Bruce was unusually demanding and wickedly mischievous. Finally, Rand exclaimed, "He's as bad as his grandmother," and scooped Bruce up on his shoulders.

"They both love you, and want all your attention," Alana commented.

"Martha may want everything her own way, but love?" Rand snorted derisively. "Don't be ridiculous."

"She does love you, Rand, despite what you think." It suddenly became terribly important to Alana that Rand understand his mother. Among all the complexities at Bluejay, this one area at least could be eased. The terrible coldness with which Rand treated Martha was upsetting, reminding Alana of her own stupid, maudlin dramatics with her gentle father.

"But she does, Rand. She loves you; she loved your father," Alana insisted passionately. Rand threw her a look of utter disbelief, then deliberately turned his attention to Bruce. He put the boy down on the grassy forest floor, wrestling with him until Bruce was squealing with excitement. Alana felt frustrated and impotent, and desperately determined to make this stubborn man understand.

"Damn you, Rand, will you listen to me?" she shrieked, fighting the tears burning behind her eyes. "Martha told me she waited too long to tell your father, and she just can't find a way to be different with you. She wants to, I know, but you're so awful to her, so cold," Alana gulped, knowing she was describing her own behavior just as much as Rand's, and then something broke within her. Inside, she exploded. Great, gulping sobs tore her, sobs she'd never allowed to surface at the time of her father's death, feeling she didn't deserve their painful, yet comforting release. Now, she cried like a child, mouth open, nose running, gulping and choking.

Rand sprang up, shock and concern evident in his expression, wrapping his long arms around her, patting her back in clumsy comfort.

"Don't, honey, don't cry like that. I'll be different with her, I promise..."

Bruce stared at his teacher, his own chin quivering, and wrapped his arms around her, copying his father's patting. The two males sat her down, wet Rand's handkerchief in the creek, mopped her face with the icy water, sending rivulets trickling down her shirtfront. Bruce sat on her lap, watching her expression closely until, with the amazing perception of the deaf, he sensed she was better. He gave her cheek a final pat, and raced off to chase Tad into the water.

Alana slumped into the comforting circle Rand's arms created around her.

"Better now?" he asked softly, and when she nodded, too exhausted even to talk any more, he crushed her against him in silent empathy. "I'm not sure it'll work, but I give you my solemn promise I'll try harder with Mar—with mother," he assured her. Then, he turned her chin up gently and kissed her, a wonderfully tender, healing kiss that told her more than any words could that he understood. They were interrupted suddenly by Bruce, tackling his father from behind and nearly choking him, and shortly after that, they straggled reluctantly home again.

Martha met them with impatient displeasure, demanding Rand explain financial statements she was checking, and Bruce upset an entire quart of milk over himself, the kitchen floor and Tad. Usually, Rand disappeared grimly into his study, slamming the door in the midst of Martha's tirades. Tonight, he helped mop up floor and child and dog, calmly agreeing with his mother's litany about Bruce and discipline.

"You're absolutely right, mother. The kid's a holy terror. What do you think we should do with him?"

Martha was, for the first time since she'd arrived, wordless. Rand flashed Alana a conspiratorial wink and raised his eyebrow in amazement as Martha took a deep breath and immediately began to defend her grandson.

BUT WHEN THE DAY of Lissa's birthday party arrived, it was Rand who was defensive.

"If I thought those kids were going to cause Bruce problems about his hearing aids or deafness, I'd forbid you to take him."

Alana had explained reasonably, "There'll only be a few children there, four- and five-year-olds. Bruce loves

Lissa, and he's so eager to go." Bruce clutched his gaily wrapped and already bedraggled gift and tugged impatiently on Jenny's arm.

"We will take good care of him, Boss," Jenny assured Rand.

The party was a rowdy success, and Alana couldn't help but compare the robust and confident imp Bruce had become with the shy and introverted child she'd met in Vancouver. Katy had hired a pony, and Bruce lorded his "horse sense" over the Elkford children.

In the past few days, Bruce had also set out to charm his grandmother. Alana grinned, remembering. Martha being Martha, the process was slow, but Bruce was winning. Martha went on waging war about Tad being kept outside, but it was beyond her to resist a freshly bathed, pajama-clad boy climbing trustfully into her lap at bedtime.

Which meant that she and Jenny would have not just Rand to contend with, but Martha as well, Alana concluded wearily as she steered slowly up Bluejay's driveway after the party. Bruce was asleep on Jenny's lap, filthy, bruised and exhausted. "Boss will be plenty mad with us when he sees that eye," Jenny predicted. That, Alana silently agreed, was probably the understatement of the year. She felt exactly like a child being sent to the principal's office.

Lissa had given a concise report on the battle, stomping up to Katy and Alana where they sat sipping lemonade.

"Steven punched Bruce," she'd puffed, exactly like an outraged mother. "He shoved my Bruce, and Bruce fell down, and he got up, and then," Lissa took an immense gulp of air to prepare for the climax, "Bruce punched

Steve so hard he got a nosebleed, and Bruce got a black eye. What magic sign means fight, Lana?"

Stopping now to open the gate, Alana steeled herself for the confrontation sure to come. If anyone could ask Bruce, Alana was certain he would insist he'd just had the best day of his life. He'd screamed bloody murder when Jenny tried to load him in the car to come home. He and Steven were busy digging up the dirt under the trailer to make roads for their trucks, won as party favors. Finally, Jenny smacked his bottom to stop the tantrum, and Alana had sternly insisted he pay attention as she promised that Steven could come to visit Bluejay soon.

Rebelliously, Alana left the gate open. Martha had gone to Elkford with Rand, at his invitation—for an afternoon of shopping and a lunch at the local hotel. Chances were they hadn't yet returned, so they could shut the damn gate.

Jenny was as subdued as Alana when they pulled into the driveway and stopped. It had been an exhausting party. Bruce still snored gently.

"Let's open the car windows and let him nap out here," Jenny decided, sliding out from under the sleeping child. They quietly closed the car doors, and they were half across the yard when Jenny said, "Funny, Boss must have locked Tad in the shed."

They could hear the dog whining pitifully. Alana strolled slowly, waiting for Jenny as she detoured to free the animal. The air was hot and still, and Alana bent to sniff at Jenny's roses. It was then that she saw Tom.

He lay in a crumbled heap just beside the roses, on the path near the door. Horrified, frozen, Alana saw his aluminum crutch dangling pathetically from a bush nearby. His old brown hat lay near his head. He didn't move. A red stain was coloring the pinned-up leg of the jeans that covered his stump.

Alana screamed, and screamed again. Jenny came running, and when she saw Tom, she began to moan, "My God, oh my God."

They dropped to their knees beside him, and he moved a hand and flopped it down again.

"Water, teacher, get some water," Jenny ordered and Alana scrambled up. As she raced for the kitchen, she saw Rand's truck drive up. Tom was struggling to sit, groaning and rubbing his head. Filling a pitcher, Alana hurried back out, fear and relief at seeing Rand making her weak. He took over, competently and efficiently. He held Tom's head as Jenny sponged, cradling Tom's back against his shoulder. Tom was pasty white, and the water made his grizzled hair stick to his forehead. His eyes focussed first on Jenny, then on Rand. He became wildly excited.

"Did ya get him, Boss? Did ya catch the bugger?"

"Take it easy, relax," Rand said. His forehead puckered in a frown. "Catch who, Tom?"

Tom's head thrashed from side to side. He reached up and pushed away the cloth, wiping his face with his sleeve.

"I heard the dog, see, goin' crazy in the shed. Figured I'd come over and let him out. Then I heard this noise from the house—and I knew all of you were out." A grimace of pain twisted Tom's face, and he rubbed the back of his skull.

"He jumped me from behind. Knocked the damn crutch out from under me. Didn't even get a good look at him." Tom's voice was stronger, and now he thumped a fist into the grass in utter frustration.

"Damn it all to hell, anyway."

Jenny had hurried into the house. Now Rand ordered, "Alana, go and phone David." Tom protested loudly that he was fine, didn't want no damn doctor, and his voice followed Alana as she headed for the kitchen phone. Jenny stood in the doorway, her narrow dark eyes stretched as wide as they'd go, hands knotted in front of her.

"He went through the whole house, teacher. All the cupboards, all the drawers. Bruce's room, yours, mine. What was he looking for? What could he want at Bluejay? He never touched the money on my dresser, either."

Her voice rose to a wail, and tears poured down her round cheeks.

"Why did he have to hurt my poor Tom?"

It was a good question, thought Alana later, after things had settled down. David had arrived promptly, bringing a stout elderly doctor he introduced as Dr. Monroe. Alana was surprised to see Martha with them—she'd been too preoccupied to even ask where Rand's mother was.

The doctors made a quick examination, and quietly loaded a protesting, angry Tom into their station wagon, equipped with a foam mattress and obviously used as a makeshift ambulance.

Alana heard Dr. Monroe quietly tell Rand, "That stump was injured by the fall he took. I'm going to insist he sees a specialist, probably in Vancouver. We'll keep him in the clinic overnight and fly him down tomorrow. Could you pack some clothes and such for him?"

Jenny, too, was close by and heard the doctor's words.

"Tom will never agree to go. I will go with him, talk and make him see how important this is. He's a very stubborn man."

After that, things happened very quickly. Jenny, with Rand's help, packed clothing from Tom's cabin, and then she hurried to pack a bag for herself. Martha thoughtfully took Bruce out for a walk when he awoke, away from the confusion. Jenny came downstairs, her own brown suitcase in one hand, Tom's old brown Stetson in the other. She wore a black pantsuit, and a yellow and black spotted blouse. For Jenny, the outfit was nearly somber.

Grasping Alana's hand in her own, Jenny said, "Damn, teacher, too many things happen all at once." Then, with a sob, she wrapped her arms around Alana. Her shiny black braids atop her head came just under Alana's chin, and tears dripped into them from Alana's own wet cheeks. They hugged fiercely.

Alana had made a hurried telephone call, and fortunately reached Grace. Now she told Jenny, "My friend and her mother will meet you tomorrow in Vancouver. You're to stay at my apartment with Grace—it's close to the hospital where Tom will be." Alana gave her a card with the information. Jenny began to protest, but Alana held a finger over her friend's lips.

"Just hurry back home, both of you, okay?" The last words squeaked up as Alana's concern for these friends brought a flood of tears. How she had come to love this little woman. And Tom, too.

Martha and Bruce were returning from their walk as

Jenny ran down to the truck where Rand was waiting to drive her into Elkford. The doctors had hurried off with Tom several minutes earlier. Alana watched from the doorway as Jenny gave Bruce a long hug and kiss. Then, with great dignity, Jenny spoke to Martha for several minutes. Amazingly, the two women, one tall and thin, one short and plump, clasped hands. Rand put Jenny's case in the truck, and they drove off.

Martha made tea for Alana and herself, fixing a milky mug for Bruce as well. Her face held a bemused expression.

"Do you know what Jenny Chan said to me, Alana?" Alana shook her head.

"She said she was leaving Bruce in my hands, that she knew I would take good care of him and love him for her until she returned." She met Alana's eyes over the steaming teacup.

"That's word for word what I told her so many years ago when—when I left Randall with her to return to England." She shook her head wonderingly. "Ironic, isn't it, how circular life can be?"

Later that evening, Alana had reason herself to marvel at the circuitous routes of fate. Rand had waited for a report on Tom—he would need further tests—and arranged for tickets on the early-morning flight for Tom and Jenny. Now he slumped in an armchair, rubbing the back of his neck with a weary hand. And Bruce rushed at him from the kitchen where Martha had made him eggs for his supper.

Since the party, Bruce's black eye had developed into a classic shiner. Clambering up on his father's knee, he wore blue flannelette pajamas with a red T-shirt over them bearing a Superman emblem on the chest. Around him floated an old red tablecloth, the nearest thing Alana had been able to find as a cape. It was fastened at the neck with a huge diaper pin. On his feet were cowboy boots, and his feathery curls shone white-blond in the light. The purple swelling was even more obvious and shocking due to the barely faded bruise on his forehead from his fall several weeks before. Double hearing aids perched jauntily behind miniscule ears, and all around his mouth were yellow traces of egg.

Rand stared hard for several thumping heartbeats. Alana steeled herself for the explosion. Impervious to any problems, Bruce excitedly demonstrated the trucks he'd won at the birthday party. Rand took his son's small chin in his hand, turning it gently to one side and then the other. He raised an enquiring eyebrow at Alana, his expression so carefully bland she couldn't guess his real reaction. She felt her usual telltale blush begin, and she cursed it bitterly. Stay cool, she urged herself. It's perfectly natural for kids to fight. Rand must understand that. Calm, cool, collected Alana Campbell.

Her voice came out unnaturally loud and highly pitched, and in an instant she could actually feel her eyes snapping at him, daring him to contradict her.

"Well, the other boy was trying to look at Bruce's hearing aids, so Bruce punched him in the nose. It was a perfectly normal fight between little boys, and Bruce had a marvelous time, and just because there was a little...skirmish, is absolutely no reason for you to—why, Jenny and I had to drag Bruce away from that party kicking and screaming, he was having such fun, and finally, Jenny smacked his bottom, he fought us both, I've told you he has to have playmates, he needs other children..." Gradually she wore down, the words coming slower and further apart. At last, she stopped.

"Violence, teacher? Do I actually hear you condoning violence?" Rand's eyebrow was now nearly at his hairline, his expression one of exaggerated amazement.

"For heaven's sake, Rand, if you think that's violence—"

Suddenly, she stopped short. Were his chocolate eyes actually laughing at her?

Indignantly, she went on, "He bruised both Jenny and I with his boots, and a small smack on his bottom..." Her voice trailed off. Uncomfortably, she remembered a similar conversation with Rand, the very day she'd arrived. Hadn't she lectured him primly for spanking Bruce? Heavens, she'd told him—hadn't she said condoning violence made him... Her own words sprang up to haunt her. Had she really said Rand was as civilized as a tree trunk?

Mortified, she refused to meet Rand's eyes. Her whole upper body felt as though it were on fire. She kept her eyes riveted on Bruce, and the absolutely incongruous spectacle he made, his Superman cape spreading out over Rand's knees, pajama bottoms sagging so his bottom gleamed out, the black eye, and the mouth pursed and spraying Rand as he made the spattering noise small boys always used for truck sounds. Steven had taught it to him.

A hysterical giggle bubbled in her throat. It popped out, and then she and Rand were laughing helplessly. Martha came in, stared from one to the other, and stated firmly, "Both of you are hysterical. You need a strong cup of tea."

It was a sort of safety valve, that laughter, decided

Alana later. It kept them from dwelling on Tom, or Jenny, or themselves. She stood at the door to her bedroom. The drawers were spilled on the floor, the closet ransacked, her picture of Johnny a puddle of broken glass on the floor. The senseless chaos gave her a feeling of foreboding, an unreasonable nameless fear.

What was the intruder looking for? Why ransack Bruce's room, Alana pondered, sweeping up glass shards. Against her will, Alana remembered Martha telling her of Interpol, of smuggling, of Lindsay.

Rand came quietly up behind her just then, pulling her back against him, encircling her fiercely with his arms. Alana turned blindly and gratefully toward him, desperate to blot out with sensation the ugly suspicions she couldn't subdue. She raised her mouth eagerly to welcome his kiss, but Martha's step sounded just then on the stairs. Alana stumbled back, out of Rand's arms, trembling from his touch.

"There's no damn way to get one private second in this house," gritted Rand. He stalked off down the hall, and Alana began to put her room in order, working furiously hard to avoid her conviction that what had happened today was part of the ominous puzzle surrounding Rand. Whoever had broken in had been watching the house. Today was the first time Alana could remember everyone being out at the same time. Except for Tom.

In bed that night, thinking of Tom, cold fear started in her toes and worked its way up her body. Attacking Tom had been the work of a desperate and ruthless person. Surely it wasn't feasible that Rand would have any part of a scheme that might injure Tom, or anyone for that matter. But what if Rand were hiding something for Lindsay, something—her every instinct rebelled at that point, and she gave herself a mental shake. The whole thing was ridiculous!

She heard Rand's quiet steps passing her door several times, and she realized he was on guard, watching over Bluejay and those he loved.

Alana sent out a silent plea to the one person she felt might be able to sort out the tangled web of intrigue knotting itself around their lives. Hurry, Johnny, please hurry, she whispered desperately. Outside her door, Rand's footsteps paused, waited, and then reluctantly moved away.

CHAPTER ELEVEN

THE NEXT MORNING was torpid with August heat. Rand left late for work, assuring the women he would visit the RCMP office and request a watchful eye be kept in the area. He and the doctors had reported Tom's assault the evening before, and an investigation was underway.

Alana was tossing a ball with Bruce in the meadow when a sporty blue convertible pulled into the yard, and a tall man in jeans, cowboy hat low on his forehead, stepped lithely out and started toward them.

Tad made his usual show of bravery, and Alana bent to grab his collar. There was something about the way the man moved—she set the dog free, and in two leaping bounds was in her brother's arms.

Martha was hurrying over from the house, and Johnny rapidly whispered, "Easy, sis, don't blow my cover. Let me do the talking."

Martha bustled curiously up, and Johnny extended his hand, charmingly grinning, saying, "I'm an old friend of Lana's, my name's John Kelly. I was in the area, and decided to drop in and see how she is. How do you do, Ms...?"

Alana regained her composure enough to introduce Martha and Bruce, aware of the curious glances Martha was sending her as they ambled toward the house.

"What is your vocation, Mr. Kelly?" Martha demanded.

"Insurance," John answered smoothly. "I'm in the insurance business, have to travel a great deal."

"How long have you known Alana?" Martha pursued, her astute gaze flicking from one to the other.

"We've been...close friends...since we were just kids, right, Alana?" She nodded, desperate to get Johnny alone. But Martha was delighted to have a stranger to entertain, and she made tea, regaling Johnny with the history of Bluejay and the production of the mine.

Finally, she wore down. Bruce went off for a nap, and Martha decided she, too, would rest for an hour. Alana felt nearly ready to burst with frustration by the time she was finally alone with her brother. She led him impatiently down the path to the lakeshore, and they sat on the dock.

Johnny pulled her toward him in a rough hug. "Well, squirt, you got yourself in a fine mess this time, huh?" He gave her an assessing stare. "You're thinner, and I get the feeling things aren't as amusing as you tried to pretend in your letter. Good thing I know you so well, sis. Good thing, too, I was between assignments. The Officer in Charge and I did some checking on the information you gave me in your letter, and he decided to fly me back here. I'd rather no one knew I was your brother, for a while...just in case you happened to brag about me being in the Force. It's more effective if everybody just thinks I'm an old romance. That way, I can keep a close eye on things and nobody's suspicious. Now. Just how well d'you know this Evans character, anyway?"

The demanding tone of his voice and his question irritated Alana. She tilted her chin stubbornly.

"I'm not telling you one thing till you answer my questions, Johnny Campbell. I have to know what's going on here, who attacked poor Tom, who Lindsay Ross is, why—"

Johnny held both hands up. "Slow down, Red, and I'll start from the beginning. Just promise you won't interrupt."

His voice was serious when be began.

"Interpol is working on a huge smuggling operation based in Hong Kong; a well-organized group who uses stewardesses to transport gems to contacts in North America where they're fenced and sold at enormous profit. The stewardesses are paid well, but they're only couriers—mules, we call them—used to carry the stones through customs. Lindsay Evans-Ross was a mule, dutifully turning her loads over to the syndicate men on this side, getting paid a fair chunk of dough for her trouble. She was caught once, but charges were dropped for lack of evidence. Anyway, she got mixed up with a real bad dude called George Krane. He was an ex-airline pilot, small-time crook, who decided to cash in on the big money the gems were worth. He convinced Lindsay Ross to bring in a load, avoid the courier and disappear with him, probably to South America. But the plan backfired."

Alana was quite still, hardly able to breathe. She didn't want to hear anything more, terrified of what Johnny would say next. Because she knew, any moment, the story would implicate Rand. She remembered Rand saying, "I didn't fly high enough for her. She took off with a pilot."

"Interpol was trailing her, trying to nail the big guys

behind the operation. She threw up a smoke screen in London, and they lost her temporarily, only to have her turn up in Vancouver. Without the jewels, and without Krane. Nobody seems to know where he is." Johnny paused, staring off at the mountains, the shimmering haze hovering over the lake in the afternoon stillness.

Alana's voice was strained. "And the—the jewels she had? Where are they?"

"The RCMP think she freaked when she found out she was being followed. They figure she gave them to a man she met in Vancouver, to keep for her till she can pick them up. Or maybe to fence, who knows?"

"Rand," Alana whispered hopelessly. "You think she gave them to Rand."

Johnny nodded, wrapping an arm around her shoulders. "How well do you know this guy anyway, Alana? What's your relationship with him besides teaching his son?" When she didn't answer, Johnny said impatiently, "The RCMP checked his room at the hotel in Vancouver, went over his stuff with a fine-toothed comb: no jewels. Maybe she mailed the parcel here, to him. I called in to the detachment in Elkford before I came, and heard about the attack on Saunders yesterday. To me, that suggests that Krane believes the stuff is hidden here, and wants it back. Krane could be hiding out somewhere in this valley. Lindsay lived here, she'd know of places to hide."

He turned her body toward him, hands on her shoulders in entreaty. "When your letter came, and the O.C. briefed me on what was going on, I damned near had a cardiac arrest. The last thing I need is my kid sister mixed up in something like this. My first reaction was to come and take you out of here, quick. But the O.C. insists things have gone too far, that any sudden changes now might be dangerous. They don't want to spook Krane. The authorities want him, because he knows the people at the top. Lindsay's on her way here right now, and they figure she'll lead them to the jewels and to him." Johnny forced Alana to meet his eyes, holding her shoulders gently but firmly.

"The unknown quantity in this whole mess is Evans. Is he, or isn't he involved? Do you know him well enough to be sure, one way or another?"

How well did she know Rand? She knew his body, had mapped it with her hands. She knew him as her beloved, his prickly surface, his inner gentleness. She knew she loved him.

But Rand did still care for Lindsay. He obviously knew of her criminal activities, he had been with his ex-wife in Vancouver and again in Calgary, within a few weeks. A film of ice seemed to spread through her chest, in the region of her heart. Johnny's logic led in one direction: Rand was, for his own reasons, helping his former wife.

How well did she know Rand? Well enough to know he didn't love her or trust her enough to explain what really was going on. Black despair overwhelmed her, and she slumped into her brother's arms.

Water lapped noisily beneath them as the dock tilted suddenly, and Rand, face like a thundercloud, stood over them.

"Martha said you were probably down here," he growled, his burning gaze memorizing Johnny's arms around her, her face pressed close to his chest. Rand's fists flexed and closed again, and Alana scrambled to her feet. Johnny rose leisurely, his big rangy body seemingly relaxed, but Alana knew he was watching carefully for the flicker in Rand's eyes that would preface attack, and she could feel the steely muscle tense in the arm Johnny slung so casually around her shoulders.

Rand was jealous. The knowledge gave Alana a twinge of satisfaction; she had tormented herself so often over Rand and his dealings with Lindsay, it was a neat turnabout now to recognize his anger for what it was. She felt that way only for a moment, however. Then, she wished desperately she could introduce her brother honestly, watch these two strong, determined men learn to respect and like each other. It couldn't be, not now.

Johnny held out a hand, and Rand took it as she made introductions, but the handshake was a token gesture. Battle lines were drawn on both sides for different reasons, and Alana was placed—helpless as any chess pawn—directly in the middle.

THE SPAN OF DAYS Alana would later term "the watching time" began. Martha and Alana struggled to fill the huge chasm created by Jenny's absence. It took them all their time to accomplish a quarter of the chores Jenny did alone. Johnny was around every day, arriving before Rand left in the morning, leaving after he came home each evening. Rand made no pretense at friendliness with Johnny, but Bruce adopted the chestnut-haired giant as his hero. Johnny's fluent signing helped, and Bruce followed him around every second he was free from lessons.

Alana drew pictures, explaining to the child where Jenny and Tom were. During one conversation with her brother she confided her guilt and remorse about her father, and his response completed the healing process begun when she'd talked with Rand.

"I talked to dad just before he went home that time,

and he said you were going through a bad stage, but that he was proud of your strength." Johnny reached an affectionate hand to tousle her hair. "Hell, Red, dad understood you. He'd never believe you were ashamed of him. He knew you loved him." With his words, Alana at last began to forgive herself.

Martha warmed to Johnny's charm. What female could resist him, Alana smilingly wondered. Johnny cheerfully took over many of Tom's chores, and the calm few days sped past, marred only by Rand.

Rand was avoiding her. He'd explained tersely that he was having problems with the electrical system at the mine. Several times she heard him come home late at night, open Bruce's door, then pause outside her own door as though about to enter. Each time, she lay breathlessly waiting, body drawn tight as a bow string. Every cell longed to have him come to her, but her mind frantically warned him to stay away. She was simply not good at subterfuge, and Johnny had warned her against confrontation. Yet she knew she had to at least discuss with Rand his plans for Bruce for September, because she knew now she had to leave Bluejay when summer was over.

Katy visited several times, her small car overflowing with children. Bruce was proving to be a social butterfly. He responded now to Tad's bark, loud music, and of course his beloved alarm clocks that Alana used for auditory training.

"I've registered for night school," Katy told Alana on one visit. "Running away's not the answer, David's convinced me."

"How do you feel about him?" Alana ventured.

Katy shrugged nonchalantly. "Oh, I can take him or

leave him. I can't eat or sleep. Every song is for him. His kisses make the fillings in my back teeth shiver." She tossed her mane of hair. "He doesn't really bother me at all." The women looked at each other and burst into giggles.

Katy was naturally curious about Johnny. "He's an absolute hunk. If it weren't for David, I'd give you some competition, Alana. It's clever of you to make Rand jealous, it's time he started living again." She glanced hesitantly at Alana. "It *is* Rand you care for, isn't it? Selfishly, I'd love it if you stayed here. There's a special-ed teaching position open at the school, and an older deaf girl will be starting classes this September." Martha chose that moment to serve tea, and Alana avoided answering as Katy turned the conversation to the upcoming yearly celebration.

"Coal Miner Days is the biggest event of the year here. You all have to come. Bruce will love it, and my mother would be grateful, Martha, if you'd help her with the judging at the food booths."

"Any fool can see I'm better at judging food than cooking it," Martha stated dryly, and Alana had to laugh. She and Martha had the same method for menu planning; a can and a can opener.

"I'll speak to Randall. Bruce should experience a carnival," Martha said emphatically, her eyes resting indulgently on her grandson.

Rand agreed, another indication of his growing rapport with his mother. The two were still furiously opposed much of the time, but now their disagreements were tempered with a small measure of affection on both sides.

Lessons began to be centered around red lines on the

calendar leading to that final day in August. The parade was on September first, the beginning of the three-day gala, and Bruce became more and more excited as the adults found ways to tell him of the event.

Somehow, the date became a deadline for Alana, marking the end of the waiting time. Her contract with Rand ended the first week in September.

The days slipped by until the red marks on Bruce's calendar showed no more spaces. It was Friday. The parade would be the following morning.

Before he left that afternoon, Johnny took Alana aside and said, "Things are starting to happen, and I don't want you going to the carnival without me. So wait for me in the morning." Before Alana could question him, Rand came around the corner and glared at them. Johnny glared back and left soon afterward.

After dinner, Rand said unexpectedly, "I'll help Martha clean up, Alana. You have half an hour to get ready. Katy's singing tonight, and she told me to bring you."

Martha firmly took the plates Alana held. "Hurry up, my dear," she directed. "It's time Randall learned to wash dishes."

Alana showered, splashed on lemon cologne and talc. It was aeons since she'd worn anything but shorts or jeans. She pulled on white lace bikini panties, and surveyed her closet. There was one deceptively simple wrap dress, a soft swiss cotton in a bold blue and green geometric print. She swirled it around her, pleased that it reduced her waist to minute proportions. It was a romantic dress. Alana smoothed on lip gloss, adding a touch of cosmetics from the box Rand had given her. That seemed so long ago, those first confusing days at Bluejay. She'd wanted to bolt back to the city, away from Rand. And now? She met her own silvery gaze in the mirror, and her lips moved as she quoted to herself, "Better to have loved and lost, than never to have loved at all."

Could you lose what you'd never had? Rand hadn't pretended to love her. He'd been brutally honest with her about that, at least. As for the rest? She pushed it one last time into the Pandora's box of her consciousness, and firmly shut the lid.

Tonight, there was just her and Rand, she thought happily as they sped along in the Fiat toward Elkford. The crimson and gold spill of sunset from the high mountains bathed them in radiance. Rand's long arm snaked over and around her, impeded by the bucket seats. Still, his callused fingers raised goosebumps of sensation as they trailed restlessly up and down the bare flesh of her upper arm.

"Why the hell are you avoiding me, Alana?"

"Me?" she sputtered. "It seems it's the other way around, Rand."

A scowl creased his forehead. "There's no choice, with Martha and Bruce around every minute, not to mention your lovelorn salesman friend. How long is he staying, anyway? Doesn't he have work to do?"

Alana managed to laugh lightly. "I do believe you're jealous, Rand."

He turned toward her. "Damn right I'm jealous. There's a lot to straighten out between us, teacher. There are things I still don't have answers for, but I want to talk to you about them anyway. Should we stop somewhere now, or wait till later?"

A cramp of fear convulsed her. "Can we leave it till later?" she asked, feeling the need to procrastinate.

He nodded, pulling the car into a paved parking area

beside a log structure spilling out music and people, and soon she was seated close to Rand's side in the smoky, ear-splitting clamor of Elkford's favorite and only watering hole.

Black Jack's Tavern took a lot of getting used to. Rand ordered a glass of wine for her, beer for himself, and they sat companionably absorbing the tumultuous atmosphere.

Then, Katy was on the stage. She sent Rand and Alana a wide smile and a thumbs-up greeting. She wore faded blue jeans and a dramatic white satin shirt with billowing sleeves caught into narrow cuffs. A gay red scarf emphasized her lovely face, and the dark hair made her look gypsylike. Through the hubbub, her soft, husky voice calmly commanded the room. She introduced herself, and struck a dramatic chord on her guitar.

What happened next took Alana's breath away. Her song was a ballad, "You and Me against the World." Katy's voice purred and sobbed, ringing with the clarity of a flute played by an expert. Katy didn't just sing; she became her song. She threw her head back, letting the music possess her.

"When all the others turn their backs and walk away, you can count on me to stay..."

The words tore at Alana's heart. They were every lonely person's dream of a lover who cared enough to stand alongside through life's storms. Katy's voice and the lyrics drew tears from Alana's eyes. Rand watched her, reaching out to stroke a finger down each wet track, detouring to trace the sensitive outline of her lips. He grasped her hand in his, and a bond of silent passion and understanding flowed between them.

Katy began a medley of other tunes, romantic and slow.

"Dance?" Rand suggested. Alana nodded, and then she was in his arms, eyes level with his lips, his hands firm on the small of her back. He pressed her tight to the muscles of his body.

They hadn't danced together before. They had shared the most intimate of moments, yet had not had the chance to enjoy casual social contact. How she longed for hours to talk with Rand, explore their differences, their similarities. Why, it could take a lifetime—and they only had tonight. If only tonight would never end.

She gave herself up to his embrace, floating under the spell of Katy's seductive voice. The graceful, lithe male body led, controlled her own, teasing, promising with its rhythm and its pressures, cradling and protecting with its rough tenderness. Rand's lips were in her hair. It was difficult to tell whether the excited hammering in her ears was her own pulse or a vibration of his. The lights were dim. A smoky haze enveloped them, permeated by the lyrics of Katy's songs. Rand's body heat seared through the thin cotton of her dress. He bent closer, lips tickling her ear. Slow, heady sparks ignited and the resulting flames coursed upward, meeting in the center of her abdomen.

She wanted him—how she wanted him! His fingers circled her rib cage until they touched the underside of her breasts. Alana drifted in a cocoon of sensation, eyes closed, savouring the delight of being held in the arms of the man she adored.

"Teacher, you're driving me crazy," he breathed. "I can't wait to get you alone—shall we leave, soon?"

She nodded, and they moved slowly through the

crowded tables to reclaim her purse and shawl, intimacy pulsing between them.

In the next second, it shattered. A cultured voice from behind Alana's shoulder purred, "Rand, I've searched all over for you, darling." The heavy odor of expensive perfume enveloped the table, and the healthy color slowly faded from Rand's face. Shutters seemed to drop, masking the expressive warmth of a moment ago, and he stiffened with shock.

Alana didn't need Rand's terse introduction. Lindsay Evans-Ross was beautiful, awesomely so with her blond nordic coloring, her hair drawn high in a smooth chignon, wisps curling forward over her ears. Makeup flawless; features composed. She wore a dark skirt and a wheat-colored silk sweater over lush breasts.

"I hate to intrude," she went on, "but Rand and I have urgent business to discuss. Perhaps we could drive you home, Miss Campbell?"

Alana felt ill, trapped in undercurrents, blazingly aware that here was the woman Rand loved, the mother of his son, more beautiful than Alana cared to admit, and smoothly sophisticated. She was perfectly groomed, gold jewelry at neck and ears and wrist, making Alana acutely aware of her own simple cotton dress, her stockingless legs, her undoubtedly rumpled hair.

"That won't be necessary." Johnny's voice had never sounded so welcome. He was suddenly at Alana's side, a comforting arm around her, ingenuous grin intact.

"Lucky I happened to drop by. Three's a crowd, and all that." He glanced at Lindsay, then centered his attention on Rand.

"Seems you have more females than you can handle, so if Alana agrees, I'll see her safely home." He quirked an inquiring eyebrow at Alana, as Rand snapped, "Sorry, Alana's here with me."

Lindsay placed a languid hand on Rand's arm. "But we have very private matters to discuss, Rand. Don't you think—?"

Rand seemed about to explode with rage. Alana gave him a cold glare, and sweetly smiled up at Johnny, scooped up her shawl and purse, and was outside the tavern before she could draw a deep breath.

"Thanks, Johnny," she breathed as he hustled her into his car, started it and wheeled out of the parking lot. "How did you—?"

"I told you, I'm keeping a close eye on you. Besides, I want to give Evans a chance to tip his hand. Lindsay is pretty desperate. She knows the police are closing in."

Alana's face burned as she realized that had she left the tavern with Rand, Johnny would have been closely observing their actions. But by leaving, she'd set Rand up. There was no winning.

"I'm taking you back to Bluejay, but I want you to pack your things and leave with me tonight," Johnny instructed. "Krane is a dangerous character, and he's sure to be around now that Lindsay's on the scene. They want those missing gems, and it's pretty certain Evans is holding them for his ex-wife. I don't want you anywhere around when the trouble starts."

Weariness and despair enveloped her. It was an effort to think, but she managed to say, "You're forgetting one important thing in all this, Johnny. Rand would never let anything happen to his son, or his mother. If he is planning anything, it will be far way from Bluejay. I'm here as a teacher for Bruce, and my contract runs another week. This is my work, Johnny, as important to me as yours is to you. Besides," she finished illogically, "I promised Bruce I'd take him to Coal Miner Days tomorrow, and you know how excited he is."

Johnny drove in silence, finally reluctantly saying, "Tomorrow, okay, I'll be close. But tomorrow night, you leave." He was adamant, and Alana accepted his decision finally. In Bluejay's driveway, he planted a brotherly kiss on her forehead. "I'll be watching, so rest easy," he assured her. "See you in the morning."

After he drove off, Alana couldn't stand to go into the house. A light was burning in the living room; she couldn't talk to Martha tonight. She wandered down to the water, and spread her shawl on the damp grass, shoulders slumped with misery. The soft darkness was alive with sounds of trees and forest, and Bluejay Lake shone like a width of silver paper under the yellow moon. But Bluejay's peace was only a facade, she mused bitterly, covering a maelstrom of intrigue. And even the facade was shattered a few minutes later when Rand drove his car in with a roar, squealed it to a halt, and slammed the door. Alana saw him stride to the house, then heard a low conversation, the angry tones of his voice carrying in the silent night, and Martha's softer response. Then, he stood again in the doorway.

"Alana. Alana, I want to talk to you." The peremptory order echoed out over the water, repeating and repeating: you, you, you.

Slowly, she covered the short distance to the door, where Rand's large and unmoving bulk stood silhouetted against the light of the room behind him, waiting. Waiting, for her.

CHAPTER TWELVE

HE STOOD ABSOLUTELY STILL as she drew hesitantly near. Then, without warning, hands reached out and grasped her shoulders, almost lifting her off her feet with the controlled savagery of his grip. The muted light behind him showed enough of his face to show her he was in a blistering rage. She smelled a trace of whisky on his breath, and his eyes shone down on her with a glitter almost feral in the moonlight.

"Where in damnation have you been? What did you think you were doing, walking out on me that way?"

She realized she was shaking, from anger, shock, fear and the maddening, overpowering desire his touch could always ignite—even the ruthless touch of callused fingers gripping her slender arms.

"Take your hands off me," she ordered, but her voice was less than convincing. She wanted to slide one short step forward, raise her arms, encircle his neck. She pulled back, remembering Lindsay, the jewels, all the things Rand hadn't told her. Then, defeatingly, came the knowledge that now she, too, was unable to be honest.

"I didn't think you'd notice I was gone," she said pettishly. "Or have your forgotten all about Lindsay?"

"I wish to God I *could* forget," he gritted. "But I can't."

His admission confirmed what she suspected. Obviously this bond between them could never be broken. Rand would always respond when Lindsay called him. Any woman foolish enough to love Rand would suffer the same as Alana had, because if he ever had to choose between them, he would choose Lindsay.

Rand seemed to emanate danger, poised like some wild animal over her, intent on attack.

"Are you going to start explaining?" He yanked her forcefully against him, holding her there effortlessly.

With a last shred of defiance she twisted to glare up at him. "I don't owe you any explanations. You told me once your life had complications you couldn't explain. Well, maybe my life does, too."

She felt him flinch. Then he brought his hard mouth down on hers with punishing force, crushing her arms between their bodies. His sinewy strength held her captive, arms wrapped across her back pressing her harder and still harder to his heated length. She forced her mouth away, turning her head frantically from side to side. Relentlessly, he pursued her, brushing her face with his soft, tickling mustache, flicking a tongue in her ear, nibbling gently, tracing her cheek with his lips.

Despite everything, she met his lips with her own. Her arms rose as much as his embrace allowed, tracing the heated flesh under his open shirt, feeling the pulse of blood pounding through him, wandering till her fingers locked in his hair, twisting into its soft, curling mass. Her pulse took its rhythm from the full, rapid pace of his, and she felt the strength of his desire hotly through her thin cotton dress. His hands slid down, caressing and pressing her closer.

"Alana, my Alana," he groaned, "God, how I want you. When you walked away with that—that cowboy, I felt like killing both of you." He punctuated his words with hot, quick kisses down her neck. "You belong to me, Alana."

The words broke the web of arousal he'd spun around her. Want and have, but never love. Belong, but never marry. In a frenzy, she tore away, using both hands to shove as hard as she could at his chest. Staggering back several steps, she held up a cautionary hand as he moved toward her, his expression puzzled. This time, it was the absolute cold certainty in her voice that stopped him.

"That's not enough, Rand." To her surprise, the words she needed were there and she spoke them without hesitation. "I want you, too." The wild pounding of her heart, the aching need he roused in her were unnecessary reminders of how much. "But I want more. At first, I thought what you had to offer would be enough, but it's not. I want a wedding, and babies and a man who loves me completely, belongs to me body and soul...as my husband. Who doesn't put another woman's needs ahead of mine." The words poured from her, and Alana realized their truth. Her future seemed an aching, empty void before her, and Rand's face twisted with pain, his hand reaching toward her, then falling back to his side. What she was voicing was what she'd always known in her soul. There simply couldn't be another way for her.

Sadly, she admitted, too, that neither could there be another way for Rand. Like his father before him, Rand was trapped. Not by money, but by his own nature. He was as tied to Lindsay as his father had been to Martha. Unlike Jenny, Alana couldn't settle for being the other woman in his life. She was an all or nothing person, and with a dreadful sense that a giant fist was crushing her heart, she admitted it would have to be nothing.

Rand made no effort to stop her as she slowly moved past him and up the stairs. Before she reached her room, she heard his truck start and drive off. There was no plainer way to tell her that he could not accept her terms.

Weeping, she strode up and down the comfortable room, arms wrapped around herself to contain the agony.

Sometime in the hours that followed, she roughed out letters of application for substitute teaching jobs in Vancouver. With the generous salary Rand had paid her, and bonuses he'd insisted on adding when Bruce began to make such astonishing progress, she could afford to work part-time for a while.

Thoughts of Bruce brought fresh storms of weeping, staining the careful words she'd penned. Against her every firm resolution, against all the rules she set for herself with pupils, she'd managed to grow to love not only her employer, but his son as well. Bruce was more than ready to begin preschool in Elkford. Katy would do an excellent job of helping him integrate. The only stumbling block would be Rand. Impulsively, she drew a clean sheet of notepaper from the box, and scribbled a note to him, an objective, yet deeply personal account of how difficult it had been for her deaf parents to send Johnny and herself off every summer to stay with their grandparents. The trips had begun when she and Johnny were babies, because Alan Campbell and his wife understood their children had to learn to speak. So they sent them away, loving them enough to let them go, knowing they must learn to survive in a hearing world.

Alana tried to make Rand understand that the same was true of Bruce; he had to learn to function in a hearing world. Rand had to set him free. She sealed the letter without rereading it, afraid she'd lose the courage to remain impersonal and would scrawl across the bottom, I Love You. Instead, she managed a cool, Sincerely, Alana.

The trouble was, in a way Bruce had become her child. When the summer began, he'd seemed a small wild thing to be tamed with love and language. The countless hours she'd spent with Bruce stretched in her mind like an idyll, hours in the tree house, at the lake, monitoring the growth of the kittens, laughing at Tad's facade of bravery, sharing the excitement of finding a way to communicate. Sign language. The language of love. What a tragedy, Alana mourned wearily, that Rand had never really learned it.

Finally she fell asleep from exhaustion, but it seemed only moments before her bedroom door burst open, and a pajama-clad bundle of energy and excitement landed full force on her bed. Alana delayed the inevitable and feigned sleep, but Bruce stroked her face until she opened eyes heavy from tears and still drugged with sleep. He grinned at her, as only a four-year-old can grin at six in the morning.

"Time to get up," he related, agile fingers flying. "Today we go car, see miners, eat ice cream, watch father. Big fun!"

The flow of clearly signed words and the absolute delight on his cherub's face with its aureole of shining hair, his cleft chin so like Rand's, nearly brought a fresh storm of tears. Controlling them with an effort, she gave him a hug and sent him off to wash and dress, playfully timing him with his beloved alarm clock. Feeling weary, drained and full of pain, she dragged herself up to meet the day, knowing it would be one of the last she would spend at Bluejay.

Rand and Martha were leaving early. Rand was involved in the mine rescue competitions, and Martha was judging the food bazaar. Mindful of Johnny's instructions, Alana would wait until later in the morning to leave with Bruce. She explained to Martha she was coming with Johnny. Rand overheard, gave her one smoldering glance and ordered, "Bring the Fiat. I may have to stay late, and I want you to have your own vehicle." He looked tired and withdrawn as he hurried out to the truck.

The only problem, Alana realized several hours later, was that Rand must have the car keys in his pocket. Bruce was dancing up and down in an agony of impatience, waiting for her, and Johnny tapped his fingers restlessly on the car metal as she dumped the contents of her purse on the grass in a desperate search.

"Isn't there a spare set?" Johnny finally suggested, and Alana hurried to the cupboard door in the kitchen where Jenny kept a neat set of hooks with labelled keys. But the hook labelled "Fiat" was empty.

On impulse, she pointed at the empty hook, raising her hands helplessly to Bruce.

Understanding leaped into the long-lashed eyes, and he grabbed her hand, heading at full gallop for the tree house.

The keys were there, under a fresh box of biscuits Martha had searched for just yesterday. The little diary lay forgotten, and Alana touched it tenderly. One of Bruce's alarm clocks had joined the other treasures and the brown teddy bear in the Mountie uniform.

Alana shook her head at Bruce. "You're a packrat, rascal," she muttered. She replaced his collection and hurried back to Johnny.

With his sports car trailing close behind, Alana and Bruce soon arrived in Elkford. The town had assumed a Mardi Gras atmosphere, and the usually quiet streets were bubbling with activity. Alana parked, and with Johnny's assurance he would be nearby, she and Bruce found a spot to watch the parade.

Alana was unable to respond to what should have been an exhilarating occasion. Unless she kept a firm rein on her thoughts, replays of all last night's events ran through her mind, and the agony of her hopeless love for Rand would overcome her.

With a crash of drums and a blare of trumpets, the parade began. She settled Bruce firmly against her legs, holding his shoulders to prevent him from dashing into the street to gape at the approaching spectacle. His body quivered with excitement.

As the elaborate pageant slowly passed, he tugged at her hand, ordering with urgent fingers that she "Look, see," banging on her denim-covered knee until she responded correctly. She'd pulled on a practical one-piece jump suit, and it just might withstand what looked to be a long, long day.

When the parade ended, Bruce raced to the nearest hot dog stand. He wanted chips and a jumbo with everything on it, and she bought coffee for herself. As she sat sipping it, Katy and Lissa joined them.

"It's just a matter of time till those two get violently ill," Katy remarked philosophically, watching Lissa devour the same items as Bruce. She studied Alana. "You look as wiped out as I feel. That was an interesting evening. If you left with Johnny just to make Rand jealous, you sure succeeded. He looked black enough for murder after you'd gone."

"He had Lindsay there to entertain him." Alana said waspishly, and Katy shook her head.

"She didn't stay long. She and Rand had what looked to be a heated argument, and she left."

Alana yearned to pour out the whole complicated mess to Katy. If ever she'd needed a friend to confide in, the time was now, but she dared not breathe a word. She couldn't even tell Katy she was leaving Bluejay. Well, she vowed, she would make this final time together as happy and carefree as possible, a day to remember. She linked her arm through her friend's.

"Let's see how long it takes these two dynamos to wear us down," she suggested, and Katy gave her arm an affectionate squeeze. Shyly, she confided, "David's asked me to marry him. He's offered to loan me the money to go to school full-time, with me as collateral, of course." Her face was a dusky rose.

"Sounds wonderful to me," Alana managed, wishing with all her soul that it could be this way for her and Rand. She was happy for Katy, though. It was comforting to know that someone she cared for might just live happily ever after.

The women allowed themselves to be dragged to the midway set up in a vacant lot. Bruce and Melissa ecstatically sampled every single ride, and after their third circuit, Katy said firmly, "Enough. I've got motion sickness from watching the merry-go-round. Let's go see how Mrs. Evans is making out judging the home fair." She caught Alana's eye and they both giggled at the thought of Martha, barely able to boil water, judging the food exhibits.

"Then I think we should take these two rascals to the trailer for short naps. Before I collapse," Katy added.

Children in hand, they made their slow way to the huge tent set up to shelter displays of food, gardening and local artwork.

Flushed and excited, Martha was in her element. "One needn't be an expert at something in order to simply judge it," she insisted, taking nibbles of multi-colored cakes and pies. She slipped several huge cookies to Melissa and Bruce.

"How's Randall's team doing in the mine rescue competitions?" she demanded.

"We'll go and check for you," Katy promised, but the children had found a fish pond where for a nickel they could snag a parcel full of surprises. Racing after them, Katy called, "You go see the Mine Rescue, and I'll keep these two supplied with money. They won't appreciate Mine Rescue anyhow."

Reluctantly, Alana started toward the exit, wishing she didn't have to see Rand today. The pain she felt each time she thought of last night could only intensify around Rand.

Wandering past the flowers and the crafts, she slowed where a small corner had been set aside for the display of local photography and watercolors.

She casually scanned the wildlife photos and breathtaking scenes of mountains and lakes. Her eyes were drawn toward a framed black and white photo, austerely simple among the lavish color and ornate gilt of the other pictures.

Unconsciously, she gasped and moved closer until she stood directly before it.

In the photo, sunlight dappled down through huge pines, scattering light and shade over a newly constructed wooden footbridge, stretched across a small brook in the forest. The camera had caught two people, sitting on the roughly hewed planks, dipping bare toes in the water. Engrossed in each other, their expressions were lovingly intent, the child's wide eyes riveted to the woman's smiling instruction. She looked young and rather hoydenish, her face dramatically expressive and lit with sunlight. She was turned slightly away from the camera, toward her small companion. Her long legs were bare, slender in cut-off jeans. She was making a graphic sign with her hands for the boy whose hearing aids rested so obviously behind each ear. His arms were lifted in a replica of hers, one arm bent across in front of him, the other at right angles to it, forming a suspended V with his fingers on the underside of his bent arm. The simple black lettering under the frame titled it Bridges, but anyone familiar with sign language would already have read the word from the graphic hand positions so clearly portrayed. It was a picture of Alana and Bruce. Instantly, she remembered the afternoon it had been taken, the impromptu little picnic, the camera clicking as Rand took photo after photo.

She stood as though paralyzed, unaware of the people passing or of their curious glances. The simple picture eloquently embodied all the summer had meant. The meticulous building of a bridge of language for Bruce, and the love that grew like a bridge between her and Rand and their differences, spanning the loneliness and discontent in her soul at summer's start to the feeling of completeness she now had.

The utter peace of the tranquil scene was Bluejay's mystical charm, the spell of enchantment the Elk Valley had cast on those who lived in and loved its isolation, its unspoiled beauty and the protection its high mountain walls promised from the outer world.

The photo shimmered as tears filled her eyes. What did it mean to have Rand exhibit proudly this very personal picture, hung here for the people he knew to see? His son's hearing aids were very evident. Perhaps, she mused, Rand had now fully accepted Bruce's deafness. Perhaps he was ready now to set Bruce free, allowing him to be anything and everything his potential allowed. The longer she studied the photo, the clearer its message became. It spoke of understanding, acceptance...and love. Surely the message was there for herself as well as for Bruce. And she suddenly wanted to let Rand know she understood...that in so many ways, the summer had been a perfect bridge for all of them. She hurried now, through the thickening crowd to where the serious mine rescue competitions were in progress.

As she neared the large, roped-off area, the tone of the spectators changed. The crowd here was quiet, intensely observing the teams and applauding in a restrained way at their success. This was no game. In a mining community, lives depended on the efficiency and expertise of the mine rescue teams. Rand had explained that all the teams were isolated "in lock up," he'd called it, before they competed, allowed to see only the officials until their turn came at solving the complex and elaborate problems the judges had devised.

Alana was impressed at the well-constructed stage set of mocked-up mine shafts, overturned vehicles and contrived chaos created to symbolize the reality of mine disaster. Horns and whistles sounded, and men in gas masks and coveralls scrambled around bodies whose faces were smeared with coal dust and fake blood. The authenticity of the actors and the scene made Alana shudder, and the atmosphere was one of intense drama.

This was only an exercise, but every person watching knew how easily it could become reality.

Inching through the crowd, Alana shivered again, this time from the suddenly cool breeze. The lowering clouds overhead had thickened ominously. It was about to rain on Coal Miner Days. Where in this crowd could Rand be?

Then she caught a glimpse of his tall frame, towering above the people around him. He was moving slowly away from where Alana was, head bent politely to hear whatever was being said by the person he was with, still hidden from Alana by the crowd. Just then, the exercise in the rescue area came to a finish. The crowd applauded, but Rand paid no attention, his arm grasping the silk-clad sleeve of the woman he was with.

The crowd had suddenly parted, but Alana stopped short where she was, heart pounding and stomach sick. Lindsay stood close beside Rand, wearing skin tight designer jeans and a lavender-blue silk shirt. They sauntered along together, Lindsay leaning slightly on the tall figure at her side, a couple obviously looking for a place away from the crowd where they could be alone.

Alana turned and ran, as fast as the crowd allowed. How many times, she wondered bitterly, did she have to be shown? How could she have mistaken a simple picture of an appeal from Rand, a desire for a bridge between them? It had been an accident, a coincidental matching of subject and title. Frantically, she elbowed people aside to allow her to pass, to leave behind the bridges Rand had burned.

"Hold on, Red. Slow down." Johnny's arm snaked out, pulling her to a sudden halt. "You're tough to follow, running that way." His grin was relaxed and amiable, but his eyes flitted warily across the crowd. "Where's Bruce?" he asked anxiously.

She pointed to the food tent. "Over there, with Katy. Johnny, I have to—" but he was already moving rapidly away.

"Johnny," she cried desperately. He halted briefly, saying, "Can't wait—where'll you be for the next hour?"

She related the plan for naps at Katy's trailer, and told him the location.

"Stay right there," he ordered emphatically. "Wait for me or Evans to come for you. He's okay, by the way. I'll explain later." He was gone, moving rapidly through the crowd.

What was that supposed to mean? Alana stared after him angrily. She'd been about to tell Johnny that Rand was with Lindsay, and anything but okay. Damn men! She stomped over to Katy and the exhausted children.

But once inside Katy's cozy home, Alana knew there was little chance of Bruce settling for a nap. He was nervously charged with energy, cranky and uncontrollable. He whined, disturbing Lissa, already settling for sleep. He made the sign for "home" and "car" over and over.

Alana's own emotions and nerves were in chaos, and she understood Bruce's pathetic need for the quiet and familiarity of Bluejay. Finally, she gave in. Grateful that Katy understood the eccentricities of four-year-olds, she retrieved the car. Squinting up at the lowering gray sky, she took Bruce on her hip and dashed through the light rain.

"I'll tell Rand where you are," Katy promised, and Alana felt guilty as she remembered Johnny's orders. *"Stay there. Wait for me or Evans."*

Well, she wasn't going to wait for Rand, ever again, and Johnny would simply have to understand there were times one couldn't argue with a hysterical little boy who wanted his own bed. She drove off through the quickening downpour, eager to get home.

By the time she arrived at Bluejay's driveway, the storm had begun in earnest. The summer afternoon had darkened almost to dusk, the rain was sheeting down in gray frenzy. There had been several rumbles of thunder, and lightning played across the sky above the mountains. With each mile, Alana had welcomed the pull of Bluejay, the promise of a quiet haven where she could let her numbed being relax in the hours before the others returned. She needed time to gather her pride around her and steel herself for the final meeting with Rand, when she would tell him she was leaving.

She turned off the engine gratefully. Bruce sat beside her in a half stupor, his eyelids threatening to close any instant.

"Guess we're just not good party people, tiger," she whispered to him, grabbing his hand and scampering through the downpour to the front door.

Tad was barking frantically from the shed as Alana scrabbled in her purse for the house key. But Bruce had already thrown the front door wide. Strange, Alana mused, ducking in out of the rain. She thought she'd locked it. But the confusion with car keys—she slammed the door behind her, and banged sharply into Bruce, nearly knocking him over. He was staring wide-eyed at the man in the middle of the living room.

Dark-haired, he was slightly shorter than Alana, with the powerful build of an ex-wrestler gone to fat. He had on gray trousers and a navy rain slicker, still dripping on the rug. Reaching out, he clicked on the overhead light, and Alana noticed a large ring on his finger.

Instinctively, Alana reached down and wrapped both arms around Bruce's shoulders, pulling him tight against her trembling legs.

His voice came quiet, so she almost had to strain to hear. "Only the two of you?" Alana felt her head nod up and down, and she swallowed convulsively, wondering what there was about him that could terrify her so totally.

"Who—what are you..." she croaked, but the question was answered before she could finish.

The sound of hurrying footsteps came from the stairway, the tap-tap of a woman's heels. A low throaty voice floated down. Unlike her companion, Lindsay Evans-Ross sounded tense and upset. "I watched from the window, George. There's only her and the kid." Lindsay appeared from the stairs, and her gaze flicked dispassionately over Alana and Bruce. Even through her fear, Alana registered the utter indifference Lindsay showed for Bruce. For heaven's sake, this was her son! Alana suddenly felt hugely grateful that Bruce didn't understand that the woman before him was his natural mother. He pressed closer to Alana, shy with these strangers and sensing Alana's nervousness.

Lindsay's silk blouse was rumpled, and there was a stain on the front of her jeans. But it was her face that drew Alana's gaze. She looked old...and hard. Tight lines connected her nose and the corners of her mouth.

"Find it?" His voice was still soft, but the glance he shot Lindsay wasn't. She shook her head 'no,' and looked almost frightened.

Alana didn't move. There was a catlike quality about

George—what had Johnny called him? Krane, that was it, George Krane. Dangerous, Alana's senses warned.

"Ask the kid where the hell he put it, then. Go on, ask him," he ordered Lindsay.

Lindsay didn't even bother to glance at Bruce.

"He doesn't talk. He's deaf and dumb," Lindsay said offhandedly.

As if her senses had suffered a blow with a hammer, everything in Alana crashed to a halt, quivered with shock, and jerked into life again. But now the fear that had immobilized her was gone, swept away by simple rage.

That good old epithet, the same one which had transformed her into a punching, kicking harridan in school, had made her fling an expensive diamond into the ocean, affected her the same way now, but the years had taught her subtlety. She lowered her eyes, afraid the bright fury she felt would be reflected there. The paralysis of the last moments was gone. Her mind worked at top speed.

They were searching for the missing gems. The cache was here at Bluejay, after all. The rest of the complicated matter was unimportant now to Alana. The only thing that mattered was the small shy boy clutching her hand. She had to make certain there was no danger for Bruce. Her heart hammered. She had to get Bruce out of here. Then she would try to help them find whatever they were searching for, and maybe they'd go. She thought no further.

Bruce glanced up several times, searching Alana's face for reassurance. Alana tapped his chest gently with a forefinger, praying she could attract his attention to her hands. Deliberately, she met George's cold eyes, keeping his attention centered on her voice and words as she made herself say quaveringly, "I'll—I'll help you find whatever it is you need. Just...please...don't hurt us."

To Bruce, she spelled "dog" over and over, praying he'd understand and respond.

He did, almost instantly. "I go Tad?" he queried with quick signs.

Shooting a pleading, embarrassed glance at the two now staring at Bruce's motions, she gave a tiny laugh.

"He has to visit the bathroom. Could I—"

Just as she'd hoped, Krane shook his head. "Tell him to go by himself," he ordered. "You stay here and tell us where that bloody toy is."

Toy? But there wasn't time to dwell on what he meant, because she was already signing to Bruce, "Get Tad. Run and hide. Play game. Hide."

Alana knew that with the beloved dog with him, Bruce would have less fear of the storm raging outside. Was there any chance the others might come home? How long could she distract these two? What would happen when—but she forced her mind to deal with each instant separately, and she turned as Bruce tore out of the room, trying to shield him from the menace of the man and woman standing there.

Quickly, Bruce had the door open, and had disappeared outside before they realized where he was headed. Krane made a quick movement toward the door, but Alana stepped in front of him, chattering fast and nervously, "He—he nearly always goes outside, he'll be back in a minute, you know how kids are. Let me help find the—"

Lindsay interrupted. "For God's sake, George, forget the kid. Let's find the stuff and get out of here. I hate this place, it makes me nervous."

"This mess is your fault, Lindsay. Hiding jewels in the back of a teddy bear, then being dumb enough to mail it here."

"They were after me! I told you, I was scared. You always said it was safe, that I'd never get caught. It was the only plan I could think of, there at the airport. And it worked, didn't it?" Her cool sophistication was slipping, tension evident in her nervous movements. "Rand didn't know, he'd never suspect I'd hide anything at his precious ranch."

Rand hadn't known. Everything else faded as that fact spread through Alana's consciousness, and a huge weight dropped from her heart.

Then the door behind Alana crashed open, and a wet bundle of growling fur shot past her, straight at Lindsay and Krane. Bruce followed Tad. The dog was making his low, ominous growl, doing his mad dog act. Lindsay's scream ripped through the air. Alana snatched Bruce into her arms, and raced out the open door. She had no plan beyond getting her and Bruce far away from the house and Krane.

She was already among the evergreens when the shot came. It was a muted, soft implosion of noise, not at all the bang Alana had always believed a gun made. But neither was there any mistaking it. Had they killed Tad? Convulsively, her arms tightened around Bruce, and a whimper of fear escaped her lips.

Thunder rumbled as if echoing the gunshot, and a flash of white lightning illuminated a small silver float plane moored at Bluejay's dock. That explained the puzzling fact that there had been no car in the driveway. Krane had flown here.

Alana blessed the strong runner's legs that carried her

and Bruce along the wooded path. She'd veered onto the almost hidden trail to the tree house. Wet branches whipped Alana's face, and she turned Bruce to her shoulder for protection. Once, she stumbled on a tree root, staggering ahead with giant crazy strides until she caught her balance. And a tiny, inner voice screamed out silently with every gasping breath, "Rand, please come home, we need you, Rand." Bruce's arms were tight around her neck.

The huge old tree was before her, and with arms that shook almost uncontrollably, she boosted Bruce and scrambled up the ladder, dragging it after her. Bruce was frightened and about to burst into tears. She attempted an expression of mischievous fun, placing her finger on her lips in the old sign for silence. He studied her warily, not quite believing this was a game, but at least not bursting into loud wails. She heard Krane's voice yell something, but it was lost in the thunder.

She must keep Bruce calm and quiet, focus his attention on something beside her own barely controlled panic. The trunk wasn't locked—they'd been in too much of a rush that morning. She lifted the lid and found the bag of cookies, handing them to Bruce. Petulantly, he waved them away, still too full of the junk food he'd gobbled all day. Replacing the bag, searching for something, anything to amuse him, her fingers touched the teddy bear.

Like a flash of the lightning illuminating the trees around her, Alana suddenly understood. The teddy bear Krane had mentioned. It hadn't come from Grace after all. Lindsay had sent it in some desperate moment. And somewhere, in some airport bathroom doubtless, she'd sewn the gems inside—and mailed it to her son!

Alana lifted it gingerly, as if it might explode in her grasp. Her shaking fingers stripped off the tiny red coat, tracing the seam down the toy's back. Lindsay had done a surprisingly good job. The stitches were tight and even.

Bruce was exploring the trunk and Alana felt relieved, hoping he'd stay quiet, just until—until what? Closing her eyes, listening hard for Krane, Alana prayed. Please, God, let Rand come home.

The wind was increasing and it rocked the platform gently. The rain drummed on the tin roof, and the crude walls protected them from the wet. But the whispering of trees and rain also masked the sounds Alana strained to hear. Where were her pursuers? They'd never leave without the thing they'd come for. But they'd never find it, because ironically it was here in her hand. How long could she stay hidden? How long till someone came home?

She imagined she heard a car. Could they be taking the car, leaving? Every nerve stretched taut, she listened and listened. If only she could hear them... but there was only the wind. She shut her eyes tight, concentrating.

A branch snapping close by made her stiffen. Her eyes opened wide with fear. She made a stealthy move toward Bruce, crouched on his knees on the old rug in front of the trunk. Before she could reach him, she saw with horror that he held the alarm clock they'd used so often. His small fingers were pulling at the alarm button. His mischievous grin told her he'd seen her closed eyes and was about to awaken her. She lunged, but the clamoring jangle rose above the storm, strident in its summons. Alana's scream broke free as Krane's head and shoulders appeared over the platform's edge.

His hair was flattened grotesquely by the rain, his features twisted with rage. He was panting, and his hand held a snub-nosed gun pointed straight at her head.

Like a naughty child trying to placate an adult, she stretched the stuffed toy out toward him, placing herself between Krane and Bruce. Again, she imagined she heard car doors slamming, men's voices.

"Hand that to Lindsay," the deadly soft tones instructed. Forcing herself nearer the opening where Krane was, Alana reached down. Lindsay snatched the bear from her hand. Krane lowered himself, giving Lindsay a small pocketknife with which she ripped the toy open, and triumphantly drew out a bulky plastic-wrapped bundle. Krane snatched it, shoving it into the pocket of his navy raincoat.

"Now get back to the plane," he barked at Lindsay. She hesitated a brief second, staring up at Alana and Bruce.

"Don't—" she began to say to Krane, but he snarled at her, and she turned and hurried off, her heels catching on the rough earth.

Alana's heart seemed about to burst from her chest with terror. Why didn't he leave? What more did he want?

"Get down here," he ordered.

Forcefully, Alana signed, "Lie down. Stay here," at Bruce. Then she started down the rope ladder.

She was never sure exactly what happened next. There was a crashing from the woods; Rand hurled himself at Krane as Alana screamed, "The gun, he's got a—"

She didn't hear the shot, but a burning began to flower in her right shoulder. As though a giant fist had punched her, she reeled, fell heavily to the ground. Everything slowly spun.

Rand's voice roared fury, frustration. Krane's footsteps thundered in her head as he charged heavily through the underbrush, racing for the lake. Then, peace descended. Rand's arms cradled her tightly to his chest, tenderly lifted her from the dank smelling dirt.

"My darling, my darling, he's hurt you—"

Mixing with the delight of Rand's voice she heard the sputtering of an airplane engine on the lake. It caught, faded, caught again. Men's voices shouted frantically back and forth over the roar, and the thunder and the rain. Then came a noise drowning out other sound as the pilot skimmed the lake for takeoff. It reached a crescendo, faltered, rose again...

Or was the roaring only in her head? Alana felt boneless, totally at peace. Nothing mattered, Bruce was safe—she could hear him making his sleepy humming sound up in the tree house above her. Rand had heard her silent message, he'd come when she needed him. She'd known he would. Alana floated, cradled tight to the warm body of the man she loved.

Irritatingly, a tongue of pain licked at her shoulder. She moved restlessly close to Rand's chest, and it crashed over her in a rush of white-hot agony. The world became a swirling haze. Rand's voice shouted desperately over and over, and Johnny seemed to answer. Then, there were harsh, angry words and she was jostled, making her cry out, making her lonely because Johnny held her now instead of Rand. But everything was going far away, and the lovely dark tunnel beckoned, drawing her into silence without pain, and darkness without time.

CHAPTER THIRTEEN

SHE WAS FAR FROM BLUEJAY when she woke. Rand was gone, and Johnny was taking her to Vancouver. The drugs she'd been given numbed her brain, and she wondered muzzily why they didn't also numb her heart. Semiconscious, she knew Johnny was right in his decision to transfer her to Vancouver. Her reasons for leaving hadn't changed, and wouldn't.

Johnny talked to her a lot, each time she awoke during the mechanics of being moved from one vehicle to the other, and finally onto the plane.

"The Cessna crashed," he told her once. "Both of them were killed, on some high mountain range beyond the Valley. Krane didn't let the engine warm up long enough, and as he was lifting off the lake he grazed his propeller and floats on the tips of some evergreens. The plane exploded."

So Lindsay was dead. Alana could only feel repugnance. In Alana's opinion, some people were evil, and Lindsay was one of them. Krane was definitely another. Shuddering, she asked, "What did he want with me, Johnny? Why didn't he leave the tree house when Lindsay did?"

Johnny tugged the gray blanket closer under her chin. His bearded face was grim. "I think he was going to get you out of the way and take Bruce with them as hostage, to guarantee their escape. Don't think about it now, Red. It's over."

She nodded. It was over. She slept.

For most of the following week, she was only groggily aware. Tubes in her arms hurt, and Johnny told her over and over to lie still, that she was in hospital, that she'd lost a lot of blood, and please, would she just lie still?

Finally, she woke and knew the grogginess was gone. Autumn sun spilled in dusty windows, visitors talked in the corridors, cleaning women rattled past. This was a big city hospital, and Johnny lounged on the straight-backed chair beside her bed.

He'd shaved his beard. Half his face was tanned, the other, where the beard had been, was white. He still had the drooping mustache, however. He gave her an appraising look, and grinned when she struggled to sit up, demanding he find her a mirror and hairbrush.

"That's the ticket, Red," he encouraged. "Now, just start an argument and I'll know for sure you're better."

A thin-faced stranger with spikes of hair shooting in every direction stared back at Alana from the mirror. She gave up. Johnny asked gently, "Feel up to talking, sis? There's a lot of answers I need for my report."

She nodded. Best to get it over with, the post mortem of that last, horrible day at Bluejay. Maybe, by remembering now for Johnny she could then begin to forget. She smiled sadly. Someday. The pain in her chest had nothing to do with her shoulder.

Briefly, she related exactly what had happened after she'd seen Johnny in the crowd at Coal Miner Days. Like a movie strip, the events rewound before her mind's eye. Once, she cried out, "He shot Tad. My God, he shot Tad, I forgot—"

"The dog was fine," Johnny assured her, pushing her back on the pillow. "He'd gotten creased with a bullet, all right, but all that hair saved him. It just knocked him cold." The strain of the last days showed as he added, "Both of you were lucky, Lana. Another few inches, and you—" He stopped abruptly. "Go on," he encouraged.

She relived the flight through the woods, the awful moment Bruce had set off the alarm.

"Lucky he did," Johnny said. "Rand knew immediately where you were. We were wrong in our suspicions about him, of course. After I left you at Bluejay that night, he went to the RCMP office in Elkford. Told them Lindsay had tried to blackmail him, and when that didn't work, she made threats about Bruce. Rand had suspected she was still mixed up in the smuggling, even after the charges had been dropped that time. Anyway, Lindsay was worried she and Krane might not find the toy, and they needed money to get away. I think she believed Rand still loved her, would never turn her in." Johnny moved restlessly on the hard chair, then got up to prowl the room, ending by the window.

"Krane was hiding out, just as we suspected, in a fishing cabin not far from Bluejay. He was watching the ranch closely, waiting for a time to hunt for that ridiculous bear with its load of gems."

"That's who hit Tom," Alana shuddered. It was Krane she'd seen in the woods, the day she'd jogged and climbed the fence.

Now Johnny scowled at her in exasperation. "If only you'd do as you're told once in a while, Lana. I told you to stay put at your friend's trailer, and you drove back to Bluejay. Rand was trying his best to get Lindsay to confide in him. She'd made another bid for money—he figured she was scared of Krane, maybe ready to back out. But she disappeared, and he went to check on you. He alerted the police office right away when he found you gone, and they radioed me. Rand got to Bluejay first, heard that crazy alarm. I saw Lindsay dashing for the plane, Krane after her. I couldn't catch them, and then Rand came running with you in his arms, bleeding all over the place. Things got a little heavy. I went a bit crazy, I guess, accused Rand of all sorts of things." Johnny rubbed his chin ruefully.

"You're not the only Campbell with a temper, Red. Truth was, I was furious with myself for not keeping a closer eye on you. God, I should know you're not to be trusted." He dodged a tissue box she flung. She was trying to keep him from guessing how desolate his words were making her.

"Another thing, Lana. I'm afraid I didn't get around to telling him you were my sister. I figured I'd let you straighten it out later. Rand phones the hospital about forty times a day, anyway, so now you're mobile you can talk to him. The nurses are impressed with his persistence." Johnny eyed his sister, concern and compassion on his face. "Hope I didn't wreck anything important for you sis. You muttered a lot when you were out of it."

Alana shook her head emphatically. It was best, this abrupt physical separation with Rand. Hadn't Rand told her all she could expect was one day at a time? The days had simply come to an end.

Johnny was scribbling notes in his small black book. He closed it now. "When Tom Saunders gets back from his honeymoon, I'd like to talk with him. Until then, this gives me what I need."

"Tom? Honeymoon?" Surely she'd misunderstood. "Tom Saunders?"

"Yeah, I called the hospital he'd been in. They said he'd been fitted for a new leg, discharged and married, all in one week. Then, I talked with Grace." Johnny looked defensive as Alana's eyebrows shot up. "Well, I knew she'd want to know how you were. She told me Tom and a lady called Jenny Chan were married and took off for Hawaii." He added, "Grace is one foxy lady. I promised her lunch as soon as you were on the mend."

For some people, at least, there had been a happy ending.

Grace burst in within the hour, clutching a huge bouquet Alana suspected had been filched from various gardens along the way. Scanning Alana's bandages and pale features, Grace enveloped her in a careful bear hug.

Then, she regaled Alana with the tale of Jenny's wedding which seemed to have involved most of Vancouver's Chinatown, because Grace had persuaded Jenny to contact some of her relatives at last.

"We went to City Hall," Grace concluded. "Tom walked up all those steps, that leg they fitted him with is a wonder, it's called a Seattle foot, less painful or irritating than other limbs have been. Jenny wore an electric-blue pantsuit, and they got married." Grace gave a deep, contented sigh, wriggling her silk-chemise-clad body with the delight of a true romantic. Johnny looked quite smitten as he led her out for lunch.

As their voices faded, so did Alana's brief respite from the aching loneliness, the hopelessness she felt. Her shoulder hurt, and when a nurse gave her a pain shot, she fell into a restless sleep.

An aide woke her, plugging in a telephone and saying

archly, "This man simply won't believe we're taking good care of you, so I told him to ask you himself." Rand. Alana struggled into wakefulness, her heart hammering, and accepted the receiver.

"Alana?" The voice was husky, tentative. "They say you're getting better." He cleared his throat nervously.

Her voice was weaker than she wanted it to be. "Hello, Rand. Yes, I'm feeling much stronger." She cursed the social trap they'd tumbled into, these polite noises without real meaning.

He must have sensed her discomfort, because he blurted next, "You do know the plane crashed, and—" his voice caught, and he tried again "—Lindsay's dead?" The query hung between them.

Sadness that he should be so hurt overcame her. "Yes, I know. I—I'm sorry, Rand." What else was there to say? The ghost of the lovely blond woman fluttered between them, the woman who'd been his wife. Lindsay Evans-Ross.

Rand's voice was troubled. "The only thing I feel is the most incredible relief. Her death has set me free, Alana. I feel as though I've been trapped in a mine tunnel, shut off from pure air and sunshine. But with it comes the most agonizing guilt. How can you be relieved that someone is dead?" As though embarrassed at revealing himself, he hurried on, "I didn't mean to trouble you with that, Alana. I really phoned to tell you—" Blood pounded in her ears so she could hardly hear, and the long-distance line faded and recovered. "I called to thank you for my son. You saved his life, protected him." This, then, was why he'd phoned. To thank her. A polite gesture to a teacher. Tears of weakness and disappointment spilled out of her eyes.

"I love Bruce," she managed to whisper. "I'd never let anything hurt him." The tears came faster. "I'm very tired now, Rand. Thank you for calling. Good night." She heard him saying something as she hung up, but it was cut off.

"No more calls, please," she ordered the nurse. Feeling empty of everything but tears, she let them slip down her cheeks and off her chin, wetting the bandage, the sheet, her gown, on and on and on.

After that, she made up her mind to get well, to find a job—Grace mentioned a temporary teaching job at the school where she was secretary and Alana applied for it. She would put the memories all behind her.

Weeks later, she stood uncertainly in front of eight restless deaf students, her usually nimble fingers clumsy as she tried to explain a word that confused them, from their reading lesson.

Outside the window, Vancouver rain fell in an endless gray drizzle. One of the overhead neon tubes was flickering bright, dim, bright. Alana frowned up at it, irritated. She barely avoided a show of bad temper when her problem student, a ten-year-old boy called Shawn, asked for the twentieth time when his regular teacher, Miss Hardy, would be back. Alana knew it was natural for the class to miss the petite young woman with the wide smile and twinkling eyes whom Alana was replacing. Children were naturally attached to their teachers, and Alana sensed that Miss Hardy brought a lighthearted joy to this classroom which Miss Campbell, despite her pathetic attempts at cheeriness, just couldn't match.

Handing out printed worksheets, Alana sank down behind her desk, gazing blankly out at the downpour.

She had to get hold of herself. The anger she felt at the malfunctioning light, her impatience with Shawn, her disgust at the weather; they signaled emotional upset. Physically, she'd recovered quickly—oh, she was still weak at times, and certainly she was much thinner than she'd ever been. The rust-colored velour dress she was wearing revealed the bones in her hips, the concave flatness of her stomach.

It wasn't losing weight that bothered her. She'd lost something inside, some vital life-force that had always purred along inside like a trusty, quiet motor, but that now had ground to a halt, and wouldn't start again.

She'd tried. She'd gone to a play last weekend, donned her jogging gear for a run around the park. But she'd walked out of the play during the first act, quit her run before she'd gone even a mile. Worst of all, these children sensed her depression and were disturbed by it.

"Be happy, smile," they signed each morning hopefully. The truth was she'd lost even the sense of joy and accomplishment her job had always brought. It was a blessing she hadn't been able to get a permanent position. At least with many different classes, her lack of enthusiasm wouldn't seriously affect one group. Share the misery, she grimaced to herself. Even the city she'd always loved now irritated her—the gas fumes, the noise, the traffic. She was homesick for a valley far away.

Katy had phoned two nights ago. Jenny had sent a card from Hawaii, and Martha had forwarded it with a long affectionate letter, telling Alana that Bruce had started kindergarten, and Martha planned to return to England as soon as Jenny was back. She even said Tad was all over his soreness. Bruce sent his love, and they all missed her and felt dreadful about what had happened. No one mentioned Rand at all, and he'd never written or phoned again. Katy had ended her call by saying, "If you ever want to come back, Alana—" and for several choking moments Alana fought the too-ready tears.

"Leaving was—was my choice, Katy," she'd tried to explain.

Katy had sighed, the sound whispering over the miles of distance between them. "I miss you," she said then, adding shyly, "David sends his love."

When she hung up the phone, Alana collapsed on the corduroy sofa. If only it were Rand who sent his love.

For some strange reason, her dreams at night were always happy—scenarios of long, idle days with Bruce and always, somewhere out of the picture but close by, of Rand. In her dreams, he loved her, he told her so over and over and there were no complications. Bluejay was bathed in sunshine, the lake rippled cheerily in the breeze, Jenny sang tending her roses.

Alana would wake, isolated in her small apartment, aware of strangers just beyond the walls in other isolated rooms, and she would remember the joy of running with Rand in the early mornings, of Bruce landing in her bed with his alarm clock, of Jenny bringing coffee. And she would have to get up, shaking off the dreams, to face another rainy day. Why did it seem to rain every single day?

Alana glanced at her watch. There was another endless half hour to this rainy day, and the neon tube was flickering again. The children were carrying on spirited silent conversations, ignoring the work she'd given them to do. They knew their teacher was far too distracted to notice them.

A wave of shame shot through her. She was giving them less than they deserved. Surely her professional pride should insist she maintain order, capture their interest, use her skills to help them learn. They needed something now to vent their pent-up energy. Was ten too old for action songs? Of course not, she chided herself.

Eight pairs of observant eyes centered on her as she got quickly to her feet. She clapped her hands, beginning with an old favorite they all recognized—You put your left hand in, you take your left hand out, you put your left hand in and you shake it all about—

They giggled delightedly, following her ever increasing speed, unaware of her tuneless singing. *Good thing they can't hear me,* she thought wryly, belting out "You do the hootchy kootchy and you shake yourself about," suiting actions to words with a vengeance. The air of bored grayness that had hung like a cloud over the classroom was gone, and her students watched her expectantly, enjoying themselves. After a moment's thought, she started again.

"If you're happy and you know it, clap your hands, if you're happy and you know it, then your face will surely show it—"

Her hands flowed through the words of the song, her voice breaking in spite of her best intentions. It was a song she'd taught Bruce, and it was a mistake to sing it now. Her face would reveal anything but happiness if she relaxed her frozen features even slightly. Concentrating, she didn't hear the classroom door open and quietly close behind her. She saw the children's eyes centering somewhere else, their singing hands slowing and then stopping altogether. Alana whirled around, some sixth sense belatedly working...and there stood Rand.

Raindrops shimmered in his wood-brown curls. The shoulders of his beige raincoat were wet. The dark, angular face was thin, the lines beside his eyes and mouth deeply etched. Absently, his eyes drinking her in, he raised a hand up, rubbing the rain from his hair, ending with a gesture that convinced her it really was him, that weary, frustrated hand on the back of his neck. Then he shrugged off the coat, draping it carelessly on a chair. Still his eyes devoured her, the hard lips quirking slightly upward as she babbled, "How—where—when—" She was frozen, yet burned. She knew her banging heart would show through her dress.

"Grace told me where you were, and I talked to your brother, too. She put him on the phone. Mother and Jenny and Katy have all told me what they thought of me. Bruce wants you back—fast."

Her voice barely worked. "So you came because they sent you?" Her chin shot up, and she felt her eyes narrow. How could he do this, walk in here and tell her—

He shook his head slowly, once, from side to side. She felt herself memorizing again the way his eyebrows quirked up at the corners, how his ears lay molded and flat to his head. Behind her, the class was silent, but she knew their fingers were busy, assessing the scene.

"You should know by now I'm far too stubborn to listen to good advice," he said. "We're alike that way, you and I. No, I came to tell you something myself." His hands were now rammed in the pockets of his brown trousers, forcing apart the tweed sports coat, baring the expanse of chocolate colored shirt that exactly matched his eyes.

Steeling herself against hurt, she watched him draw his hands from his pockets, lift them self-consciously, and with his huge, callused, clumsy fingers he spelled her name. A-L-A-N-A. The effort showed on his face, and he nodded, watching his fingers carefully as though they might refuse to do his bidding. Drawing a deep breath, he began again. With the small finger of his right hand, he made the "I" sign against his chest. Then he made fists with both hands, slowly raising them, crossing them over his heart as though holding someone dear against him. Her breath caught, and stopped. It was the deaf sign for "love." He impaled her then with his eyes, slowing and emphatically pointing at her with his index finger. "You."

In case she hadn't understood, he went through it again, and yet again, stuttering in sign language. "I...love...you, I...love...you, I...love..."

The words he'd insisted no woman would hear him say. He'd stuck to that promise. She wasn't hearing them. Randall Evans was making her see them, using the signs of love.

The endearing, crazy, stumbling message went on. His hand swung down in an arc. "Will...you." She dared not move. Time hung suspended, the flickering neon overhead marking the seconds. His right fingers slid over the third finger of his left hand, sliding on an invisible ring. A tiny quiver shot over her, and it seemed her own finger tingled with an invisible band. "Marry." Almost humbly, his hand rested on his own chest. "Me."

Behind her, the classroom erupted. Sixteen adolescent hands clapped with glee. Alana whirled to face them, her face burning. The girls were chortling with joy, bouncing excitedly up and down in their seats. Some of the boys had their hands over their eyes, peeking through in pantomimes of horror. Shawn and several followers were making violent gagging sounds and clutching their throats. The dismissal bell flashed red, and with relief she excused them all, her face burning with waves of rich color. The problem was now they didn't want to go. The girls grilled her.

"You will marry with him?" "We will see you marry?" "When?" "You will wear what dress?" and "You love him?"

Most of their lightning fast signs had escaped Rand, but this final query didn't. A strained, almost frightened expression crossed his face, totally unlike his usual amiable self-confidence. Until now, Alana had neatly sidestepped the questions, trying to maintain some semblance of control. She smiled softly at the child who'd asked her about love, and nodded her head up, down, emphatically. Making a fist, she nodded it as well. Yes, yes, she loved Rand Evans. Today, yesterday, for months now, it had been the single thing she knew for sure. Rand's pent-up breath whistled slowly out.

At last, the room was empty. Rand was propped on one corner of her desk, quietly watching her every move. The door slammed behind the last curious face, and hesitantly she turned toward him. There were so many questions, so many answers necessary. But at this moment, nothing was more important than the compelling force that drew her slowly into his beckoning arms. He bent his head to hers, and a small pulse throbbed in his temple. His hands rose to her shoulders, paused. He touched the place where only a small dressing remained, hidden by her clothing. She felt him shudder. Then his hands drew her fiercely into him, closer, tighter, the sinews in his arms steel bands that would never release her again.

"Alana, teacher, beloved, I'm sorry." Brokenly, he whispered, "Darling, I'm so sorry. I'm to blame for this, for all of it. For—" he touched her shoulder with his lips "—for everything. If only you'll give me the chance, I'll spend the rest of my life making it up to you."

Nothing would ever matter again but this, the joy of being here in his arms. Words were so difficult for him; perhaps it was just a macho image men like him adapted, the facade of being physically strong, silent, unemotional; what they felt was required of them. She would penetrate that barrier—teach him to be open with her, as he had taught her the wonders of physical love. His voice was ragged when he whispered in her ear, "You are going to marry me, teacher?"

She drew a hand away and made the "Yes" sign. She drew out of his embrace, and the room was cold. She blurted out the words before she lost her courage.

"What took you so long, Rand? Why didn't you come before?" A childish gulp caught the last word, and she swallowed convulsively... and waited.

He was giving her so much now—couldn't she just accept, not demand explanations? But she needed to understand, to exorcise the pain she'd kept inside all these long weeks.

"I'm a coward, darling," he admitted at last, fumbling for the cigarette package outlined in his shirt. He shook one out, snapped the match on a strong, blunt fingernail, exhaled smoke in a faint blue cloud, and stubbed the cigarette out in the roots of a plant on her desk.

"And damn it, I have to stop smoking if I'm going to

marry a jogger." Taking her fingers in his, he stroked each one separately, staring down at her hands. He pressed a kiss into her palm.

"First, there was Lawrence. He's very ill, and his daughter's death had been hard on him. I've spent a great deal of time with him. Most of all, I've done a lot of thinking. You were right, darling; I'd locked my feelings up and thrown away the key. Something happened to me during my marriage, knowing Lindsay didn't want my child, terrified she'd abort him. Then, the divorce nearly broke me financially. And when I suspected Bruce was deaf, brought him down for testing, she phoned, demanding still more money, threatening custody proceedings. I—I wanted to strangle her, Alana."

She'd believed Rand loved Lindsay. She listened quietly, shocked at how far she'd been from the truth.

"Suddenly, you walked into my life. I was bitter, angry...scared about Bruce. And falling in love with you. There wasn't room in my life for love. Lindsay made a rotten scene that night, and the next day I found you in the park, bounding along like a wild thing." His half smile, the adoration on his face, was more than she could resist. She wrapped her arms around his neck.

"I was ashamed, frightened," he went on, holding her close. "I felt if you knew the shoddy details of my marriage, you'd despise me. You see, I'd started to suspect Lindsay was in far more serious trouble than ever before. Later, when I was about to tell you everything, John was there, and I thought he was your lover. I'd seen his picture in your room. I was insane with jealousy. But there wasn't time for explanations, knowing what hell Lindsay was causing." He rubbed his lips across her forehead, his mustache tickling in a wonderfully familiar way. "I didn't know until he phoned a few days ago that John was your brother." He drew away and looked down at her accusingly.

"He was working undercover. He made me promise," she said weakly, loving the heat of his breath in her ear.

"When you were in the hospital I asked you on the phone how serious you were with him, and you hung up on me," he accused gently.

"Oh! That must have been what I didn't hear—the line was so bad."

"Anyway, I want a full report on any other relatives, so I know what to expect." His arms tightened around her till she thought her ribs would crack.

"And I want you to teach me sign language. It took me forever to learn enough to propose."

"Forever is exactly how long we have," she said.

THEY WERE MARRIED AT BLUEJAY, on a sunny afternoon when autumn was burning crimson and gold and copper, lavishing its reflected fire over the watery mirror of the lake. The ceremony was in sign language and in speech. Reverend Fred Grange, an old friend of Alana's, flew out from Vancouver to perform the wedding, bringing a group of Alana's friends with him. Their surprise arrival was one of Rand's wedding gifts to her. The other was a photo named Bridges.

"We are here in God's magnificent cathedral," began Reverend Grange, "to join this couple in the holy sacrament of marriage."

They stood under the spreading arms of the cedar tree on Bluejay's front lawn. Tom had arranged chairs in a circle for the guests. The clear, skillful signs of the minister combined with his sonorous voice to unite the two languages in which he was adept, joining them in a union of communication. The clamorous jays added noisy counterpoint to the faint breeze rustling the surrounding forest.

"Marriage is a joining, the closing of a circle."

Beside Alana, Rand was unbearably handsome in his dark suit. His deep brown eyes read Alana's admiration and love in her expressive face.

"If you marry me in sign language," she'd teased, "it'll be impossible to get out of. I don't know any lawyers who speak it."

"That's exactly right," Rand had replied, not smiling. "Married for eternity. That's how long I'll love you."

"The symbol of marriage is this ring, an unbroken sphere of love." It glinted in the sunlight as Tom held it out, standing proud and unsupported, balancing easily on his new leg and beaming with the task of being Rand's best man.

"That unbroken ring of love will expand, encompassing Bruce in this union, enfolding him within the circle of the new family."

Bruce stood close beside the minister, proudly holding the Bible so Fred Grange's hands were free to spell their message. It mattered not at all that Bruce held the Holy Book upside down, or that Trefusus Antropus Denningham chose that moment to escape the shed to which he'd been banished. He dashed wildly to Bruce, tail wagging insanely, settling with several short victorious barks at the minister's feet. Bruce giggled.

"What if we should have other deaf children,

Alana?" Rand had awakened her in the dark hours before morning, stroking her shoulder apologetically, kissing her fingertips, needing to share the demons of the night. "I can't promise you our children will be able to hear," he whispered.

"If they're deaf, I guess we'll cry first," she mumbled sleepily. "Silence isn't always golden, my dad used to say. But we're so lucky, you and I. We've been allowed to share both worlds. And of course, we already speak the language, the signs of love," she added, just before his lips devoured hers.

Now, Alana handed her casual bouquet of wild autumn flowers and Jenny's roses to Grace, her maid of honor. With a shaking voice but supremely confident fingers, she spoke and signed her vows. "I, Alana, take you, Rand—"

Her simple ivory-toned dress of crepe-backed satin caught at every lightbeam, shimmering around her in rainbows from the tears in her eyes. Its long narrow sleeves formed lily points at her wrists, and a narrow braided band encircled her forehead in a formal echo of a jogging headband. It disappeared in the tousled curls she'd brushed so carefully, before Johnny had led her across the lawn to where Rand was waiting, and whispered, "Well, Red, it took some doing on my part, but I'm finally getting you married off." Then, unthinkingly, he'd reached a loving hand up and rumpled her hair.

With deep-toned absolute confidence in his voice, but with uncertain, shaking fingers, her beloved now spoke and signed his vows.

"I, Rand, take you, Alana—"

Alana could hear Martha sobbing loudly in her seat just behind them.

"I always cry at weddings," she'd warned just before the ceremony began.

"You can use my clean hanky, Missus Martha," Lissa had volunteered.

Amid the laughter, Rand had reached long arms out to Martha and Jenny, drawing both women close to his chest.

"Mothers always do," he'd rumbled. "I expect both of you to cry."

Somewhere close, perhaps among the shimmering birch trees on the lakeshore, Alana imagined her father's spirit lingered to bless this, her wedding day.

Fluidly, the signing fingers of Reverend Grange completed their silent benediction. It was a full minute before his voice repeated the message his signs had made.

"I now pronounce you," he said, "husband...and wife."

A hand strummed slowly down a guitar and Katy's voice rose, triumphant and free, soaring to the mountain peaks and bouncing back, as Rand's kiss welcomed Alana home.

**April's other absorbing
HARLEQUIN *SuperRomance* novel**

SPANGLES by Irma Walker

When she was in the cage with her cats, lion trainer Tanya Rhodin had the upper hand. So why, when it came to Wade Broderick, did she feel so out of control?

The millionaire businessman had run away to the circus to fulfil a boyhood fantasy, but when the colour and pageantry of the travelling show faded for him, he would leave.

The circus was Tanya's whole world. She knew it would be folly to become involved with an outsider. But Wade made her aware of a hundred new feelings . . . and one of them was love.

A contemporary love story for the woman of today

These two absorbing titles
will be published in May
by

HARLEQUIN
SuperRomance

WINDWARD PASSAGE by Christina Crockett

Miranda Calvert had worked hard the past five years. She owned her own business, her own home—going back to Florida presented problems.

The Southern Ocean Racing Conference was not her only reason for returning. She had left behind an angry father and an ex-fiancé—it was time to clear the air.

Meeting Walker Hall complicated matters. Captain of *Persistence*, he was as determined to win her love as he was to win the race. Miranda was caught between her past and future—with only her heart as her guide....

THE UNMASKING by Emilie Richards

Mardi Gras was magical, but Bethany Walker also loved its more practical aspect—as a mask maker, it was her most profitable time of year. After Justin Dumontier had deserted her and their unborn daughter, she had lived on the edge of poverty, and she vowed it would never happen again.

Now Justin was back, threatening her independence, igniting painful feelings of betrayal. Bethany knew reconciliation with him was impossible.

But, like one of Bethany's masks, the bitterness was merely a façade disguising their loving passion. And, in the fantastic spirit of Mardi Gras, anything seemed possible....

2 BOOKS FREE
Discover
Harlequin SuperRomances
Sensual and Spellbinding, Dramatic and Involving...

Strong stories with unpredictable plots... fascinating characters... gripping suspense... exotic locations. By becoming a regular reader of Harlequin SuperRomances you can enjoy FOUR superb new titles every other month and a whole range of special benefits too: your very own personal membership card, a free monthly newsletter packed with exclusive book offers, competitions, recipes, a monthly guide to the stars, plus extra bargain offers and big cash savings.

**AND an Introductory FREE GIFT for YOU.
Turn over the page for details.**

Fill in and send this coupon back today and we'll send you
2 Introductory SuperRomances yours to keep FREE

At the same time we will reserve a subscription to Harlequin SuperRomances for you. Every other month, you will receive the FOUR latest novels by leading Romantic Fiction authors, delivered direct to your door. You don't pay extra for delivery. Postage and packing is always completely Free. There is no obligation or commitment — you only receive books for as long as you want to.

What could be easier? Fill in the coupon below and return it to
HARLEQUIN, FREEPOST, P.O. BOX 236, CROYDON, SURREY, CR9 9EL.
Please Note:- READERS IN SOUTH AFRICA write to
Harlequin S.A. Pty., Postbag X3010,
Randburg 2125, S. Africa.

HARLEQUIN PRIORITY ORDER FORM

To:- Harlequin, Freepost, P.O. Box 236, Croydon, Surrey, CR9 9EL.

Please send me my 2 SuperRomance titles absolutely FREE. Thereafter please send me the four latest SuperRomances every other month, which I may buy for just £6.00 postage and packing free. I understand I may cancel my subscription at any time, simply by writing to you. The first two books are mine to keep, whatever I decide. I am over 18 years of age.

Please write in BLOCK CAPITALS.

Signature_____

Name_____

Address_____

_____Post code_____

SEND NO MONEY — TAKE NO RISKS.
Please don't forget to include your Postcode.

Remember, postcodes speed delivery. Offer applies in UK only and is not valid to present subscribers. Harlequin reserve the right to exercise discretion in granting membership. If price changes are necessary you will be notified.
Offer expires May 31st 1986.

4SR   EP13F